I AM NUMBER FOUR
The Lost Files
The Legacies

PITTACUS LORE

PENGUIN BOOKS

PENGUIN BOOKS

Published by the Penguin Group
Penguin Books Ltd, 80 Strand, London WC2R ORL, England
Penguin Group (USA) Inc., 375 Hudson Street, New York, New York 10014, USA
Penguin Group (Canada), 90 Eglinton Avenue East, Suite 700, Toronto, Ontario, Canada M4P 2Y3
(a division of Pearson Penguin Canada Inc.)
Penguin Ireland, 25 St Stephen's Green, Dublin 2, Ireland (a division of Penguin Books Ltd)
Penguin Group (Australia), 707 Collins Street, Melbourne, Victoria 3008, Australia
(a division of Pearson Australia Group Pty Ltd)
Penguin Books India Pvt Ltd, 11 Community Centre, Panchsheel Park, New Delhi – 110 017, India
Penguin Group (NZ), 67 Apollo Drive, Rosedale, Auckland 0632, New Zealand
(a division of Pearson New Zealand Ltd)
Penguin Books (South Africa) (Pty) Ltd, Block D, Rosebank Office Park,
181 Jan Smuts Avenue, Parktown North, Gauteng 2193, South Africa

Penguin Books Ltd, Registered Offices: 80 Strand, London WC2R ORL, England

www.penguin.com

This collection first published in the United States of America by HarperCollins Publishers 2012
This edition first published in Great Britain by Penguin Books 2012

002

I Am Number Four: The Lost Files: Six's Legacy, copyright © 2011 Pittacus Lore
I Am Number Four: The Lost Files: Nine's Legacy, copyright © 2012 Pittacus Lore
I Am Number Four: The Lost Files: The Fallen Legacies, copyright © 2012 Pittacus Lore
All rights reserved

The moral right of the author has been asserted

Set in 12.5/14.75pt Garamond MT Std
Typeset by Jouve (UK), Milton Keynes
Printed in England by Clays Ltd, St Ives plc

Except in the United States of America, this book is sold subject
to the condition that it shall not, by way of trade or otherwise, be lent,
re-sold, hired out, or otherwise circulated without the publisher's
prior consent in any form of binding or cover other than that in
which it is published and without a similar condition including this
condition being imposed on the subsequent purchaser

ISBN: 978–1–405–91262–4

www.greenpenguin.co.uk

MIX
Paper from
responsible sources
FSC
www.fsc.org   FSC™ C018179

Penguin Books is committed to a sustainable
future for our business, our readers and our planet.
This book is made from Forest Stewardship
Council™ certified paper.

ALWAYS LEARNING

PEARSON

Contents

Six's Legacy   1

Nine's Legacy   83

The Fallen Legacies   201

I AM NUMBER FOUR
The Lost Files
Six's Legacy

I

Katarina says there is more than one way to hide.

Before we came down here to Mexico, we lived in a suburb of Denver. My name then was Sheila, a name I hate even more than my current name, Kelly. We lived there for two years, and I wore barrettes in my hair and pink rubber bracelets on my wrists, like all the other girls at my school. I had sleepovers with some of them, the girls I called 'my friends.' I went to school during the school year, and in the summer I went to a swimmers' camp at the YMCA. I liked my friends and the life we had there okay, but I had already been moved around by my Cêpan Katarina enough to know that it wasn't going to be permanent. I knew it wasn't my *real* life.

My real life took place in our basement, where Katarina and I did combat training. By day, it was an ordinary suburban rec room, with a big comfy couch and a TV in one corner and a Ping-Pong table in the other. By night, it was a well-stocked combat training gym, with hanging bags, floor mats, weapons, and even a makeshift pommel horse.

In public, Katarina played the part of my mother, claiming that her 'husband' and my 'father' had been killed in a car accident when I was an infant. Our names, our lives, our stories were all fictions, identities for me and Katarina to

3

hide behind. But those identities allowed us to live out in the open. Acting normal.

Blending in: that was one way of hiding.

But we slipped up. To this day I can remember our conversation as we drove away from Denver, headed to Mexico for no other reason than we'd never been there, both of us trying to figure out how exactly we'd blown our cover. Something I said to my friend Eliza had contradicted something Katarina had said to Eliza's mother. Before Denver we'd lived in Nova Scotia for a cold, cold winter, but as I remembered it, our story, the lie we'd agreed to tell, was that we'd lived in Boston before Denver. Katarina remembered differently, and claimed Tallahassee as our previous home. Then Eliza told her mother and that's when people started to get suspicious.

It was hardly a calamitous exposure. We had no immediate reason to believe our slip would raise the kind of suspicion that could attract the Mogadorians to our location. But our life had gone sour there, and Katarina figured we'd been there long enough as it was.

So we moved yet again.

The sun is bright and hard in Puerto Blanco, the air impossibly dry. Katarina and I make no attempt to blend in with the other residents, Mexican farmers and their children. Our only regular contact with the locals is our once-a-week trip into town to buy essentials at the small store. We are the only whites for many miles, and though we both speak good

Spanish, there's no confusing us for natives of the place. To our neighbors, we are the gringas, strange white recluses.

'Sometimes you can hide just as effectively by sticking out,' Katarina says.

She appears to be right. We have been here almost a year and we haven't been bothered once. We lead a lonely but ordered life in a sprawling, single-level shack tucked between two big patches of farmland. We wake up with the sun, and before eating or showering Katarina has me run drills in the backyard: running up and down a small hill, doing calisthenics, and practicing tai chi. We take advantage of the two relatively cool hours of morning.

Morning drills are followed by a light breakfast, then three hours of studies: languages, world history, and whatever other subjects Katarina can dig up from the internet. She says her teaching method and subject matter are 'eclectic.' I don't know what that word means, but I'm just grateful for the variety. Katarina is a quiet, thoughtful woman, and though she's the closest thing I have to a mother, she's very different from me.

Studies are probably the highlight of her day. I prefer drills.

After studies it's back out into the blazing sun, where the heat makes me dizzy enough that I can almost hallucinate my imagined enemies. I do battle with straw men: shooting them with arrows, stabbing them with knives, or simply pummeling them with my bare fists. But half-blind from the sun, I see them as Mogadorians, and I relish the chance to tear them to pieces. Katarina says even though I am only thirteen years old, I'm so agile and so strong I could easily take down even a well-trained adult.

One of the nice things about living in Puerto Blanco is that I don't have to hide my skills. Back in Denver, whether swimming at the Y or just playing on the street, I always had to hold back, to keep myself from revealing the superior speed and strength that Katarina's training regimen has resulted in. We keep to ourselves out here, away from the eyes of others, so I don't have to hide.

Today is Sunday, so our afternoon drills are short, only an hour. I am shadowboxing with Katarina in the backyard, and I can feel her eagerness to quit: her moves are halfhearted, she's squinting against the sun, and she looks tired. I love training and could go all day, but out of deference to her I suggest we call it a day.

'Oh, I suppose we could finish early,' she says. I grin privately, allowing her to think I'm the tired one. We go inside and Katarina pours us two tall glasses of *agua fresca*, our customary Sunday treat. The fan is blowing full force in our humble shack's living room. Katarina boots up her various computers while I kick off my dirty, sweat-filled fighting boots and collapse to the floor. I stretch my arms to keep them from knotting up, then swing them to the bookshelf in the corner and pull out a tall stack of the board games we keep there. Risk, Stratego, Othello. Katarina has tried to interest me in games like Life and Monopoly, saying it wouldn't hurt to be 'well-rounded.' But those games never held my interest. Katarina got the hint, and now we only play combat and strategy games.

Risk is my favorite, and since we finished early today I think Katarina will agree to playing it even though it's a longer game than the others.

'Risk?'

Katarina is at her desk chair, pivoting from one screen to the next.

'Risk of what?' she asks absently.

I laugh, then shake the box near her head. She doesn't look up from the screens, but the sound of all those pieces rattling around inside the box is enough for her to get it.

'Oh,' she says. 'Sure.'

I set up the board. Without asking, I divvy up the armies into hers and mine, and begin placing them all across the game's map. We've played this game so much I don't need to ask her which countries she'd like to claim, or which territories she'd like to fortify. She always chooses the US and Asia. I happily place her pieces on those territories, knowing that from my more easily defended territories I will quickly grow armies strong enough to crush hers.

I'm so absorbed in setting up the game I don't even notice Katarina's silence, *her* absorption. It is only when I crack my neck loudly and she neglects to scold me for it – 'Please don't,' she usually says, squeamish about the sound it makes – that I look up and see her, staring openmouthed at one of her monitors.

'Kat?' I ask.

She's silent.

I get up from the floor, stepping across the game board to join her at her desk. It is only then that I see what has so completely captured her attention. A breaking news item about some kind of explosion on a bus in England.

I groan.

Katarina is always checking the internet and the news for mysterious deaths. Deaths that could be the work of the Mogadorians. Deaths that could mean the second member of the Garde has been defeated. She's been doing it since we came to Earth, and I've grown frustrated with the doom-and-gloom of it.

Besides, it's not like it did us any good the first time.

I was nine years old, living in Nova Scotia with Katarina. Our training room there was in the attic. Katarina had retired from training for the day, but I still had energy to burn, and was doing moores and spindles on the pommel horse alone when I suddenly felt a blast of scorching pain on my ankle. I lost my balance and came crashing down to the mat, clutching my ankle and screaming in pain.

My first scar. It meant that the Mogadorians had killed Number One, the first of the Garde. And for all of Katarina's web scouring, it had caught us both completely unaware.

We waited on pins and needles for weeks after, expecting a second death and a second scar to follow in short order. But it didn't come. I think Katarina is still coiled, anxious, ready to spring. But three years have passed – almost a quarter of my whole life – and it's just not something I think about much.

I step between her and the monitor. 'It's Sunday. Game time.'

'Please, Kelly.' She says my most recent alias with a certain stiffness. I know I will always be Six to her. In my heart, too. These aliases I use are just shells, they're not who I really am. I'm sure back on Lorien I had a name, a real name, not just a number. But that's so far back, and I've had so many names since then, that I can't remember what it was.

Six is my true name. Six is who I am.

Katarina bats me aside, eager to read more details.

We've lost so many game days to news alerts like this. And they never turn out to be anything. They're just ordinary tragedies.

Earth, I've come to discover, has no shortage of tragedies.

'Nope. It's just a bus crash. We're playing a game.' I pull at her arms, eager for her to relax. She looks so tired and worried, I know she could use the break.

She holds firm. 'It's a bus *explosion*. And apparently,' she says, pulling away to read from the screen, 'the conflict is ongoing.'

'The conflict always is,' I say, rolling my eyes. 'Come on.'

She shakes her head, giving one of her frazzled laughs. 'Okay,' she says. 'Fine.'

Katarina pulls herself away from the monitors, sitting on

the floor by the game. It takes all my strength not to lick my chops at her upcoming defeat: I always win at Risk.

I get down beside her, on my knees.

'You're right, Kelly,' she says, allowing herself to grin. 'I needn't panic over every little thing –'

One of the monitors on Katarina's desk lets out a sudden *ding!* One of her alerts. Her computers are programmed to scan for unusual news reports, blog posts, even notable shifts in global weather – all sifting for possible news of the Garde.

'Oh come on,' I say.

But Katarina is already off the floor and back at the desk, scrolling and clicking from link to link once again.

'Fine,' I say, annoyed. 'But I'm showing no mercy when the game begins.'

Suddenly Katarina is silent, stopped cold by something she's found.

I get up off the floor and step over the board, making my way to the monitor.

I look at the screen.

It is not, as I'd imagined, a news report from England. It is a simple, anonymous blog post. Just a few haunting, tantalizing words:

'Nine, now eight. Are the rest of you out there?'

There is a cry in the wilderness, from a member of the Garde. Some girl or boy, the same age as me, looking for us. In an instant I've seized the keyboard from Katarina and I hammer out a response in the comments section. 'We are here.'

Katarina bats my hand away before I can hit Enter. 'Six!'

I pull back, ashamed of my imprudence, my haste.

'We have to be careful. The Mogadorians are on the hunt. They've killed One, for all we know they have a path to Two, to Three –'

'But they're alone!' I say. The words come out before I have a chance to think what I'm saying.

I don't know how I know this. It's just a hunch I have. If this member of the Garde has been desperate enough to reach out on the internet, looking for others, his or her Cêpan must have been killed. I imagine my fellow Garde's panic, her fear. I can't imagine what it would be like to lose my Katarina, to be alone. To consider all I deal with . . . *without* Katarina? It's unimaginable.

'What if it's Two? What if she's in England, and the Mogs are after her, and she's reaching out for help?'

A second ago I was scoffing at Katarina's absorption in the

news. But this is different. This is a link to someone *like me*. Now I am desperate to help them, to answer their call.

'Maybe it's time,' I say, balling my fist.

'Time?' Katarina is scared, wearing a baffled expression.

'Time to fight!'

Katarina's head falls into her hands and she laughs into her palms.

In moments of high stress, Katarina sometimes reacts this way: she laughs when she should be stern, gets serious when she should laugh.

Katarina looks up and I realize she is not laughing at me. She is just nervous, and confused.

'Your Legacies haven't even developed!' she cries. 'How could we possibly start the war now?'

She gets up from the desk, shaking her head.

'No. We are not ready to fight. Until your powers are manifest, we will not start this battle. Until the Garde is ready, we must hide.'

'Then we have to send her a message.'

'Her? You don't know it's a she! For all we know, it's no one. Just some random person using language that accidentally tripped my alert.'

'I *know* it's one of us,' I say, fixing Katarina with my eyes. 'And you do too.'

Katarina nods, admitting defeat.

'Just one message. To let them know they're not alone. To give her hope.'

'"Her" again,' laughs Katarina, almost sadly.

I think it's a girl because I imagine whoever wrote the message to be like me. A more scared and more alone version of me – one who's been deprived of her Cêpan.

'Okay,' she says. I step between her and the monitor, my fingers hovering over the keys. I decide the message I've already typed – 'We are here' – will suffice.

I hit Enter.

Katarina shakes her head, ashamed to have indulged me so recklessly. Within moments she is at the computer, scrubbing any trace of our location from the transmission.

'Feel better?' she asks, turning off the monitor.

I do, a little. To think I've given a bit of solace and comfort to one of the Garde makes me feel good, connected to the larger struggle.

Before I can respond I'm electrified by a pain, the likes of which I've only known once before; a lava-hot lancet digging through the flesh of my right ankle. My leg shoots out from beneath me, and I scream, attempting to distance myself from the pain by holding my ankle as far from the rest of me as I can. Then I see it: the flesh on my ankle sizzling, popping with smoke. A new scar, my second, snakes its way across my skin.

'Katarina!' I scream, punching the floor with my fists, desperate with pain.

Katarina is frozen in horror, unable to help.

'The second,' she says. 'Number Two is dead.'

Katarina rushes to the tap, fills a pitcher, and dumps it across my leg. I am nearly catatonic from the pain, biting my lip so hard it bleeds. I watch the water sizzle as it hits my burned flesh, then it floods the game board, washing the army pieces off onto the floor.

'You win,' I say, making a feeble joke.

Katarina doesn't acknowledge my attempt at wit. My protector, she has gone into full-on Cêpan mode: pulling first-aid supplies out from every corner of our shack. Before I know it she's applied a cooling salve to my scar and wrapped and taped it with gauze.

'Six,' she says, her eyes moist with fear and pity. I'm taken aback – she only uses my real name in moments of extreme crisis.

But then I realize that's what this is.

Years had passed since One's death, without incident. It had gotten easy to imagine it was a fluke. If we were feeling really hopeful, we could imagine One had died in an accident. That the Mogadorians hadn't caught our scent.

That time is over. We know for sure now. The Mogadorians have found the second member of the Garde, and killed him or her. Two's message to us, to the world, was the last thing he or she would ever do. Their violent death was now written across my skin.

We know two deaths is no fluke. The countdown has truly begun.

I almost faint, but pull myself to consciousness by biting my lip even harder. 'Six,' Katarina says, wiping the blood from my mouth with a cloth. 'Relax.'

I shake my head.

No. I can never relax. Not ever.

Katarina is straining to keep her composure. She doesn't want to frighten me. But she also wants to do the right thing, to honor her responsibilities as a Cêpan. I can tell she's torn between every possible reaction, from outright panic to philosophical cool; whatever is the best for me and for the fate of the Garde.

She cradles my head, wipes the sweat from my brow. The water and the salve have taken the sharpest edge off the pain, but it still hurts as bad as the first time, maybe worse. But I won't comment on it. I can see that my pain, and this evidence of Two's passing, is tormenting Katarina enough.

'We'll be okay,' says Katarina. 'There are still many others . . .'

I know she is speaking carelessly. She doesn't mean to put the lives of the Garde before me – Three, Four, and Five – ahead of my own. She is just grasping for consolation. But I won't let it pass.

'Yeah. It's so great others have to die before me.'

'That's not what I meant.' I can see my words have upset her.

I sigh, putting my head against her shoulder.

Sometimes, in my heart of hearts, I use a different name for Katarina. Sometimes to me she's not Katarina or Vicky or Celeste or any of her other aliases. Sometimes – in my mind – I call her 'Mom.'

4

We're on the road an hour later. Katarina white-knuckles the steering wheel of our truck through country roads, cursing her choice of hideaway. These roads are too rough and dusty to go faster than forty miles per hour, and what we both want is the speed of a highway. *Anything* to put as much distance as possible between us and our now abandoned shack. Katarina did what she could to scrub our tracks, but if what we imagine is true – the Mogadorians killing Two seconds after we saw her fatal blog post – then they moved fast, and they could be racing towards our abandoned home right now.

As I watch the fields and the hills pass through the passenger window, I realize that they could already be at the shack. In fact, they could already be following us on the road. Feeling like a coward as I do it, I crane my neck and look through the rear window, through the dust trail our truck kicks up in our wake.

No cars trail us.

Not yet, at least.

We packed light. The truck was already loaded with a first-aid kit, a lightweight camping set, bottled water, flashlights, and blankets. Once I was ready to walk again, all I had to do was pick out a few items of clothing for the road and retrieve my Chest from the lockbox under the shack.

The panic of flight gave me little time to feel the searing pain of my second scar, but it returns to me now, lacerating and insistent.

'We shouldn't have responded,' says Katarina. 'I don't know what we were thinking.'

I look at Katarina for signs of judgment on her face – after all, I'm the one who insisted we write back – and I'm relieved to find none. All I see is her fear, and her determination to get us as far away as possible.

I realize that in the confusion and haste to flee I forgot to notice if we turned north or south at the crossing at the edge of Puerto Blanco.

'US?' I ask.

Katarina nods, pulling our most recent passports from the inside pocket of her army jacket, tossing mine into my lap. I flip it open and peer at my new name.

'Maren Elizabeth,' I say aloud. Katarina puts a lot of time into her forgeries, though I usually complain about the names she chooses for me. When I was eight and we were moving to Nova Scotia, I begged and begged to be named Starla. Katarina vetoed the suggestion. She thought it was too 'attention getting,' too exotic. I almost laugh to think about it now. A Katarina in Mexico is about as exotic as you can get. And of course she's keeping it. Katarina has grown attached to her *own* name. Sometimes I suspect that Cêpans aren't so different from parents after all.

Maren Elizabeth . . . it's no Starla, but I like how it sounds.

I reach down and cradle my calf, just above the throbbing scars on my ankle. By squeezing my calf I can muffle the pain of my sizzled flesh.

But as the pain fades, the fear returns. The fear of our present situation, the horror of Two's death. I decide to let go of my calf, and I let my leg burn.

Katarina refuses to stop the car for anything but gas and pee breaks. It's a long trip, but we have ways to pass the time. Mostly we play Shadow, a game that Katarina made up during our previous travels, out of our desire to keep training even when we couldn't do physical drills.

'A Mogadorian scout races at you from two o'clock, wielding a twenty-inch blade in his left arm. He swings.'

'I crouch,' I say. 'Dodge left.'

'He swings around, the blade above your head.'

'From the ground, a kick to the groin. A leg sweep, from his right side to his left.'

'On his back, but he grabs your arm.'

'I let him. I use the force of his grip to swing my legs free, up, and then down to his face. Step on his face, pull my hand free.'

It's a strange game. It forces me to separate the physical from reality, to fight with my brain and not my body. I used to complain about games of Shadow, saying it was all made up, that it wasn't real. Fighting was fists, and feet, and heads. It wasn't brains. It wasn't words.

But the more Shadow we played, the better I got at drills, especially hand-to-hand drills with Katarina. I couldn't deny that the game made good practice. It made me a better fighter. I have come to love it.

'I run,' I say.

'Too late,' she says. I almost complain, knowing what's coming. 'You forgot about the sword,' she says. 'He's already swung it up and nicked your flank.'

'No he didn't,' I say. 'I froze his sword and shattered it like glass.'

'Oh did you, now?' Katarina is tired, eyes bloodshot from ten straight hours of driving, but I can see I'm amusing her. 'I must've missed that part.'

'Yeah,' I say, starting to grin myself.

'And how'd you pull off that feat?'

'My Legacy. It just kicked in. Turns out, I can freeze stuff.'

This is make-believe. I have yet to develop my Legacies, and I have no idea what they'll be when they arrive.

'That's a good one,' says Katarina.

5

We crossed the US border hours back, without a hitch. I have never understood how Katarina manages to make such incredible forgeries.

Katarina is pulling us into a dusty pit stop off the highway. There's a tiny, single-story motel, an old-fashioned and decrepit diner, and a gas station, newer and brighter than the other two buildings.

It is barely dusk when we step out of the truck. The faintest pink of sunrise creeps over the horizon, just enough to add a strange hue to our flesh as we stumble out onto the gravel.

Katarina curses, getting back into the car. 'Forgot to get gas,' she says. 'Wait here.'

I do as I'm told, watching her pull the truck from the motel parking lot towards one of the pumps. We have agreed to rest up at the motel for a day or two, to recover from our grueling, fifteen-hour drive and the shock of recent events. But even though we'll be here for some time, the tank must be filled: that's Katarina's policy.

'Never leave an empty tank,' she says. I think she says it as much to remind herself as to educate me.

It's a good policy. You never know when you'll have to leave in a hurry.

I watch Katarina pull up to the pump and start filling the car.

I examine my surroundings. Through the front window of the diner across the lot, I can see a few grizzled-looking truckers eating. Through the scent of exhaust and the faint odor of gas fumes from the pumps, I can smell breakfast food in the air.

Or maybe I'm just imagining it. I am incredibly hungry. My mouth waters at the thought of breakfast.

I turn my back on the diner, trying not to think about food, and look at the town on the other side of the fence from the pit stop. Houses only a step up from clapboard shacks. A ragged, desolate place.

'Hello, miss.' Startled, I whizz around to see a tall, gray-haired cowboy strutting past. It takes me a second to realize that he's not starting a conversation, merely being polite as he passes. He gives a little nod of his ten-gallon hat and proceeds past me into the diner.

My heart rate is up.

I had forgotten this aspect of the road. When we're settled in a place, even a remote one like Puerto Blanco, we get to know the local faces. We know, more or less, who to trust. I've never seen a Mogadorian in my life, but Katarina says that most of the Mogadorians look like anyone else. After what happened to One and Two, I feel a deep unease all around me, a new alertness. A roadside rest stop is especially troublesome in that everyone is a stranger to everyone, so no one raises any eyebrows, not really. For us that means anyone could be a threat.

Katarina has parked the car and approaches me with a weary grin.

'Eat or sleep?' she asks. Before I can answer, she's raised her hand hopefully. 'My vote for sleep.'

'My vote is to eat.' Katarina deflates at this. 'You *know* eat beats sleep,' I say. 'Always does.' It is one of our rules of the road, and Katarina quickly accepts the verdict.

'Okay, Maren Elizabeth,' she says. 'Lead the way.'

6

The diner is humid with grease. It is barely six a.m. but almost all of the booths are full, mostly with truckers. While I wait for our food I watch these men shovel hearty, well-syruped forksful of breakfast meat – sausage, bacon, scrapple – into their mouths. When my food finally comes I find myself more than holding my own. Three pancakes, four strips of bacon, a side of hash, one tall OJ.

I finish with a rude belch that Katarina is too tired to chastise me for.

'Do you think . . . ?' I ask.

Katarina laughs, anticipating my question. 'How is that possible?'

I shrug. She nods, and calls the waitress over. With a guilty grin, I order another stack of pancakes.

'Well,' says the waitress, with a dry smoker's cackle, 'your little girl sure can put it down.' The waitress is an older woman, with a face so lined and haggard you could mistake it for a man's.

'Yes, ma'am,' I say. The waitress leaves.

'Your appetite will never cease to amaze me,' Katarina says. But she knows the reason for it. I train constantly, and though I'm only thirteen years old I already have the tightly muscled body of a gymnast. I need a lot of fuel, and am not ashamed of my appetite.

Another customer enters the crowded diner.

I notice the other men give him a suspicious glance as he makes his way to a booth in the rear. They looked at me and Katarina with similar suspicion when we first entered. I took this place for a way station, filled with strangers, but apparently *some* strangers are worthy of suspicion and others aren't. Katarina and I are doing our best, dressed in generic American mall clothes: T-shirts and khaki shorts. I can see why we stand out – apparently they have a different definition of 'generic' here in the far reaches of West Texas.

This other stranger is harder to figure, though. He's dressed the part, more or less: wearing one of those Texas ties, with the dangly strands of black leather. And like the rest of the men here, he's wearing boots.

But his clothes seem somehow out-of-date, and there's something creepy about his thin black mustache: it looks straight at first glance, but the more I consider it, something about it just seems *crooked*.

'It's impolite to stare.' Katarina, chiding me again.

'I wasn't staring,' I lie. 'I was looking, with interest.'

Katarina laughs. She's laughed more in the past twenty-four hours than she has in months. This new Katrina is going to take some getting used to.

Not that I mind.

*

I stretch out luxuriantly on the hotel bed while Katarina showers in the bathroom. The sheets are cheap, polyester or rayon, but I'm so tired from the road they may as well be silk.

When Katarina first pulled the sheets down we found a live earwig under the pillow, which grossed her out but didn't bother me.

'Kill it,' she begged, covering her eyes.

I refused. 'It's just an insect.'

'Kill it!' she begged.

Instead, I swept it off the bed and hopped into the cool sheets. 'Nope,' I said stubbornly.

'Fine,' she said, and went to shower. She turned the faucets on, but stepped out of the bathroom again a moment later. 'I worry –' she started.

'About what?' I asked.

'I worry that I haven't trained you well.'

I rolled my eyes. ''Cause I won't kill a bug?!'

'Yes. No, I mean, it's what got me thinking. You need to learn to kill without hesitation. I haven't even taught you to hunt rodents, let alone Mogadorians . . . you've never killed anything –'

Katarina paused, the water still running behind her. Thinking.

I could tell she was tired, lost in a thought. She gets like that sometimes, if we've been training too gruelingly. 'Kat,' I said. 'Go shower.'

She looked up, her reverie broken. She chuckled and closed the door behind her.

Waiting for her to finish, I turned on the TV from the bed. The previous tenant had left it on CNN and I'm greeted with the site of helicopter footage of the 'event' in England. I watch only long enough to learn that both the press and English authorities are confused as to what exactly *happened* yesterday. I'm too tired to think about this; I'll get the details later.

I shut off the TV and lay back on the bed, eager for sleep to take me.

Katarina steps out of the bathroom moments later, wearing a robe and brushing out her hair. I watch her through half-closed eyes.

There is a knock on the door.

Katarina drops her brush on the bureau.

'Who is it?' she asks.

'Manager, miss. I brought ya some fresh towels.'

I'm so annoyed by the interruption – I want to sleep, and it's pretty obvious we don't need fresh towels since we only just got to the room – that I propel myself right off the bed, barely thinking.

'We don't need any,' I say, already swinging the door open.

I just have time to hear Katarina say, 'Don't –' before I see him, standing before me. The crooked mustache man.

The scream catches in my throat as he enters the room and shuts the door behind him.

7

I react without thinking, pushing him towards the door, but he flings me back easily, against the bed. I clutch my chest and realize with horror that my pendant is out from under my shirt. In plain view.

'Pretty necklace,' he growls, his eyes flashing with recognition.

If he had any doubt about who I am, it is long gone.

Katarina charges forward but he strikes her hard. She crashes against the TV set, smashing the screen with a bare elbow, and falls to the ground.

He pulls something from his waist – a long, thin blade – and raises it so quickly I don't even have time to stand. I see only the flash of his blade as he swings it down – straight down, like a railroad spike – into my brain.

My head floods instantly with warmth and light.

This is what death feels like, I think.

But no. The pain doesn't come.

I look up – *how can I see?* I think. *I'm dead*. But I do see, and realize that I'm covered, from head to toe, in hot red blood. The Crooked Mustache Man still has his arm outstretched, his mouth is still frozen in victory, but his skull has been split open, as if by a knife, and his blood is spilling out across my knees.

I hear Katarina wail – it's such a primal noise that I can't tell if it's a cry of grief or a scream of relief – as the man, emptied of blood, turns quickly to dust, collapsing in on himself as an ashy heap.

Before I can take a breath, Katarina is up, shedding her robe and throwing on clothes, grabbing our bags.

'He died,' I say. 'I didn't.'

'Yes,' Katarina replies. She puts on a white blouse, which she instantly ruins with the blood from her elbow, shredded from the TV screen. She throws it out, blots the blood from her elbow with a towel, and puts on another shirt.

I feel like a child, speechless, immobile, covered in blood on the floor.

That was it – the moment I've been training for my whole life – and all I managed was a feeble, easily deflected shove before getting tossed aside and stabbed.

'He didn't know,' I say.

'He didn't know,' she says.

What he didn't know is that any harm inflicted on me out of order would instead be inflicted upon my attacker. I was safe from direct attack. I knew it, but I also didn't *really* know it. When he stabbed me in the head, I thought I was dead. It took seeing it to believe it.

I reach up and touch my scalp. The flesh there is unbroken, it's not even damp . . .

29

There's the proof. We are protected by the charm. As long as we stay apart from each other, we can only be killed in the order of our number.

I realize his blood has now turned to dust along with his flesh. I am no longer drenched in it.

'We have to go.' Katarina has shoved my Chest into my arms, her face pressed right up to mine. I realize I've spaced out, gone to a place inside my own head, reeling from the shock of what just happened. I can tell from the way she says it that this is the third or fourth time she's repeated it, though I am only just hearing her.

'*Now*,' she says.

Katarina drags me by the wrist, her bag slung over her shoulder. The hot asphalt of the parking lot burns the soles of my shoeless feet as we rush outside towards the truck. I carry my Chest, which feels heavy in my arms.

I have been preparing for battle my whole life, and now that it's come all I want is to sleep. My heels drag, my arms are heavy.

'Faster!' says Katarina, pulling me along. The truck's unlocked. I get into the passenger seat as Katarina tosses our stuff in the bed of the truck and hops into the driver's seat. No sooner has she closed her door than I see a man racing towards us.

For a moment I think it's the motel manager, chasing us for fleeing our bill. But then I recognize him as the cowboy from before, the one who gave me the polite nod of his cowboy hat. There's nothing polite about the way he's racing towards us now, his fist upraised.

His hand smashes through the glass of the passenger door and I'm sprayed with glass. His fist closes around the fabric of my shirt and I feel myself lifted out of my seat.

Katarina screams.

'Hey!' A voice from outside.

My hand scrambles, looking for something, anything to keep me in my seat. It finds only my unbuckled seat belt, which gives easily as the Mog starts pulling me through the window. I feel Katarina's hand clutching the back of my shirt.

'I'd think twice 'bout that!' I hear a man's voice shout, and soon I am released, falling back into the seat.

I am breathless, my head spinning.

Outside the truck, a crowd has formed. Truckers and cowboys, ordinary American men. They've encircled the Mog. One of them has a shotgun raised, pointed right at him. With a wry, bitter smile, the Mog lifts his arms in surrender.

'The keys.' Katarina is panicking, near tears. 'I left them in the room.'

I don't think, I just move. I don't know how long the Mog will be contained by the protective mob, our saviors, but I don't care: I race back to the room, swipe the keys off the night table, and head back out into the heat of the parking lot.

The Mog is kneeling on the ground now, surrounded by angry men.

'We called the cops, miss,' says one of them. I nod, my

eyes teary. I'm too keyed-up even to say thanks. It's strange and wonderful to consider that none of these men know us but they came to our aid, yet frightening that they don't understand this Mog's true power, that if he hadn't been instructed to keep a low profile he'd have torn the skin clean off each of their bodies by now.

I get in the car and hand Katarina the keys. Moments later, we pull out of the lot.

I turn back for one last glance and lock eyes with the Mog. His eyes brim with reptilian hate.

He winks as we pull away.

8

Katarina was wrong. I have killed before. Years ago, in Nova Scotia.

It was early winter and Katarina had released me from our studies to go play in our snowy backyard. I took to the yard like a demon, running circles in the snow in my baggy clothes, leaping into snowbanks and aiming snowballs at the sun.

I hated my cumbersome jacket and waterproof pants, so once I was sure Katarina had turned from the window I shed them, stripping down to my jeans and T-shirt. It was below freezing outside, but I've always been tough about the cold. I continued to play and race when Clifford, the neighbors' St Bernard, came bounding over to play with me.

He was a huge dog and I was small then, even for my age. So I climbed on top of him, clutching the warm fur of his flank. 'Giddyup!' I squealed and he took off. I rode him like a pony, running laps around the yard.

Katarina had recently told me more about my history, and about my future. I wasn't old enough to fully understand, but I knew it meant I was a warrior. This sat well with me, because I had always felt like a hero, a champion. I took this ride with Clifford as another practice run. I imagined chasing faceless enemies around the snow, hunting them down and taking them out.

Clifford had just run me to the edge of the woods when he stopped and growled. I looked up and saw a pale brown winter rabbit darting between the trees. Seconds later, I was on my back, tossed off by Clifford.

I picked myself up and dashed after Clifford into the woods. My imaginary chase had become a very real one, as Clifford ran after the darting rabbit and I followed him.

I was delirious, breathless, happy. Or I was, until the chase ended.

Clifford caught the rabbit in his jaws and reversed course, back to his owners' yard. I was equally dismayed by the end of the pursuit and by the likely end of the rabbit's life, and I now stalked after Clifford, attempting to command the rabbit's release.

'Bad dog,' I said. 'Very bad dog.'

He was too content with his achievement to pay me any mind. Back in his yard, he happily nuzzled and nipped the damp fur of the rabbit. It took shoving him forcibly from the rabbit's body for him to give it up, and even then he snapped at me.

I hissed at Clifford, and he grumpily padded off in the snow. I looked down at the rabbit, matted and bloody.

But it wasn't dead.

All of my hardness gave way as I lifted the light, furry beast to my chest. I felt its tiny heart beating furiously, at the brink of death. Its eyes were glassy, uncomprehending.

I knew what would happen to it. Its wounds were not deep, but it would die of shock. It wasn't dead now, but it was past life. The only thing this creature had to look forward to was the paralysis of its own fear and a slow, cold death.

I looked to the window. Katarina was out of sight. I turned back to the rabbit, knowing in an instant what the kindest thing to do was.

You are a warrior, Katarina had said.

'I am a warrior.' My words turned to frost in the air before my face. I grabbed the gentle creature's neck with both hands and gave it a good hard twist.

I buried the rabbit's corpse deep beneath the snow, where even Clifford couldn't find it.

Katarina was wrong: I have killed before. Out of mercy.

But not yet out of vengeance.

9

Katarina pulls the truck off the dirt road and we get out. It's been a day of straight driving and it's now three in the morning. We're in Arkansas, in the Lake Ouachita State Park. The park entrance was closed so Katarina broke through a chain barrier and snuck the truck in, off-roading in the dark of the woods until we came to the main camp road.

We've been here before, though I don't remember it. Katarina says we camped here when I was much younger, and that she had thought it would make a good burial site for my Chest, if it ever came to that.

It has, apparently, come to that.

Outside the truck I can hear the lake lapping weakly at the shore. Katarina and I walk through the trees, following its sound. I carry the Chest in my arms. We've decided it's too cumbersome and too dangerous to hold on to. Katarina says it must not fall into Mogadorian hands.

I don't press her on this point, though there is a dark implication to this task that haunts me. If Katarina thinks it's come to the point of burying the Chest to keep it safe, then she must think our capture has become likely. Perhaps inevitable.

I shiver in the cool of the night, while swatting mosquitoes away. There are more of them the closer we get to the water's edge.

We finally come to the shore. In the middle of the lake, I see a small green island, and I know Katarina well enough to know what she's thinking.

'I'll do it,' she says. But she only barely gets the words out. She is exhausted, on the brink of collapse. She hasn't slept in days. I've barely slept either, only a few quick minutes here and there in the car. But that's more than Katarina's had, and I know she needs rest.

'Lie down,' I say. 'I'll do it.'

Katarina makes a few weak protests, but before long she's lying on the ground by the shore. 'Rest,' I say. I take the blanket she brought out to use as a towel and instead use it to drape her, to hide her from the mosquitoes.

I strip off my clothes, then grab the Chest tight and step into the water. It's bracing at first, but once I'm submerged it's actually fairly warm. I begin an awkward doggy paddle, using one arm to stroke through the water and the other to clutch the Chest.

I've never swum at night before, and it takes all of my will not to imagine hands reaching up from the murky depths to grab at my legs and pull me under. I stay focused on my goal.

I arrive at the island after what feels like an hour but is more likely ten minutes. I step out of the water, trembling as the air hits my bare skin, and walk awkwardly over the stones littering the shore. I walk to the center of the small island.

It is nearly round, and probably less than an acre, so it doesn't take long to reach.

I dig a hole three feet deep, which takes considerably longer than the swim out. By the end my hands are bleeding from clawing through the rough dirt, stinging more and more with each barehanded shovel through the soil.

I place the Chest in the hole. I am reluctant to let it go, though I have never seen its contents, never even opened it. I consider saying a prayer over it, the source of so much potential and promise.

I decide against praying. Instead, I just kick dirt into the hole until it's covered, and smooth over the mound.

I know I may never see my Chest again.

I return to the water and swim back to Katarina.

10

It's been a week since we arrived in upstate New York. We're at a small motel adjacent to an apple orchard and a neighborhood soccer field. Katarina has been plotting our next move.

There have been no suspicious announcements on the news or on the internet. This gives us some measure of hope for the future of Lorien, and also that the Mogadorians' trail on us has gone cold.

It's silly but I feel ready to fight. I may not have been back at the motel, but I am now. I don't care if I don't have my Legacies. It is better to fight than to run.

'You don't mean that,' she says. 'We must be prudent.'

So we wait. Katarina's heart has gone out of training but we still do as best we can, push-ups and shadowboxing in our room during the day, more elaborate drills out in the unlit corners of the soccer field at night.

During the day I'm allowed to wander through the orchards, smelling the sweet rot of fallen apples. Katarina has told me not to play on the soccer field during the day, or talk to the children who practice on it. She wants to continue to keep a low profile.

But I can watch the field from behind a tree at the edge of the orchard. It's a girls' team playing today. The girls are all in purple jerseys and bright white shorts. They're about my age. From beneath the shade of the apple tree I wonder what it would be like to give myself to something as light and inconsequential as a game of soccer. I imagine I'd be good at it: I love being physical, I'm strong and quick. No: I'd be great at it.

But it's not for me to play games of no value.

I feel envy creep up my throat like bile. It's a new sensation for me. I am usually resigned to my fate. But something about this time on the road, about the near miss with the Mogadorians, has opened me to hating these girls with their easy lives.

But I choke it down. I need to save my spite for the Mogs.

That night we allow ourselves to watch a little TV before bed. It is a luxury Katarina usually denies me, as she thinks it rots my brain and dulls my senses. But even Katarina softens sometimes.

I curl up next to Katarina on the queen bed. She's turned the TV to a movie about a woman who lives in New York City and complains about how hard it is to find a good man. My attention wanders quickly away from the screen to Katarina's face, which has gone soft with attention to the film's plot. She has succumbed to it.

She catches me looking at her, and turns red in an instant. 'I'm allowed to be sappy sometimes.' She turns back to the screen. 'I can't help it. He's handsome.'

I look back at the TV. The woman is now yelling at the

handsome man about how he's a 'sexist pig.' I've seen very few movies in my life but I can already guess how this one ends. The man is handsome, I suppose, though I'm not as transfixed by him as Katarina is.

'Have you ever had a boyfriend?' I ask her.

She laughs. 'Back on Lorien, yes. I was married.'

My heart seizes, and I blush at my own self-absorption. How could I have never asked her this before? How could I not have known that she had a husband, a family? I hesitate before asking another question, because I can only assume her husband died in the Mogadorian invasion.

My heart breaks for my Katarina.

I change the subject. 'But since we've been on Earth?'

She laughs again. 'You've been with me the whole time. I think you'd know if I had!'

I laugh too, though my amusement is mixed with sadness. Katarina couldn't have had a boyfriend even if she wanted one – and it's all because of me. Because she's too busy protecting *me*.

She raises an eyebrow. 'Why so many questions all of a sudden? Do you have a crush? Seen any cute boys out on the soccer field?' She reaches over and pinches my side, tickling me. I squirm away, laughing.

'No,' I say, and it's the truth. Boys practice out there some days and I watch them, but usually just to measure their athleticism and reflexes and to compare them to my own. I don't think I could ever *like* any of them. I don't think I could love anyone who wasn't locked into the struggle with

41

me. I could never respect someone who wasn't part of the war against the Mogs, to save Lorien.

Back on the TV, the woman is standing in the rain, tears streaming down her face, telling the handsome man that she's changed her mind, that love is all that matters after all.

'Katarina?' I ask. She turns to me. I don't even have to say it out loud; she knows me well.

She switches the channels until we find an action movie. We watch it together until we fall asleep.

The next day after drills and studies I make it back out to the orchard. It's a warm day and I dodge from the shade of one tree to another as I stroll. I walk over mushy, sweet-stinking apples, feeling them turn to goop beneath my feet.

Despite the heat of the sun, the air is crisp and pleasant today, not too hot or cold. I feel weirdly happy and hopeful as I tramp around.

Katarina is booking us plane tickets to Australia today. She thinks it'll make as good a hiding place as any. I'm already excited for the journey.

I turn, ready to walk back to the motel, when a soccer ball comes rolling past me, scudding over broken apples. Without thinking I leap forward and hop on it with one foot, stopping it in its tracks.

'You gonna give that back or what?' Startled, I turn around. A pretty girl with a chestnut ponytail stares at me from the edge of the orchard. She's dressed in soccer clothes and her mouth is open, smacking on bubble gum.

I step off the ball, pivot around it, and give it a quick kick, right to the girl. I use more strength than I should: when she clutches it with her hands, the force of the impact nearly sends her off her feet.

'Easy!' she yells.

'Sorry,' I say, instantly ashamed.

'Good kick, though,' says the girl, sizing me up. 'Damn good kick.'

I am on the field moments later. The girls' team was short a player for scrimmage and the gum-chewing girl, Tyra, somehow convinced the coach to let me play.

I don't know the rules of soccer but I pick them up soon enough. I owe Katarina for that, for keeping my brain sharp enough to process rules quickly. The coach, a dour, squat lady with a whistle in her mouth, puts me in as a fullback and I quickly establish myself as a force. The girls on my team catch on fast and soon enough they're putting up a wall, forcing the other team's forwards to run past me on the right side of the field.

Not one of them gets through without losing their hold on the ball.

Before I know it I'm covered in sweat, blades of grass sticking to the sweat on my calves – fortunately, I wore high socks today, so no one can see my scars. I'm dizzy and happy from the sun and the appreciative cheers of my teammates.

There's a reversal to my left. Tyra's seized the ball from a charging opponent before getting chased by another member of the opposing team. I'm the only free player and she manages to kick the ball right at me.

Suddenly, almost the entire opposing team is on my tail. My teammates chase after them, trying to keep them away from me, as I make a mad dash with the ball towards the goal. I can see the goalie steeling herself, ready for my approach. My opponents break free of my blocking teammates. Even though I am still nearly half the field from the box, I know it's my only chance.

I kick.

The ball swings in a long, curving arc, propelled like a jet. I acted too fast, too thoughtlessly, and have aimed right at the goalie's position. I'm sure she'll catch it.

She does. But I've kicked the ball with such power that it lifts her off her feet and the ball goes out of her hands, spinning against the net behind her.

My teammates cheer. Our opponents join in; this was only a scrimmage, so they can acknowledge my skills without sacrificing too much pride.

Tyra gives me a pat on the shoulder. I can tell she's excited about having been the one to coax me out of the orchard. The coach pulls me aside and asks where I go to school. She clearly wants me for her team.

'Not from here,' I mumble. 'Sorry.' She shrugs and congratulates me on my playing.

I grin and walk away from the field. I can tell the girls are eager for my friendship, standing in a cluster and watching me depart. I imagine a different life for myself, a life like theirs. It has its charms, but I know my place is by Katarina's side.

I walk back to the motel, doing my best to wipe the grin of victory off my face. I feel a childish urge to blab about the game to Katarina, even though she told me not to play. In spite of myself I find I'm running back to the room, ready to start crowing.

The door's unlocked and I swing it open, still grinning like an idiot.

The grin doesn't last long.

There are ten men in the room – Mogadorians. Katarina is tied to the motel's desk chair, her mouth gagged and her forehead bloody, her eyes filling with tears at the sight of me.

I turn to run, but then I see them. More men, some in cars, some just standing there, all over the parking lot. There must be thirty Mogadorians total.

We've been caught.

My hands are cuffed and my legs are bound in rope. Katarina's are too, though I can't see her. The Mogadorians threw us in the back of a big rig's trailer, tied together, so the only proof of Katarina I have is the place where our spines touch.

The trailer bucks wildly and I know we are on the highway, going somewhere fast.

Katarina is still gagged, but they never bothered to gag me. Either they sensed I would stay quiet to keep Katarina safe, or they figured the roar of the road would swallow any sound I made.

I don't have any idea where we're being taken or what the Mogadorians plan to do to us once we get there. I assume the worst, but I still murmur soft, soothing things to Katarina in the dark of the trailer. I know she'd be doing the same thing for me if she could.

'It'll be okay,' I say. 'We'll be okay.'

I know we won't. I know with sick certainty that this journey will end in our deaths.

Katarina presses her back against mine, in a gesture of love and encouragement. Hands tied and mouth gagged, it's the only way she can communicate with me.

It's dark in the trailer save for a small sliver of light shining through a break in the trailer's aluminum roof. Sunlight dribbles in through the crack. Sitting in the dark, musty chill of the trailer, it is strange to think it's day outside. Ordinary day.

I'm achy everywhere, sore from sitting and too uncomfortable to sleep. In my exhausted delirium, I have the ridiculous thought that I should've stayed behind with the soccer girls. At least long enough to have some of the Gatorade the coach offered me.

Something murmurs inside the trailer. A low, guttural growl.

There is a cage, tucked up against the front of the trailer. I can dimly make out its thick steel bars in the dark.

'What is it?' I ask. Katarina mumbles through her gagged mouth, and I feel bad for asking her a question she can't possibly answer.

I lean forward, as far as I can, pulling Katarina with me. I can hear Katarina protest from beneath her gag, but curiosity pushes me forward. I stretch into the darkness, bringing my face as close to the steel bars as I can.

Another rustle in the dark.

Another captive? I wonder. Some kind of beast?

My heart fills with pity.

'Hello?' I speak into the void. The person or creature makes low whimpers of distress. 'Are you okay?'

Jaws snap with sudden force against the bars of the cage, eyes the size of fists flashing red in the dark. The breath of the beast sends my hair back. I pull away in terror and disgust, the smell so revolting I almost retch.

I try to scoot away, but the huge beast, unappeased, keeps its head pressed to the bars, its red eyes fixed on me. I know that were it not for the bars, I'd be dead already.

This is no captive. No fallen ally. This is a piken. Katarina told me about these beasts before, savage accomplices and hunters for the Mogadorians, but I had taken them for fairy tales.

Katarina helps me nudge us back towards the rear, giving me more space to pull away from the beast. As I back farther away, so does the piken, disappearing into the dark of its cage.

I know I am safe for the moment. But I also know this animal, this foul, fearsome creature, may be pitted against me in the coming days or weeks. My stomach turns in fear and helpless rage: I don't know whether to vomit or pass out or both.

I nestle my damp head against Katarina's, wishing this nightmare away.

I fall into an agitated half-sleep, awoken only by Katarina's voice.

'Six. Wake up. Six.'

I snap to.

'Your gag?' I ask.

'I worked it off. It's taken this whole time to get it off.'

'Oh,' I say stupidly. I don't know what else to say, what good it does us to speak. We are caught, without defense.

'They bugged our car. Back in Texas. That's how they found us.'

How stupid of us, I think. *How careless.*

'It was my job to think of that,' she says, as if reading my thoughts. 'Never mind that. I need you to prepare for what's coming.'

What's that? I think. *Death?*

'They will torture you for information. They will . . .' I hear Katarina succumb to weeping, but she pulls herself together and resumes. 'They will inflict unthinkable torments on you. But you must bear them.'

'I will,' I say, as firmly as I can.

'They will use me to make you bend. You can't let them . . . no matter what . . .'

My heart freezes in my chest. They will kill Katarina in front of me if they think it will make me talk.

'Promise me, Six. Please . . . they can't know your number. We can't give them any more power over the others than they already have, or power over you. The less they know about the charm, the better. Promise me. You have to.'

Imagining the horrors to come, I can't. I know my vow is all Katarina wants to hear, but I just can't.

13

I have been in my cell for three days. I have nothing in here with me but a bucket of water, another bucket to use as a toilet, and an empty metal tray from yesterday's meal.

There is not a speck of food left on the tray: I licked it clean yesterday. When I woke up in my cell three days ago it had been my intention to mount a hunger strike against my captors, to refuse all food and water until they let me see my Katarina. But two days passed with no food or water from them anyway. I had begun to imagine I'd been forgotten in my cell. By the time the food arrived, I was so far out of my mind with hopelessness that I forgot my original plan and wolfed down the slop they shoved through the little slot of my cell door.

The odd thing is that I wasn't even particularly hungry. My spirits were low but I didn't feel weak from hunger. My pendant throbbed dully against my chest during my days in the dark, and I began to suspect the charm was keeping me safe from hunger and dehydration. But even though I wasn't starving, or dehydrated, I'd never gone so long without food or water in my life, and the experience of being deprived drove me to a kind of temporary madness. I wasn't hungry or thirsty physically, but I was mentally.

The walls are made of heavy, rough stone. It feels less like a prison cell and more like a makeshift burrow. It seems to have been carved out of a natural stone formation instead of built. I take this as a clue that we're in some natural structure: a cave, or the inside of a mountain.

I know I may never find out the answer.

I have attempted to chip at the walls of my cell, but even I know there is nothing I can do. In my attempts, all I accomplished was to wear my nails down until the tips of my fingers bled.

The only thing left now is to sit in my cell and try to hold on to my sanity.

That is my sole mission: to not let my solitary confinement drive me to madness. I can let it harden me, I can let it toughen me, but I must not let it make me crazy. It's a strange challenge, staying sane. If you focus too hard on maintaining your sanity, the slipperiness of the task can only make you crazier. On the other hand, if you forget your mission, if you try to maintain your sanity by not thinking about the matter at all, you can find your mind wandering in such dizzying patterns that you wind up, again, at madness. The trick is to forge a middle ground between the two: a detachment, a state of neutrality.

I focus on my breathing. *In, out. In, out.*

When I'm not stretching or doing push-ups in the corner, this is what I do: just breathe.

In, out. In, out.

Katarina calls this meditating. She used to try to encourage me to do meditation exercises to keep my focus. She felt it would aid me in combat. I never followed her advice. It seemed too boring. But now that I'm in my cell, I find it is a lifeline, the best way for me to keep my sanity.

I am meditating when the door to my cell opens. I turn around, my eyes straining to adjust to the light coming in from the hall. A Mog stands in the light, backed by several others.

I see he's holding a bucket, and for a second I imagine he's brought fresh water for me to drink.

Instead, he steps forward and empties the bucket over my head, dousing me in cold water. It is a harsh indignity and I shiver at the cold, but it's also bracing, restorative. It brings me back to life, back to my pure hatred of these bastard Mogs.

He lifts me off my feet, dripping wet, and wraps a blindfold around my head.

He drops me again and I struggle to stay upright.

'Come,' he says, shoving me out of my cell and into the hall.

The blindfold is thick, so I am walking in total blackness. But my senses are keen and I manage a nearly straight line. I can also sense other Mogs all around me.

As I walk, my feet cold against the rough stone floors, I hear the varied screams and moans of my fellow prisoners. Some are human, some are animal. They must be locked inside cells like mine. I have no idea who they are or what the Mogs want them for. But I am too focused on my survival right now to care: I am deaf to pity.

After a long march, the Mog leading the guard says 'Right!' and shoves me to the right. He shoves me *hard*, and I land on my knees, scraping them against stone.

I struggle to get to my feet, but I am picked up before I can, two Mogs throwing me against a wall. My hands are raised and chained to a steel cord dangling from the ceiling. My torso is stretched, my toes just barely touching the ground.

They remove my blindfold. I'm in another cell; this one is lit, brightly, and my eyes feel like they will burn out adjusting from three days of nearly total darkness. Once they do, I see her.

Katarina.

She is chained to the ceiling, as I am. She looks far worse than me, bloody, bruised, and beaten.

They started with her.

'Katarina,' I whisper. 'Are you okay . . . ?'

She looks up at me, her eyes brimming with tears. 'Don't look at me,' she says, her eyes drifting down to the floor.

A new Mog enters the room. He is wearing, of all things, a white polo shirt and a crisp pair of khaki pants. His haircut is short. His shoes – loafers – scuff quietly across the floor. He could be a suburban dad, or the manager of a neighborhood store.

'Howdy,' he says. He grins at me, his hands in his pockets. His teeth are white like in a toothpaste commercial.

'Hope you're enjoying your stay with us so far.' I notice the bristly hair on his tan arms. He is handsome, in a bland

54

way, with a compact but strong-looking build. 'These caves can be awfully drafty, but we try to make it as cozy as possible. I trust you have two buckets in your cell? Wouldn't want you to go without.'

His hand reaches out so casually that for a second I think he is going to caress my cheek. Instead, he pinches it, hard, giving my flesh a twist. 'You are our guests of honor, after all,' he says, the venom at last creeping into his salesman's voice.

I hate myself for doing it, but I begin to cry. My legs give out entirely, and I dangle hard against my cuffs. I don't allow myself to sob audibly, though: he can see me cry, but I won't let him hear it.

'Okay, ladies,' he says, clapping his hands together and approaching a little desk tucked into the corner of the cell. He opens a drawer and pulls out a vinyl case, which he unwraps on the surface of the desk. The ceiling light glints off an array of sharp steel objects. He picks them up, one at a time, so I can see them all. Scalpels, razors, pliers. Blades of every kind. A pocket-size electric drill. He gives it a few nerve-shattering whirs before putting it down.

He strides over to me, putting his face right up in mine. He speaks, and his breath forces its way into my nostrils. I want to retch.

'Do you see all of these?'

I don't respond. His breath smells like the breath of the beast in the cage. Despite his bland exterior, he's made of the same foul stuff.

'I intend to use each and every one of them on you and your Cêpan, unless you answer every question I ask truthfully. If you don't, I assure you that both of you will wish you were dead.'

He gives a hateful little grin and walks back over to the desk, picking up a thin-looking razor blade with a thick rubber handle. He returns to me, rubbing the dull side of the blade against my cheek. It's cold.

'I've been hunting you kids for a very long time,' he says. 'We've killed two of you, and now we have one right here, whatever number you are. As you might imagine, I hope you are Number Three.'

I try to inch away from him, pressing my back hard against the cell wall, wishing I could disappear into the stone. He smiles at me, again pressing the dull side of the razor into my cheek, harder this time.

'Oops,' he says, tauntingly. 'That's not the right side.'

With a single dexterous motion, he reverses the blade in his wrist, the sharp side now facing me. 'Let's try it this way, shall we.'

With reptilian pleasure he brings the blade to the side of my face and swipes hard against my flesh. I feel a familiar warmth, but no pain, and watch with shock as his own cheek begins to bleed instead.

Blood flows from his wound as it splits open like a seam. He drops the blade, clutching his face, and begins stamping around the room in pain and frustration. He kicks over the desk, sending his instruments of torture scattering across the cell, then flees the room. The Mog guards who'd been standing behind him exchange indecipherable glances.

Before I even have a chance to say anything to Katarina, the Mogs move forward, unshackle me, and drag me back to my cell.

14

Two days pass. In the dark of my cell I now have more than madness and boredom to contend with. I must also work to burn the image of a bloody and broken Katarina from my mind. I want to remember Katarina as I know her: wise and strong.

I continue with my breathing exercises. They help.

But not much.

Eventually the cell door opens, and again I'm doused with cold water, gagged this time, blindfolded, and dragged back to the same cell. Once I've been chained to the ceiling, my blindfold is removed.

Katarina is right where I last saw her, as broken and battered as before. I can only hope she's been let down at some point.

The same Mog as before sits across from us, on the edge of the desk, a bandage across his sliced cheek. I can see he is straining to be as menacing as he was before. But he regards us with a new fear.

I hate him. More than anyone I have ever met. If I could tear him apart with my bare hands I would. If I couldn't use my hands, I would rip him apart with my teeth.

He sees me looking at him. He leaps forward suddenly, tearing the gag from my mouth. He wields the rubber-handled razor in front of my face again, twisting it, letting the ceiling light dance across its edge.

'I don't know what number you are . . .' he says. I cringe involuntarily, expecting him to try and cut me again, but he holds back. Then, with sadistic deliberateness, he crosses over to Katarina, pulling on her hair. Still gagged, she manages only a whimper. 'But you're going to tell me right now.'

'No!' I scream. He grins with satisfaction at my anguish, like he's been waiting for it. He presses the blade to Katarina's arm and slides it down her flesh. Her arm opens up, pouring blood. She buckles against her chains, tears flooding her face. I try to scream but my voice gives out: all that comes out is a high, pained gasp.

He makes another cut beside the first, this one even deeper. Katarina succumbs to the pain and goes limp.

With my teeth, I think.

'I can do this all day,' he says. 'Do you understand me? You're going to tell me everything I want to know, starting with what number you are.'

I close my eyes. My heart burns. I feel like a volcano, only there's no opening, no outlet for the rage filling up inside of me.

When I open my eyes he's back at the desk, tossing a large blade from his left hand to his right hand and back. Playfully, waiting for my gaze. Now that he's got it, he holds the blade up so I can see its size.

It begins to glow in his hands, changing colors: violet one second, green the next.

'Now . . . your number. Four? Seven? Are you lucky enough to be Number Nine?'

Katarina, barely conscious, shakes her head. I know she's signalling me to keep silent. She has kept her silence this long.

I struggle to keep quiet. But I can't handle it, can't watch him hurt my Katarina. My Cêpan.

He walks over to Katarina, still wielding the blade. Katarina murmurs something beneath her gag. Curious, he lowers it from her mouth.

She spits a thick wad of blood onto the floor by his feet. 'Torturing me to get to her?'

He eyes her hatefully, impatient. 'Yes, that's about right.'

Katarina manages a scornful, slow-building laugh. 'It took you *two whole days* to come up with that plan?'

I can see his cheeks turn red at the well-aimed jab. Even Mogadorians have their pride.

'You must be some kind of idiot,' she howls. I thrill at Katarina's impudence, proud of her defiance but afraid of what the consequence will be.

'I have all the time in the galaxies for this,' he says flatly. 'While you are in here with me, we are out there with the rest of you. Don't think anything has stopped us from moving forward just because we have you. We know more than you think. But we want to know everything.'

He cruelly strikes Katarina with the butt of the knife before she can speak again.

He turns to me.

'If you don't want to see her sliced into little pieces, then you better start talking, and fast. And every single word that comes out better be true. I *will* know if you're lying.'

I know he isn't playing games, and I can't bear to see him hurt Katarina again. If I talk, maybe he'll be merciful. Maybe he'll leave her alone.

It comes out so fast I barely have time to order my thoughts, so fast I barely know what I'm saying when I say it. I have one intention, but it's a murky one: to tell him everything I know that he *can't* use against me or the other Loriens. I tell him pointless details about my previous journeys with Katarina, our previous identities. I tell him about my Chest, but I don't give its burial location, claiming it was lost in our journey. Once I start talking I'm afraid to stop. I know that if I pause to measure my words he will smell my deceit.

Then he asks me what number I am.

I know what he wants to hear: that I am number Four. I can't be Three, or else they would have been able to kill me. But if I'm Four then all he'll need is to find and kill Three before he can begin his bloody work on me.

'I am Number Eight,' I say finally. I am so scared as I say it, with a desperate, cringing sigh, that I know that he's fooled. His face falls.

'Sorry to disappoint you,' I croak out.

His disappointment is short-lived. He begins to beam, victorious. I may not be the number he wanted, but he got my number out of me. Or what he thinks is my number.

I search out Katarina's eyes, and though she is barely conscious, I can see the faintest hint of gratitude in her eyes. She is proud of me for giving him the wrong number.

'You really are weak, aren't you?' He stares at me with contempt. Let him, I think. I feel a surge of superiority over him: he was dumb enough to believe my lie.

'Your relatives on Lorien, as easy as they fell, at least they were fighters. At least they had some bravery and dignity. But you . . .' He shakes his head at me, then spits on the floor. 'You have nothing, Number Eight.'

At that, he raises his arm with the blade and thrusts it, deep into Katarina. I hear the sound of bone cracking, of the knife pushing through her sternum, right into her heart.

I scream. My eyes search out Katarina's. She meets my gaze for one last instant. I will myself past my chains towards her, struggling to be there for her in her last moment.

But her last moment goes fast.

My Katarina is dead.

15

Weeks turn into months.

Some days they don't feed me, but my pendant keeps me from dying of thirst or starvation. What's harder is the absence of sunlight, the endless immersion in darkness. Sometimes I lose track of where my body ends and the darkness begins. I lose sense of my own existence, my own borders. I am a cloud of ink in the night. Black on black.

I feel forgotten. Incarcerated, with no hope of escape, and with no information that can lead them to the others, I am useless to them for now. Until they've killed the ones before me, until my extinction date.

The urge to survive has gone dormant in me. I live not because I want to but because I *can't* die. Sometimes, I wish I could.

Even so, I force myself to do the work of staying as fit and limber and as ready for combat as I can. Push-ups, situps, games of Shadow.

In these games of Shadow I have learned to play Katarina's part as well as my own, giving myself instructions, describing my imagined attackers, before I respond with my commands.

I loved this game before, but now I hate it. Still, in Katarina's honor, I continue to play.

As I was lying to the Mog, I thought I was doing it so he would spare Katarina, let her live. But as soon as I saw his knife pierce her heart I realized what I was *really* doing: hastening her end. I was giving him everything I knew so he would finish her off, so she wouldn't have to suffer anymore, so I wouldn't have to *watch* her suffer anymore.

I tell myself that was the right thing to do. That it's what Katarina would've wanted. She was in such pain.

But I've been without her so long at this point that I would give anything for another moment with her, even if she had to suffer unimaginable torments for it. I want her back.

The Mogadorians continue to test the boundaries of my conditional immortality. These trials take time to plan and construct. But every week or so I am dragged out of my cell and brought to another, jury-rigged for my destruction.

The first week after Katarina's death I was brought to a small chamber and made to stand on a sharp steel grill several feet off the floor. The door was sealed behind me. I waited for a few minutes as the room filled with noxious-looking gas, curling up from beneath the grill in green tendrils. I covered my mouth, trying not to breathe it, but I could only hold my breath for so long. I gave up, gulping in their poison, only to discover it smelled like the coolest and freshest of mountain breezes to me. Furious Mogs dragged me out of the room minutes later, pushing me quickly back to my cell, but I could see the pile of dust beside the door on the way out. The Mog who had pushed the button releasing the gas had died in my place.

The next week they tried to drown me; the week after, they tried burning me alive. None of these affected me, of course. Last week, they served me food laced so heavily with arsenic I swear I could taste each poison grain. They had brought a cake to my cell. They had no reason to treat me with dessert, and I knew at once that it was their hope to trick me with the cake – and in turn trick the charm. They hoped that if I didn't know my life was in danger, the charm wouldn't work.

Of course I suspected them at once.

But I ate the cake anyway. It was delicious.

By eavesdropping against the slot of my cell door, I later learned that not one but three Mogadorians perished from the attempted poisoning.

How many Mogadorians does it take to bake a cake? I asked myself later. Then, with malevolent satisfaction, I answered: *Three.*

I allow myself to imagine a happy outcome in which the Mogadorians, who seem to place little value even on their own lives, keep trying to kill me and end up dying in the attempt, until there are no Mogadorians left. I know it is just a fantasy, but it's a happy one.

I have no idea how long I've been here. But I have grown so hardened to their execution attempts that I am fearless as they drag me through the halls to yet another. This time I am thrown into a large, drafty space with dim lights, larger than any room I've been in so far. I know I am being watched through one-way glass or a video monitor, so I wear my face in a sneer. A sneer that reads: Bring it on.

Then I hear it. A low, guttural moan. It's so deep I can feel it, rattling through the floor. I whirl around to see, deep in the shadows of the room, a large steel cage. It looks familiar.

I hear jaws snapping hungrily, followed by the sounds of massive lips smacking.

The piken. The beast from our trip out here.

Now I am scared.

There's a bright flash. Suddenly I'm bathed in strobing red lights, and the steel bars of the cage retract.

Weaponless, I fall back against the opposite corner of the room.

Clever, I think. *The Mogs have never pitted me against a living creature before.*

The piken steps out. A four-legged monster, it stands like a bulldog the size of a rhino: forelegs bowed, mouth all dripping, sagging jowls. Massive teeth jut from its mouth like tusks. Its skin is a putrid, knobby green. It smells of death.

It roars at me, drenching me in a spittle so thick I fear I will slip on it. Then it charges.

I can't believe my own body. I'm stiff from solitary confinement, I haven't practiced combat in months, but instinct and adrenaline kick in, and soon enough I am dodging the beast like a pro, careening off corners, ducking between its legs.

The piken roars, frustrated, getting more and more worked up, battering the walls with its head.

I haven't had this much fun in years, I think, as I manage to give it a roundhouse kick across the face.

I land on the ground, beaming from my well-placed kick, but I land in one of its spit puddles and my arms and legs give out in the slime. It's a momentary lapse, but it's enough: The beast has me in its jaws.

My whole body floods with warmth, and I am sure that this is the end.

But no pain comes. The creature lets out a long whimper and then releases me from its jaws. It's a five-foot drop from its mouth to the floor and I land on my knee, which hurts worse than the bite.

I turn to see the piken sprawled out, mouth open, chest heaving powerfully. A massive crescent of puncture wounds stud its chest. It took the brunt of its own bite.

It lets out another low, pitiful moan.

Of course, I think. A Mogadorian beast is as much a Mogadorian as any of the rest. It's susceptible to the charm too.

I whirl around, trying to get the attention of whoever is watching. It is clear to me that the creature, though wounded, will live. Left to their own devices, the Mogs will nurse their beast back to health so it can live to spoil another day.

I stride over to it, remembering the rabbit I killed all those years ago in Nova Scotia. I hear the footsteps of approaching guards and know I must act fast.

67

A Mog guard bursts into the room. He wields a long blade, and is about to swing at me when he thinks twice, realizing he will only kill himself in the process.

I use his hesitation to my advantage. I leap off the ground and hit him with a high swing kick, his blade clattering to the floor. One more kick to keep him down, and then I swipe the blade from the floor.

I approach the heaving, panting beast as more guards enter the room and I bring the blade straight down, through the piken's skull.

Dead in an instant.

The guards swarm around me and drag me out of the cell. I am dazed but happy.

No mercy.

16

I have come to appreciate the tiny differences in the food they serve me. It's always the same gray slop, some protein and wheat blended into a paste and ladled onto my serving tray. But sometimes it is made with more water and less wheat, more wheat and less protein, etc.

Today is a heavy protein day. I swallow it down without joy but with some gratitude: my muscles still hurt from my battle with the piken and the guard, and I figure the protein will do me good.

I take my last bite and back into the corner.

It is dark in my cell, but there is just enough light from the foodslot that I can see my feet, and my hands, and my food tray.

Except today I can't see my hand. I can see my left one, but not my right one.

It has taken a long time to hone my vision to this state of sensitivity in the dark, so I'm furious at its failure. I wave my right hand in front of my face, twisting it left and right in my sleeve. But still all I see is darkness. I slap my face, blink, trying to bring my vision back.

But still my right hand is a void.

Finally I reach down and pick up my fork, holding it in front of my face.

I feel a thrill in my stomach as I push it down into my hand. I don't want any false hope. I know I can't *survive* any false hope.

But I can see the fork. *And I still can't see my hand.*

At that moment my cell door opens and a lowly Mog enters. He's come to retrieve my serving tray. All it takes is the light from the hallway flooding the room to confirm my suspicion.

My right hand is invisible.

My first Legacy has arrived.

I gasp. Of all the skills I could develop, this seems like the one – the only one – that might get me out of this prison alive.

The Mog grunts at me suspiciously, and I tuck my hollow-looking sleeve behind my back, hoping he didn't see. I am dizzy with joy.

He's a stupid one, and doesn't notice a thing. He lifts my tray from the floor and exits the room.

I am plunged back into darkness, and wait impatiently for my eyes to adjust to the point where I can see my new ability again. There it is. Hollow sleeve, invisible hand. I roll up my sleeve and look at my arm. My hand is completely invisible, my forearm milky, nearly translucent, but by my elbow I'm fully visible.

I can see I'll need to practice this skill.

17

It has taken two days, but I have learned to wield my first Legacy. My control is not perfect yet: sometimes my invisibility stutters, and I panic, struggling to restore it. Turning it off and on is not like turning a light switch up or down; it takes a certain kind of concentration.

Katarina's breathing exercises have come in handy. When I struggle to control my invisibility, I turn my focus to my breathing – *in, out* – and then back to the ability. After I'm able to make my hand invisible at will, I start practicing with other parts of my body. It's like flexing a new muscle – it feels strange at first but quickly feels natural. Next, I let my whole body fade out. It's no more difficult than making my hand disappear; in fact, it seems to take less precision.

I am ready.

I go fully invisible and wait for the next food drop. It takes some of my energy to maintain the invisibility, energy I wish I could conserve, but I have only that single instant for my snare to work and I can't risk them seeing me transform.

Finally, a Mog appears. The food slot opens, the tray is tossed in. It shuts.

I worry the snare hasn't worked. Maybe the Mogs don't

bother to check on me, to look for me in my cell? In which case my power is totally useless —

The slot opens again. Two beady eyes peer into the shadows, squinting.

In, out. Sometimes nerves can send me back into visibility and I can't spoil this moment. *In, out.* The worst-case scenario is them discovering my power before I can use it against them.

It is a strange thing, willing someone to see my absence.

The slot closes again. I hear the Mog walk away and my heart plummets. *Where'd he go? Didn't he notice that I'm not here —*

The door opens suddenly. Soon, my tiny cell is filled with Mogadorian guards, four in total. I press myself against the far corner, hiding. They are huddled close, conferring about my apparent disappearance. *No way out.*

One leaves and runs down the hall. His exit creates more space in the room, less chance that someone will stumble onto me, and I breathe easier.

One of them whirls his arm in frustration, and I have to duck as quickly as I can. He barely misses me. Close call.

I dodge, quiet as a cat, into the corner nearest the door. Two of the Mogs stand deep in the cell, but one of them blocks the exit.

Move, I think. *Move.*

I can hear footsteps, racing towards the cell. More Mogs. I know that all it will take is one Mog brushing my shoulder or sensing my breath for me and my new Legacy to be discovered. The footsteps are getting closer. The Mog by the door steps further into the cell to accommodate those on their way and I lunge out into the hallway.

I nearly fall on the stone floor outside my cell, but I catch my balance just in time. Flesh slapping against stone: I surely would've been discovered.

A horde of Mogs is racing down the hall towards my cell from the left. No choice but to run right. I take off, landing as delicately as I can. *Quiet as a cat.*

It is a long hall. I struggle to maintain quiet, my bare feet making only the faintest of noises as I run and run and run. At first I am scared, but then I can feel it: freedom, up ahead.

I go faster, landing on arched feet to mute the noise. My heart leaps up into my chest as I exit the hall and find myself in the center of the Mogadorian complex, a massive cavern fed by many other tunnels like the one I just came from. Closed-circuit security cameras are everywhere. When I spot them, my chest leaps with fear, but then I remember I am invisible, to cameras as well as to Mogs.

For how long, I don't know.

A siren is pulled. I should've expected that. Flashing security lights go off as the cavern is filled with the alarm's shriek. The high walls of the cave only amplify it.

I take off again, choosing a tunnel at random.

I pass other cells like mine, then steel doors that probably hold more prisoners.

I wish I had time to help them. But all I can do is run, and keep running, as long as my invisibility will hold.

I dodge left off the tunnel, passing a large, glass-windowed room to my right. It is illuminated by bright fluorescents. Inside hundreds and hundreds of computers in rows hum and sift data, no doubt looking for signs of my fellow Garde. I keep running.

I pass another laboratory, also glass-windowed, this one to my left. Mogadorians in white plastic suits and goggles stand inside. Scientists? Bomb chemists? I am past them before I have a chance to see what they're doing. I can only assume something awful.

My brain is split by the siren, and I want to close my ears. But I need my hands to keep my balance as I run, to keep my footsteps dainty and soundless. I have the strange thought that for all my bluntness, my tomboyishness, my warrior's training, I now find myself calling on such a feminine skill — being lightfooted, like a ballerina.

The tunnel feeds into another center, this one even larger than the other. I had assumed that what I saw earlier was the heart of the complex, but this is truly it: a cavernous hall half a mile wide and so dark and murky I can barely see across to the other side.

I am covered in sweat, out of breath. It is hot in here. The walls and ceiling are lined with huge wooden trellises keeping the cave from collapsing in on itself. Narrow ledges chiseled into the rock face connect the tunnels dotting the dark walls. Above me, several long arches have been carved from the mountain itself to bridge the divide from one side to the other.

I catch my breath and wipe my brow, to keep my own sweat from blinding me.

There are so many tunnels, none of them marked. My heart plummets. I realize I could run and run through this complex for days without finding the way out. I imagine myself like a rat in a laboratory maze, scampering and weaving to no avail.

Then I see it: a single pinprick of natural light, up above. There must be a way out up there. It will be a steep climb up these walls, but I can do it. As I grab the trellis to hoist myself up, I hear it.

'She *will* be found.'

It's him. Katarina's executioner.

He is speaking to a few guard Mogs, on a walkway above me. The guards tramp off. My eyes pin to the executioner as he takes a detour back into the complex.

I must choose. Between escape and vengeance. The light above beckons me like water in a desert. I wonder exactly how long it's been since I last saw sunlight.

But I turn around.

I choose vengeance.

18

I follow him through the halls on tiptoe, careful to maintain my invisibility – I've learned enough about my Legacy by now to know that any surprise or break in concentration can cause me to fade back in.

I watch as he ducks into a cell. I sneak in behind him as the door shuts.

Unaware he has company, he walks to the corner of the room and begins to tidy up. I look down. There is blood on the floor, his weapons are out. He has tortured and killed others.

I have never killed a Mogadorian before. Not counting the Mogadorians who died trying to kill me, I have only in my entire life killed a rabbit, and a piken. To my own shock, I realize I am *thirsty* for murder.

I grab a razor from his desk and approach him. The blade feels good in my hand. It feels *right*.

I know better than to give him a chance to beg, or plead, to shake me from my resolve. I clutch him from behind and slit his throat with one clean slice. His mouth gurgles and spews blood across the floor, against my hands. He falls to his knees and then bursts into ash.

I feel more alive than I've ever felt.

I open my mouth to speak. *That's for Katarina,* I'm about to say. But I don't.

I don't speak because I know it's a lie.

That wasn't for Katarina. That was *for me*.

I emerge from the complex an hour later, exhausted and struggling to stay invisible as I climb out to the mountain-top, as I run from the mountain to a hill opposite. I have to stop to rest, to adapt to the blinding midday sun.

My translucent skin bakes beneath the sun. I stare at the mouth of the complex, already hard to make out from this distance. I don't trust my memory, so I pause to memorize its shape, its precise location.

I am sure Mogs have fanned out through the complex, looking for me. And I'm sure they have crawled out of the exit, and are even right now searching through the trees along these hills.

Let them look.

They'll never find me.

I run for a few miles through trees, until I come to a road in a small mining town. I'm running barefoot, so the road slaps hard against my feet, killing my joints. I don't care; I'll get a pair of sneakers eventually.

I find a truck idling at the town's only stoplight. I lightly hop into the back of the pickup, letting the truck take me farther and farther away from the Mogadorian complex. When the trucker stops for gas a few hours later, I dash, still invisible, into the cab, rifling through his stuff. I take a handful of quarters, a pen, a couple scraps of paper, and an uneaten bag of barbecue chips.

I run behind the gas station and sit in the shade. I draw a map of the complex's entrance on one side of the paper, and a diagram of the tunnels inside as best as I can remember. It will be a long time before I put this to use, but I know my memory of their hideaway is the most valuable thing I possess, and it must be preserved.

Once I finish the diagram, I throw my head back. It's sunset, but I can still feel of the warmth of the sun on my face. I open the bag of chips and eat them in three messy bites. The salty-sweet chips taste delicious, wonderful.

I am in a motel room, at long last. For a full day I wandered, driven by the urge for shelter and rest. There was no way I could afford a room, and in my desperation I began to consider thievery. Pick a few pockets, plunk down the cash I'd need. Using my Legacy, stealing would be a piece of cake.

But then it occurred to me I wouldn't need to steal, not yet anyway. Instead I went into the lobby of a small motel, went invisible, and snuck into the hotel manager's office. I lifted the key for room 21 off the hook. I wasn't sure how I was going to get the floating key past the crowded lobby and I paused for a moment, frozen in the office. But soon the key disappeared too, in my palm.

I'd never made an object disappear before, only myself and my clothes. A hint of my Legacy's other uses.

I've been in the room for a couple of hours. So I feel less like I'm thieving, I sleep above the covers, in the chill of the room's AC.

I catch myself: I've been invisible the whole time I've been in the room, clenched from the exertion of sustaining it. It's like holding your breath.

I get up and approach the mirror across the room, letting it go. My body fills in in the mirror, and I see my face for the first time in over seven months.

I gasp.

The girl who stares back at me is almost unrecognizable. I'm hardly even a girl anymore.

I stare at myself for a long time, standing alone in the room, unattended, unaccompanied, aching for Katarina, aching for a worthy tribute to her.

But it's right there. In the new hardness and definition of my face, in the muscled curve of my arm. I am a woman now, and I am a warrior. Her love and the loss of her is etched forever in the firm set of my jaw.

I am her tribute. Survival is my gift to her.

Satisfied, I return to the motel bed and sleep for days.

19

Years have passed.

I live an unsettled life, hopping from town to town. I avoid connections or ties, and focus on developing my fighting abilities and developing my Legacies. Invisibility was followed by telekinesis, and in recent months I've discovered a new ability: I can control and manipulate the weather.

I use that Legacy sparingly, as it's an easy way to attract unwanted attention. It manifested months ago, in a small suburb outside Cleveland. I had been following a lead on one of the Garde that didn't go anywhere and, discouraged, I was ambling back towards my motel, sipping an iced coffee. My leg burst into searing pain, and I dropped my drink on the ground.

My third scar. Three was dead.

I fell to the ground in pain and in rage, and before I knew what was happening the sky above me filled with clouds. A full-on lightning storm followed.

I am in Athens, Georgia, now. It's a cool little city, one of the best I've passed through in the past couple of years. College students everywhere. I've got a bit of a vagabond roughness to my appearance that stands out in suburban areas, but surrounded by college-age hippies and music nerds and hipsters I don't look quite so unusual. This makes me feel safe.

All of my leads have gone dead, and I have yet to discover one of my kind. But I know it is coming. Time to assemble the Garde. If my Legacies are developing at this rate, I am certain the same is true of the others like me. There will be signs soon, I can feel it.

I am patient, but excited: I am ready to fight.

I wander the street, sipping the dregs of an iced coffee. It's become my drink of choice. I have resorted to pickpocketing to finance my appetites, but it's become so easy that I never have to outright fleece anyone. I just take a few bucks here or there to get by.

I am suddenly knocked by a gust of wind, practically off my feet. For a second I think I've lost control, that it's my own power that caused it. But the wind ends as soon as it began, and I realize it did not come from me. But it has swung the door of another café open.

I almost keep walking, but my eye is caught by an open computer terminal at the back of the café. I use internet cafés to keep tabs on the news, looking for items that could turn into a lead on my kind. Doing it makes me feel closer to Katarina. I have become my own Cêpan.

I chuck my empty cup in the trash outside and step into the air-conditioned chill of the place. I take my seat, and begin scanning the news.

An item from Paradise, Ohio, catches me. A teenager was

seen leaping from a burning building. New to town. Named John. The reporter mentioned how hard it was to get solid information on him.

I stand up so quickly I send the chair flying out from under me. I know in an instant he's one of us, though I don't know *how* I know. Something in that gust of wind. Something about the way butterflies are now fluttering in my stomach, brushing my insides with their wings.

Perhaps this recognition is a part of the charm, something that lets us know that a hunch is *more* than a hunch. I know.

I just know.

My heart races with excitement. He's out there. One of the Garde.

I run out of the café and onto the street. Left, right . . . I'm not sure which way to turn, how to get to Paradise as quickly as I can.

I take a deep breath.

It's beginning, I think. *It's finally beginning.*

I laugh at my own paralysis. I remember that the bus station is a mile down the road. I make a habit of memorizing all transport routes into and out of any town I visit, and the bus route out of Athens returns to my mind. The beginning of a plan to get to Paradise starts to develop.

I turn and begin the walk to the station.

I AM NUMBER FOUR
The Lost Files
Nine's Legacy

There are rules for hiding in plain sight. The first rule, or at least the one that Sandor repeats most often, is 'Don't be stupid.'

I'm about to break that rule by taking off my pants.

Spring in Chicago is my favorite season. The winters are cold and windy, the summers hot and loud, the springs perfect. This morning is sunny, but there's still a forbidding chill in the air, a reminder of winter. Ice-cold spray blows in off Lake Michigan, stinging my cheeks and dampening the pavement under my sneakers.

I jog all eighteen miles of the lakefront path every morning, taking breaks whenever I can, not because I need them, but to admire the choppy gray-blue water of Lake Michigan. Even when it's cold, I always think about diving in, of swimming to the other side.

I fight the urge just like I fight the urge to keep pace with the neon spandex cyclists that zip past. I have to go slow. There are more than two million people in this city and I'm faster than all of them.

Still, I have to jog.

Sometimes, I make the run twice to really work up a sweat.

That's another one of Sandor's rules for hiding in plain sight: always appear to be weaker than I actually am. Never push it.

It's dumb to complain. We've been in Chicago for five years thanks to Sandor's rules. Five years of peace and quiet. Five years since the Mogadorians last had a real bead on us.

Five years of steadily increasing boredom.

So when a sudden vibration stirs the iPod strapped to my upper arm, my stomach drops. The device isn't supposed to react unless trouble is near.

I take just a moment to decide on what I do next. I know it's a risk. I know it flies against everything I've been told to do. But I also know that risks are worth it; I know that sometimes you have to ignore your training. So I jog to the side of the runner's path, pretending that I need to work out a cramp. When I'm finished stretching, I unsnap the tear-away track pants I've been rocking every jog since we moved to Chicago and stuff them into my pack. Underneath I'm wearing a pair of mesh shorts, red and white like the St Louis Cardinals, enemy colors here in Chicago.

But Cards colors in Cubs territory are nothing to worry about compared to the three scars ringing my ankle. Baseball rivalries and bloody interplanetary vendettas just don't compare.

My low socks and running shoes do little to hide the scars. Anyone nearby could see them, although I doubt my fellow runners are in the habit of checking out each other's ankles. Only the particular runner I'm trying to attract today will really notice.

When I start jogging again, my heart is beating way harder than normal. Excitement. It's been a while since I felt anything like this. I'm breaking Sandor's rule and it's exhilarating. I just hope he isn't watching me through the city's police cameras that he's hacked into. That would be bad.

My iPod rumbles again. It's not actually an iPod. It doesn't play any music and the earbuds are just for show. It's a gadget that Sandor put together in his lab.

It's my Mogadorian detector. I call it my iMog.

The iMog has its limitations. It picks out Mogadorian genetic patterns in the immediate area, but only has a radius of a few blocks and is prone to interference. It's fueled by Mogadorian genetic material, which has a habit of rapidly decaying; so it's no surprise that the iMog can get a little hinky. As Sandor explains it, the device is something we received when we first arrived from Lorien, from a human Loric friend. Sandor has spent considerable time trying to modify it. It was his idea to encase it in an iPod shell as a way to avoid attention. There's no track list or album art on my iMog's screen – just a solitary white dot against a field of black. That's me. I'm the white dot. The last time we tuned it up was after the most recent time we were attacked, scraping Mogadorian ash off our clothes so Sandor could synthesize it or stabilize it or some scientific stuff I only half paid attention to. Our rule is that if the iMog sounds off, we get moving. It's been so long since it's activated itself that I'd started to worry that the thing had gone dead.

And then, during my run a couple of days ago, it went off. One solitary red dot trolling the lakefront. I hustled home that day, but I didn't tell Sandor what had happened. At best, there'd be no more runs on the lakefront. At worst, we'd be packing up boxes. And I didn't want either of those things to happen.

Maybe that's when I first broke the 'don't be stupid' rule. When I started keeping things from my Cêpan.

The device is now vibrating and beeping because of the red dot that's fallen into step a few yards behind me. Vibrating and beeping in tune with my accelerated heartbeat.

A Mogadorian.

I hazard a glance over my shoulder and have no trouble picking out which jogger is the Mog. He's tall, with black hair shaved close to the scalp, and is wearing a thrift-store Bears sweatshirt and a pair of wraparound sunglasses. He could pass for human if he wasn't so pale, his face not showing any color even in this brisk air.

I pick up my pace but don't bother trying to get away. Why make it easy on him? I want to see whether this Mog can keep up.

By the time I exit the lakefront and head for home, I realize I might have been a little cocky. He's good – better than I expect him to be. But I'm better. Still, as I pick up speed, I feel my heart racing from exertion for the first time in as long as I can remember.

He's gaining on me, and my breaths are getting shorter. I'm okay for now, but I won't be able to keep this up forever. I double-check the iMog. Luckily my stalker hasn't called in backup. It's still just the one red dot. Just us.

Tuning out the noise of the city around us – yuppie couples headed to brunch, happy tourist families cracking jokes about the wind – I focus on the Mog, using my naturally enhanced hearing to listen to his breathing. He's getting winded too; his breathing is ragged now. But his footsteps are still in sync with my own. I listen for anything that sounds like him going for a communicator, ready to break into a sprint if he sends out an alert.

He doesn't. I can feel his eyes boring into my back. He thinks that I haven't noticed him.

Smug, exhausted, and dumb. He's just what I'd been hoping for.

The John Hancock Center rises above us. The sun blinks off the skyscraper's thousand windows. One hundred stories and, at the top, my home.

The Mog hesitates as I breeze through the front door, then follows. He catches up to me as I cross the lobby. Even though I'd been expecting it, I stiffen when I feel the cold barrel of a small Mogadorian blaster pressed between my shoulder blades.

'Keep walking,' he hisses.

Although I know he can't hurt me while I'm protected by the Loric charm, I play along. I let him think he's in control.

I smile and wave at the security guards manning the front desk. With the Mog dogging my heels, we climb into the elevator.

Alone at last.

The Mog keeps his gun aimed at me as I hit the button for

89

the 100th floor. I'm more nervous than I thought I'd be. I've never been alone with a Mog before. I remind myself that everything is going just as I planned it. As the elevator begins its ascent, I act as casual as I can.

'Did you have a nice run?'

The Mog grabs me around the throat and slams me against the wall of the elevator. I brace myself to have the wind knocked out of me. Instead, a warm sensation runs down my back and it's the Mog who stumbles backward, gasping.

The Loric charm at work. I'm always surprised at how well it works.

'So you aren't Number Four,' he says.

'You're quick.'

'Which are you?'

'I *could* tell you.' I shrug. 'I don't see what it would matter. But I'll let you guess.'

He eyes me, sizing me up, trying to intimidate me. I don't know what the rest of the Garde are like, but I don't scare that easy. I take off the iMog, laying it gently on the floor. If the Mog finds this unusual, he doesn't let on. I wonder what the prize is for capturing a Garde. 'I may not know your number, but I know you can look forward to a life of captivity while we kill the rest of your friends. Don't worry,' he adds, 'it won't be long.'

'Good story,' I reply, glancing up at the elevator panel. We're almost at the top.

I dreamed about this moment last night. Actually, that's not quite right. I couldn't sleep last night, too keyed up for what was to come. I fantasized about this moment.

I make sure to savor my words.

'Here's the thing,' I tell him. 'You're not making it out of here alive.'

2

Before the Mog can react, I punch a series of buttons on the elevator panel. It's a sequence of buttons that no one in the tower would ever have reason to push, a sequence that Sandor programmed to initiate the security measures he installed into the elevator.

The elevator vibrates. The trap is activated.

My iMog floats off the floor and, with a metallic clang, sticks to the back wall of the elevator. Before the Mog can blink, he's flung backward too, pulled by the blaster in his hand and whatever other metal objects he might be hiding in his pockets. With a crunch, his hand is pinned between his blaster and the wall. He cries out.

Did he really think we wouldn't have protected our home?

The powerful magnet Sandor installed in the elevator is just one of the fail-safes my Cêpan secretly built into the John Hancock Center. I've never seen the magnet work as intended before, but I've definitely screwed around with it enough. I've spent hours with the elevator door wedged open, the magnet on, trying to bounce nickels from across the penthouse and get them to stick to the walls. Like I said, things have been kind of boring lately.

It was a good game until the tenants on the lower levels started complaining.

The Mog tries to wiggle his fingers – which are most certainly broken now – from underneath the blaster to no avail. He tries to kick at me, but I just laugh and hop away. That's the best he can do?

'What is this?' he cries.

Before I can answer, the elevator doors hiss open and there is Sandor.

I've never understood my Cêpan's affinity for expensive Italian suits. They can't be comfortable. Yet here he is, not even noon on a Saturday morning, and he's already dressed to the nines. His beard is freshly trimmed, clipped close. His hair is slicked back perfectly.

It's like Sandor was expecting company. I wonder if he was watching my run on the lakefront, and my stomach drops at the thought.

I'm going to be in deep trouble.

Sandor is twisting a silencer into the barrel of a sleek 9mm. He glances at me, his expression inscrutable, then stares hard at the Mog.

'Are you alone?'

The Mog jerks against the magnet again.

'He's alone,' I answer.

Sandor shoots me a look, and then pointedly repeats his question.

'You expect me to answer that?' snarls the Mog.

I can tell Sandor is pissed. But the Mog's answer causes a glimmer of humor to flash in my Cêpan's eyes. Sandor's mouth twitches, like he's fighting a laugh. I've sat through enough of my Cêpan's beloved James Bond movie collection to know this Mog just provided a perfect one-liner opportunity.

'No,' Sandor says. 'I expect you to die.'

Sandor raises the gun before looking at me again.

'You brought him here,' he says. 'Your kill.'

I swallow hard. I planned this whole thing out. It's been all I could think about since that red dot appeared on my iMog a couple days ago. Still, I've never killed one before. I don't feel sympathy for the bastard. It's not that at all. But this feels like a big deal. Taking a life, even if it is only a Mogadorian. Will it change me?

Whatever. I grab for Sandor's gun, but he yanks it away.

'Not like that,' he says, and drops the gun.

I don't let it hit the ground. My telekinesis developed last month and we've been practicing with it ever since.

I take a deep breath, focusing my mind, steeling myself. I levitate the gun until it is level with the Mog's head. He sneers at me.

'You don't have the ba —'

With my mind, I squeeze the trigger.

The gun releases a muffled *thwip*. The bullet strikes the Mog right between the eyes. Seconds later, he's a pile of ash on the elevator floor.

Sandor plucks the gun out of the air. I can tell he's studying me, but I can't take my eyes off the remains of the Mogadorian.

'Clean that mess up,' says Sandor. 'Then, we need to talk.'

3

I clean up what remains of the Mog as quickly as I can, not wanting to deal with building security wondering what's keeping the elevator. I scoop some of the ash into a plastic sandwich bag for Sandor. He might want it for one of his experiments.

For some reason, my hands won't stop shaking.

I figure it's because I'm rushing, that the shaking will stop once I'm done cleaning the elevator, but it doesn't. It only gets worse. I stagger out of the elevator into the living room of our penthouse, and collapse onto a white suede couch.

Yes, I killed the Mog. Yes, it was even easier than I thought it would be. But it didn't feel how I thought it would. Something could have gone wrong.

I can't shake the feeling of that Mog's fingers on my throat. Even though he couldn't hurt me, the sensation lingers. As the adrenaline drains away, all I can think about is what a stupid idea it was to engage the Mog. I'd wanted some action. I tried to be suave like the spies in those Bond movies. I think I put up a good front, not that the Mog will ever be able to tell anyone how badass I acted.

My head swims as I gaze up at the gold chandelier that

presides over the living room. I put this whole place at risk. Everything we've amassed in our years of safety, our home. Most importantly, Sandor himself. I don't feel like celebrating; I feel like puking.

Even now, Sandor could be packing our bags. We could be headed back on the road.

Before Chicago, all we did was travel. It was always hotels and motels. Sandor never wanted to put down roots. He's not much of a housekeeper – doesn't cook or clean – our needs were fulfilled by grouchy maids and room service. We spent a couple of months at the Ritz-Carlton in Aspen. I learned to ski. Sandor spent his time charming snow bunnies next to the fire. We spent some time in South America, eating the best steaks in the world. Our cover story was always the same as it is here in Chicago: Sandor is a day trader who hit a hot streak and now lives comfortably, and I'm his latchkey nephew.

I liked Aspen. It was good to be outdoors without having to worry about a crush of people and which ones might be hostile aliens.

After Aspen it was a roach motel on the outskirts of Denver. I learned to judge how safe Sandor thought we were by the luxuriousness of our accommodations. Although we could afford to live anywhere, thanks to the precious gems the nine Cêpans had left Lorien with, nice hotels meant Sandor thought we were safe enough to live it up a little; flea-bitten rattraps meant it was more important to lie low.

If I'm being honest, I liked that place too. That was where Sandor tinkered with the vibrating bed, making it powerful enough to almost toss me to the ceiling.

We moved whenever the hotel staff got to know us too well. As soon as we became a fixture, it was time to move on.

That never helped. The Mogs always caught up with us.

The last stop before Chicago was at a trucker motel in Vancouver. I still don't know how we got away that time. It was bad. Five Mogs took us by surprise there. Sandor had built weapons to keep us safe – flash bombs to blind the Mogs, a remote-control helicopter with a very real gun attached – and still we were almost overwhelmed. Sandor got slashed by one of their daggers during the fight and barely had the strength to drive us south to White Rock. There, I sat by his bedside for a week while he slipped in and out of consciousness, his fever bad enough that I thought he might have set the sheets on fire if they weren't so soaked with his sweat.

When he came to, Sandor decided there'd be no more running.

'We're going to try something different,' he told me. 'We've got the money. Might as well use it.'

I didn't know what he meant.

'We're going to hide in plain sight.'

And we used the money. The two-floor penthouse Sandor purchased in the John Hancock Center is like something out of that reality TV show where the celebrities show off their glamorous houses.

As if installing a fish tank over their king-sized bed is going to help them when the Mogadorian invasion comes. Nothing wrong with fish tanks and hot tubs, but none of that stuff's any good without weapons.

I know Sandor loves it in Chicago – and so do I. But sometimes I miss those days on the road. Sometimes it seems like we should be doing more than just training. The half-dozen flat-screen televisions, the personal chef, the fully equipped gym; all this has only made me feel soft.

Now, though, watching the sun glint off the angles of the chandelier, I realize how badly I don't want to leave this place. I rushed things. Yes, I want to take my place with the other Garde. I want to kill every Mog I can find. But for as restless as I've felt lately, I should probably try to enjoy my home for as long as I still have one. Eventually, my life will be nothing but fighting. Am I ready for that?

I take a deep breath and pick myself up. The panic I felt before is gone, replaced by a sense of dread.

I head down the hall to Sandor's workshop to face the music.

4

When I walk into his workshop, Sandor is glued to an array of
flat-screen monitors behind his desk. Various camera feeds
from around the city are on display, archived footage from
this morning frozen in time. I'm not surprised to see that
I'm on every screen, the Mog from the lakefront visible behind
me. With a few quick keystrokes, Sandor deletes the video
files, erasing my exploits from Chicago's memory banks.
When he's finished with his hacking, there will be no evidence
left of what I did this morning.

Sandor swivels around to face me. 'I get why you did it,
dude. I really do.'

My Cêpan peers at me, an array of frayed circuit boards
and dismembered computer parts spread out on the desk
between us. Stacks of unfinished or abandoned projects
leave only a narrow path of floor between door and desk;
half-finished automatons, tricked-out weapons plucked
from our arsenal, gutted car engines, and dozens of things I
can't even identify. Sandor loves his toys, which is probably
why he's developed such an affinity for Batman. Sometimes
he even calls me his 'young ward,' quoting Bruce Wayne. I
could never get into comics – too unrealistic – but I get that
when he says it it's some kind of joke.

There's no joking now. This is Sandor trying to be serious. I can tell by the way he drags his hand over his beard, searching for words. He hates that beard, but it hides the scar that the Mogs gave him in Vancouver.

'Just because I understand doesn't mean what you did wasn't stupid and reckless,' he continues.

'Does this mean we have to move?' I ask, wanting to cut to the chase.

By the look on his face, I can tell Sandor didn't even consider this. He's spooked, but moving never crossed his mind.

'And leave all this?' he gestures to the piles of in-progress gadgets. 'No. We've worked too hard to set this place up to abandon it at the first sign of trouble. And the Mog was alone. I don't think our cover's blown quite yet. But you need to promise me you won't bring home any more guests.'

'I promise,' I say, flashing a Boy Scout sign I picked up from some television show. Sandor smirks.

'It did get me to thinking,' he says, standing up. 'Maybe you're ready to take your training to the next level.'

I stifle a groan. Sometimes it feels like all I do is train, probably because *all I do is train*. Before my telekinesis developed, it was endless days of strength training and cardio, broken up by what Sandor calls 'practical academics.' No history or literature, just more skills that I could potentially use in the field. How many kids know how to set a broken bone or which household chemicals will create an improvised explosion?

Whatever complaint I might have made goes unvoiced

when Sandor brushes aside a pile of junk to reveal my Loric Chest. He rarely opens it and I've only seen him use a few of its items. I've been waiting for the day to learn everything that it contains and how to use them. Maybe I should've lured a Mog to our hideout sooner.

'Are you serious?' I ask, still half expecting to be punished.

He nods. 'Your Legacies are developing. It's time.'

Together, we open the lock on the Chest. I jostle in next to Sandor, trying to reach my hands inside. So many new toys to play with – I see some kind of spiky green ball and an oblong crystal that gives off a faint glow – but Sandor elbows me aside.

'When you're ready,' he cautions, indicating the shiny mysteries waiting inside my Chest.

Sandor hands me a plain-looking silver pipe, probably the most boring item in the whole Chest, then snaps the Chest closed before I can see anything else.

'Pretty soon your other Legacies will have developed. That means the rest of the Garde – the surviving ones, anyway – will be developing theirs too.'

I push aside the memory of the panic attack I had after killing the Mog. But Sandor is looking at me with a steely glint in his eyes. He's not playing around.

'This might be fun now, but it won't be a game forever. It will be war. It *is* war. If you want me to treat you like an adult, you need to understand that.'

'I understand,' I say. And I do. I think.

I turn the pipe over in my hands. 'What does this do?'

Before I can answer, the pipe extends into a full-length staff. Sandor takes a step back as I accidentally knock a hollowed-out computer onto the floor.

'You hit things with it,' says Sandor, glancing worriedly at his fragile gadgets. 'Preferably Mogs.'

I twirl the staff over my head. Somehow it feels natural, like an extension of myself.

'Awesome.'

'Also, I think it's time you started going to school.'

My jaw drops. In all those years traveling, Sandor never bothered to enroll me in school. Once we were settled in Chicago, I broached the subject, but Sandor didn't want to distract me from my training. There was a time when I would have killed to go to school, to be normal. Now, the idea of mixing with human kids my own age, of trying to pass as one of them, is nearly as daunting as taking down a Mog.

Sandor slaps me on the shoulder, pleased with himself. Then he hits a button on the underside of his desk.

A bookshelf littered with dusty electronics manuals makes a sudden hydraulic hiss and slides into the ceiling. A secret room, one even I was unaware of.

'Step into the Lecture Hall, my young ward,' intones my Cêpan.

5

What Sandor calls the lecture hall isn't like the classrooms that I've seen on TV. There are no desks, no places to sit at all, really, with the exception of a cockpit-looking chair built into one wall. Sandor calls it the Lectern, and he climbs into the seat behind a control panel of blinking buttons and gauges. The room is about the size of our expansive living room, all white, every surface tiled with what looks to be retractable panels.

My footsteps echo as I walk to the center of the room. 'How long have you been working on this?'

'Since we moved in,' he replies, flicking a series of levers on the Lectern. I can feel the room hum to life beneath my feet.

'Why didn't you tell me?'

'You weren't ready before,' says Sandor. 'But you proved to me today that you're ready now. It's time to begin the last phase of your training.'

I'd lured the Mog to our penthouse because I wanted to show Sandor that I was ready for more action. I'd wanted to show him that I could act independently, that I could be his partner. No more of his 'young ward' crap.

But this is just more of the same. I thought I was ready to

graduate. Instead, Sandor has decided to stick me in summer school.

Just a few minutes ago I was worried I'd made a bad decision of life-altering magnitude. Now, listening to Sandor patronize me, I'm reminded why I stayed up all night planning that Mog's demise. For all his big serious pep talk, Sandor just doesn't get me. I regretted the possibility that I'd put this place in danger to prove my readiness, but the more I watch Sandor play around with his gadgets and levers, the less sorry I feel about what I did.

'Shall we begin?' he asks.

I nod, not really paying attention. I'm tired of play-fighting. I got a taste of the real thing this morning and it might not have gone exactly as I expected, but it was still better than this. Hell, real school with soft human kids would be more exciting.

I'm part of the Garde. I have a destiny, a life to start leading. How many stupid training sessions will I have to endure before Sandor lets me start living it?

A panel on the front of the Lectern opens, discharging a trio of steel ball bearings at fastball speed. I easily deflect them with my telekinesis. This trick is played out. Sandor's been shooting objects at me pretty much nonstop since my telekinesis developed.

Before the first trio can hit the ground, though, two more panels open in the walls on either side of me, both firing more projectiles. Caught in a crossfire, I use my telekinesis to ground the ones to my left, instinctively swinging my pipe-staff in a tight arc to bat away the others.

'Good!' shouts Sandor. 'Use all your weapons.'

I shrug. 'Is that it?'

Sandor sends another volley of projectiles my way. This time I don't even bother with my telekinesis. I use the pipe-staff to deflect two of them, quickly spinning away from the others.

'How does the staff feel?'

I twirl my new weapon effortlessly from hand to hand. It feels natural, like a part of myself I didn't know was missing before today.

'I like it.'

'On Lorien, they held competitions with those things. They called them Jousts. In his younger days, your father was a champion.'

It's rare for Sandor to mention life before the Mogadorian invasion, but before I can grill him further, a section of the wall juts out at me like a battering ram. It's too heavy to stop with my telekinesis, so I throw my weight into it and roll across it.

I land on my feet, supporting myself with my staff, and am greeted by a floating drone that looks like something Sandor made by attaching a helicopter propeller to a blender. Before I can properly size up the drone, it bobs in close and zaps me with an electrical shock that sends me tumbling back over the battering ram.

The shock isn't enough to really hurt me, but it sends pins and needles through my limbs. Sandor laughs, delighted that one of his creations scored a hit.

His laughter just makes me angry.

I hop back to my feet, only to immediately duck another volley of projectiles. Meanwhile, the drone has bobbed out of staff range. I focus on it with my telekinesis.

From behind, a heavy punching bag on a chain detaches from the ceiling, slamming into me with the weight of a grown man. The wind is knocked out of me and I crash to the ground.

My face hits the floor in the fall. Instead of seeing stars, I see droplets of blood from my split lip pooling on the polished white floor. I wipe my face and scramble to one knee.

Sandor looks at me from behind his control panel, an eyebrow raised mockingly.

'Had enough?'

Still seeing red, I snarl and make a lunge for the drone. It's not fast enough. I impale it with my staff in a shower of sparks.

I shake the broken drone off the end of my staff and stare at Sandor.

'Is that all you've got?'

6

The workout in the lecture hall lasts two hours. Two hours of flying ball bearings, electrified drones made of scrap heap parts and whatever else Sandor thinks to throw at me. At some point, my mind shuts off and I just react. I'm pouring sweat, my muscles ache, but it's a welcome relief not to think for a while.

When it's over, Sandor pats me on the back. I hit the showers and stand under the hot water until my fingertips are wrinkled.

It's dark when I emerge from my bathroom. I can smell Chinese takeout in the kitchen, but I'm not ready to join Sandor yet. He'll want to talk about the training session, about what I could be doing differently and better. He won't mention this morning's Mog killing. Just like anytime we argue, it'll get ignored until we cool down and forget about it. I don't want to start the routine yet, so I stay hidden in my room.

The lights in my bedroom turn on automatically, motion sensors detecting my presence.

If I had any friends, I'm sure they'd be sick with envy of my room. I have a king-sized bed that faces a 52-inch flat-screen television, and the TV is hooked up to all three of the major video game systems. There's an awesome stereo, with speakers mounted into the walls. My laptop sits on my desk next to the Beretta that Sandor lets me keep in here for emergencies.

I catch sight of myself in the mirror. I'm wrapped in a towel, and can see the bruises and scrapes on my torso and arms, all courtesy of today's training. It's not a pretty sight.

I turn off the lights and walk over to the floor-to-ceiling windows. I press my forehead to the cool glass and look down at the city of Chicago. From this height, you can actually see the wind as it whips by the blinking lights on building rooftops. There's nonstop movement below – cars plodding along, blobs of ant-sized humans darting between them.

I did something reckless today because I thought it would prove something. Instead, it's just sucked me in deeper to the same routine. Sandor thought he was rewarding me with that Lecture Hall session, but really it was just more monotony.

I turn my gaze away from the masses of people below, out toward the dark sheet of Lake Michigan. If one of my Legacies turns out to be flying, I'm just going to take off, go someplace where there are no Mogadorians, no Cêpans telling me what to do, no anything except me and sky.

But I can't fly, at least not yet. I get dressed and join Sandor for dinner.

7

A few nights later, I dream of Lorien.

I feel energy course through me, almost like working out in the Lecture Hall, but different. It's a giddy feeling, like a never-ending sugar rush. In the dream I'm a kid. Younger than I can even remember being.

And man, am I running.

I'm booking it through the woods, my legs pumping for all they're worth. Two creatures that look like wolves but which have massive falcon wings jutting out of their backs are nipping at my heels. Chimæra. My Chimæra.

It has rained recently and the ground squishes under my bare feet. I break into a recessed clearing that's slick with bright white mud. The closest Chimæra clips my heel and I go tumbling onto my stomach, rolling through the mud, covering my clothes and face.

The Chimæra stands over me, pinning me as I pant and catch my breath. He leans down and sloppily licks my cheek.

I laugh harder than I can remember laughing in a long time. The other Chimæra cocks his head back and howls.

I roll between the Chimæra's legs and hop to my feet. I lunge at him with a guttural war cry that strains my lungs.

I wrap my arms around his neck, burying my face in his fur, and try to swing my leg over his back.

The other Chimæra gently bites the seat of my pants and pulls me back into the mud.

I dig my fingers into the wet dirt, then lob two misshapen balls of slime at the Chimæra, the stuff splattering across their snouts. They howl.

Springing to my feet, I run back the way we came. The Chimæra race behind me as I weave through the trees. I might not remember Lorien, but the young body I'm in knows it well. I'm just along for the ride as my young self tromps through stalks of knee-high grass, bare feet knowing just when to hop over errant tree roots to avoid tripping.

A campfire appears in front of me. Sitting by it, a burly man with a bushy black beard cooks our dinner over the fire, his sleeves rolled up past his thick forearms. Somehow, I know his face. My grandfather.

Next to him is a fresh-faced man I don't immediately recognize. He's dressed way too nicely for the outdoors.

It's Sandor. I guess I never realized how young he was when we were on Lorien.

My grandfather sees me coming, grinning, and has the good sense to get out of the way. Sandor isn't paying attention; he's got his eyes glued to some kind of mobile communicator. Probably messaging a girl back in the capital about watching the fireworks later. Some things don't change.

I tackle him around the knees, dragging him down into

the dirt, my mud becoming his mud. He cries out, the comm flying from his grip. I sit on his chest, my arms folded.

'Conquered,' I declare.

'Not yet, pal,' Sandor replies, his eyes lighting up. He grabs me under the armpits and lifts me up, spinning.

In the distance, from the direction of the city, there comes a low rumbling.

With that, my grandfather accidentally drops our dinner into the fire.

I wake up feeling happy and sad at the same time.

8

It's been a week since my last visit to the Lakefront and there hasn't been so much as a peep from the iMog.

I get up at dawn to find Sandor already sitting at the kitchen counter, holding a cup of coffee. That's unusual. My Cêpan normally prefers to sleep until mid-morning, sometimes not even waking up until I've returned from my run. He's always been a night owl, and it's only gotten worse since we moved to Chicago. I know that sometimes he slips out at night and comes home smelling like perfume and booze. I don't ask him about these trips just like he doesn't ask about my runs. I guess we just both need some private time – although he apparently has been keeping an eye on my private time, if the video footage he had on screen the other day is any indication.

I study his face. The bags under his eyes, the growth of beard hiding his scar; I try to find some resemblance to the young man I saw in my dream, but that person is gone. I never thought about the fact that Sandor had a life before he came here. I don't remember Lorien – at least I thought I didn't – but I know Sandor remembers it. He must miss it.

I wonder if he still sees a giddy, mud-covered menace when he looks at me. Probably not.

Sandor notices that I'm wearing my running clothes. We agreed to keep a low profile for a while, but I can't stand another day trapped in here with just the Lecture Hall, video games, and overwatched spy movies to pass the time.

'Going for your run?' he asks.

I grunt a yes, acting casual as I slug back some orange juice from the container.

'I don't think that's a great idea.'

I turn to face him. 'What are you talking about?'

'Need I remind you that last week you brought home a Mog from the lakefront? Maybe it's time to change things up.'

I slam the refrigerator door harder than I mean to, rattling our vast assortment of condiments and takeout containers.

'I'm not staying cooped up in here all day,' I state.

'You think I'm not tired of looking at that sour mug of yours twenty-four/seven?' asks Sandor, arching an eyebrow. 'Think again.'

He reaches onto the counter and hands me a laminated card.

'I got you this.'

The card is a membership for something called the Windy City Wall. There's an unsmiling picture of me in the bottom corner of the card next to my most recent alias – Stanley Worthington.

'I thought it might be good for you to get out and meet some people that aren't Mogadorian scouts. Lately you seem sort of . . .' he trails off, rubbing his beard, not sure how to proceed.

'Thanks,' I reply, and jog out the door before he can finish his thought, eager to escape. Neither of us have ever been much for sappy heart-to-hearts. I'd prefer to keep it that way.

The Windy City Wall is a sprawling rec center about twenty minutes from the John Hancock Center. I probably passed it a hundred times before today, but I'd never once considered going inside. These kinds of places were reserved for humans. And besides, I had plenty of training equipment back home.

After all these years, why had Sandor chosen now to sign me up for something like this? Now I wish that I'd let him finish his thought and tell me what I 'seem' like lately.

There's a smiley tour guide at the front desk who shows me around the center. There are basketball courts, a pool, and a gym that I'm surprised to find is as well-equipped as ours. Besides all that normal YMCA-type stuff, there are also a variety of obstacle courses, with cargo nets and old rubber tires meant to simulate various natural obstructions.

And then, of course, there is the Wall. It's no wonder the rec center takes its name from it, because it's absolutely huge, dominating an entire side of the building and rising up some forty feet from floor to ceiling. The rock is fake, and obviously there's no blue sky in this warehouse-like building, but there's still something majestic about the Wall. When my tour guide is done rambling, I head straight for it, and take my place in one of the lines, behind a bunch of kids that look just a little older than me.

Above us, a boy that I take for about seventeen is stuck in

the middle of the wall, casting around desperately for a handhold. He can't find one, and after a few seconds of flailing he drops off, his descent slowed by a safety line and cushioned by a pillowy mat.

'Is this your first time?'

I glance over my shoulder. A tall blond-haired boy about my age is smirking at me. I nod.

'Yeah.'

'This is the advanced end. You probably want to start with easy.'

'No, I don't.'

The blond kid exchanges a look with a shorter kid next to him. The short kid doesn't look as strong as his buddy, but he's compact, which should make him a better climber.

'You need a vest,' says the short kid.

I laugh. The idea of me falling off this wall after the training I've had is ridiculous. I smile at the short kid, assuming that he's joking even though both he and his friend are wearing vests.

'I don't need one of those.'

'Tough guy!' jokes the blond one.

'No, seriously, it's the rules,' says the other. 'Even if you were Sir Edmund Hillary you'd need to wear a vest.'

I stare blankly at the kid. I have no idea who he's talking about.

'He was the first person to climb Everest,' the short one explains.

'Oh,' I mumble. 'The mountain.'

Both boys snicker. 'Yeah, the mountain.'

The short kid nudges the tall one. 'Why don't you go get the new kid a vest?'

The tall kid gives me a weird look, then jogs off to an equipment rack. I realize this is one of the longest conversations with human kids I've ever had. I wonder how I'm doing.

'I'm Mike,' says the short kid, shaking my hand. 'My friend is also Mike.'

'Is everyone in this city named Mike?'

'That's funny,' says Short Mike, but he doesn't laugh. 'What's your name?'

'Stanley.' I don't hesitate, producing my alias easily, as if it's my real name – just like Sandor's drilled me to do.

Tall Mike returns and hands me a vest. I pull it over my head and they show me how to adjust the straps.

'So, Stanley,' continues Short Mike, practically interrogating me. 'Where do you go to school?'

'I'm homeschooled.'

'That explains your sparkling personality,' deadpans Short Mike.

I think he just insulted me.

Before I can respond, I notice her. She's in the next line over. Maybe sixteen or seventeen, straight black hair, and eyes to match. She's athletic looking, not like some of the flimsy girls I've seen jogging along the lakefront. She's beautiful and she's staring at me. How long has she been watching me? Has she been listening to my entire conversation with the Mikes?

When she sees that she has my attention, the girl quickly looks away, her cheeks reddening. I can't help it; I can't look away. Eventually she glances back my way and nervously flashes me a tentative smile. I can only blink in response.

Tall Mike waves his hand in front of my face.

'What?' I snap.

'It's your turn, bro.'

I turn and see the climbing instructor sarcastically tapping his watch. I step forward and he buckles the safety cords to my vest. I'm barely listening as he explains where the best handholds are, my mind too busy trying to figure out why that girl was staring at me. Instinctively, I try to straighten my mess of hair. I don't know what to think about that girl; on TV, there's always music that plays when a guy makes eye contact with a pretty girl. I'd kill for some soundtrack now.

I wonder if she likes guys from other planets who can climb walls really fast.

Guess I'll find out.

The instructor blows a whistle and I leap onto the wall. The start of my ascent is clumsy. I should've listened when the instructor explained the handholds. Even so, I quickly find a rhythm and begin swinging my body up the wall.

Is the girl watching? I have the unbearable urge to check.

I glance down. She is. She's standing right next to the two Mikes, both of them nattering at her. She ignores them, watching me. No. More than watching me. She's studying me like I'm the most interesting book in the world.

My palms are suddenly slick with sweat.

That's not good.

I realize too late that I've worked myself into the same trouble spot as the first climber I watched. I'm about half-way up the wall, but there is no handhold close enough to reach above me, and backtracking is out of the question.

There's only one handhold I can see. It'd be out of the reach of a human. With my strength, though, I can probably make it. I'll have to jump for it.

I hunker down on my footholds, putting as much weight as I can on my knees and hips, before springing upward.

I grab the handhold and my sweaty fingertips scrabble across it.

Then, it is gone. I'm falling. I can't believe this, I'm falling. Defeated by a human wall and some sweaty palms.

The mat cushions my fall. It isn't my body that's hurting, it's my ego. I lay on the mat, not wanting to get up and face the eyes of the rec center.

Her eyes.

Tall Mike peers down at me.

'Guess you did need the vest,' he says with a smirk.

Short Mike helps me off the mat, telling me it was a good first try. I'm barely listening. My eyes sweep the room, looking for the girl.

She's gone.

9

I keep my head down when leaving the Windy City Wall. I've spent pretty much my entire life in anonymity, but even when I've been on the run from killer aliens, I've never wanted to avoid attention as much as I do now. I know it's ridiculous – kids must fall off that wall all the time – yet I'm sure that everyone in the gym is secretly laughing at me.

I take the long way back to the John Hancock building and then walk past it. I keep replaying my fall in my head. I imagine seeing myself from that girl's perspective; flailing, sweaty, legs kicking uselessly at air. I pass the entire day in a daze, beating myself up, and the sun is setting when I finally decide to go home.

Sandor is in the living room when I return home, lounging in a leather recliner with some boring-looking book about advanced engineering in his lap.

'Perfect timing,' he says when I enter, waving his empty Martini glass at me.

He doesn't notice my slumped shoulders as I cross to the room's fully equipped bar. I pluck Sandor's empty glass from his hand using my telekinesis. Then I levitate bottles of gin and vermouth, mixing them through ice. The most difficult part is using my telekinesis to get the olives on the little plastic sword.

I can mix a cocktail with my mind, but I can't climb a damn wall.

When I'm finished, I walk Sandor's Martini over to him and flop down on an adjacent couch. He tastes the drink, smacking his lips.

'Pretty good,' he says. 'So, how was it?'

'Fine,' I grunt.

'Just fine? You were there all day.'

I hesitate before telling him more, but I need to confide in someone, and Sandor has way more experience with the humans – with girls – than I do.

'I fell off the wall.'

Sandor chuckles, not looking up from his book. 'You? Really?'

'I wasn't paying attention. I mean, I guess I got distracted.'

'You'll get it next time.' He shrugs.

'There won't be a next time.'

I'm silent, one arm draped across my face. Sandor must realize I'm holding back details because he finally closes his book and leans forward.

'What happened?' His voice lowers. 'Did the iMog detect something?'

'No.' I pause. 'There was a girl.'

'Ohh,' he says, drawing it out. Even with my face covered I can tell he's grinning. He rubs his hands together. 'Was she pretty?'

'She was beautiful,' I say, looking away. 'I fell because she – I don't know. She was, like, watching me . . .'

'Checking you out. Giving you the eye.'

'Shut up.'

'So a beautiful young thing saw you fall and now you're embarrassed.'

I have no comeback. When he says it like that, it sounds so juvenile, like something from one of those TV shows where humans in too much makeup mope around and make longing faces at each other. But he's exactly right.

Sandor gives my shoulder a squeeze.

''Tis but a minor setback, my young ward,' Sandor opines. 'I can tell you one thing for certain. You're not going to impress your lady by moping around here.'

'Who says I want to impress her?'

He laughs. 'Come on. Who doesn't want to impress beautiful women? Right now, in her mind, you're just a guy that bit off more than he could chew. If you don't go back, though, you become that wimp she saw fall off the wall one time. Do you want that?'

I don't even have to think about my answer.

'I'll go back tomorrow.'

10

I'm up early again the next morning, back in the Lecture Hall, dodging projectiles and batting drones out of the air with my pipe-staff even though my mind is at the Windy City Wall. Sandor doesn't take it easy on me, despite knowing that I want to be conserving my energy for a second chance at impressing that girl.

'Keep your head in the game!' he shouts at me after a mechanized tentacle trips me up.

After training, I shower thoroughly, even though I'm just getting ready for another workout. I want to look good. I even run a comb through my tangled thatch of hair. Sandor's been ragging on me to cut it forever, telling me that I look like a girl, and recommending all kinds of hair products that would give me 'maximum hold.' I've never paid any attention to his unsolicited style tips.

Only looking at myself in the steamy bathroom mirror, I wish I'd listened to him. I look like a caveman. But it's too late to do anything about my hair now. Besides, I figure showing up with a fresh haircut glistening with pomade – whatever that is – would look pretty desperate.

'Good luck,' says Sandor knowingly as I head to the elevator.

There are butterflies having a heavy artillery firefight in my stomach as I jog over to the rec center. I breeze in the door and immediately beeline for the equipment rack, grabbing a safety vest as I confidently stride toward the advanced end of the wall. I casually scan the room, looking for the girl.

She's not there. In fact, the place is nearly empty.

Ugh. It's a school day. I always forget the humans keep much different schedules than I do.

There are a few college-aged kids working out on the wall, getting envious looks from flabby older guys who are probably here on their lunch break. I join them. Might as well get a few practice runs in.

I spend an hour mastering the wall. This time I listen to the instructor, paying special attention to where the best handholds are. By the time the hour is up, I've successfully scaled the wall a half-dozen times. According to the instructor, if I shaved a few seconds off my time I'd have a shot at breaking the local record. I don't tell him that I haven't been going all out, that with my Loric strength and speed I could easily smash it.

I'm saving that performance for when the girl shows up.

There's still about an hour left before school gets out. It'd probably look pretty weird if I was already here when the other kids arrive and I decide I want to make an entrance. I imagine confidently strutting into line, ignoring taunts from the Mikes, then flying up the wall in record-setting time. While the Mikes are busy picking their jaws up off the floor,

I'll stride over to the girl, her adoring smile inviting me to talk to her. And then . . .

Well, I haven't totally planned out the talking part yet.

I buy a bottle of water from a vending machine and head outside. There's a small park across the street from the rec center, where I make myself at home on a bench – the perfect spot for a stakeout. I'm comfortable in the cool air and have a good view of the Windy City Wall entrance. I'll hide out until kids get out of school and then it'll be time for my redemption.

The thought of a stakeout causes me to make a check of my iMog. An evil red dot appearing nearby is exactly what I don't need right now. Luckily, the coast is clear.

I spend the next hour trying to think of a good opening line. All the guys in the movies and on TV have them when they approach a girl. I should've asked Sandor for one before I left. He probably has whole books filled with pick-up lines.

By the time I see the two Mikes enter the Windy City Wall, I still haven't come up with anything good. I'm stuck on climbing puns, but they all come off pretty gross, like I want to climb on her.

'Is this seat taken?' A girl's voice interrupts the conversation I'm having in my head. Distractedly, I wave at the empty space of bench next to me.

The next wall I'd like to climb is the one around your heart. How's that? Really, really cheesy.

'Hi,' the girl says, sitting down next to me.

And that's when I realize it isn't just any girl sitting inches away from me on the bench, it's *the* girl. Her cheeks are rosy in the late spring air, her black hair gently blown in the breeze. She's smiling at me. She's so beautiful, I suddenly feel like I could throw up. This wasn't the plan.

'I'm Maddy,' she says, extending her hand.

I just look at her, my mind completely blank.

So much for first lines.

Maddy squints at me. 'Sorry, I didn't mean to interrupt your, um, quiet muttering.'

Was I muttering? I must look like a crazy person. I try to recover.

'No, you're not interrupting. I was just thinking.'

'Oh,' she says, looking at me expectantly. I realize her hand is still hanging out there between us waiting for me, so I grasp it, squeezing her hand a little too eagerly.

'I'm Stanley.'

'Nice to meet you, Stanley.'

I swallow hard. This meeting is already way off track. She wasn't supposed to see me again until I'd beaten the wall and restored my pride.

I make a halfhearted gesture toward the rec center, desperately trying to recreate the scenario I'd been envisioning. 'I was about to go climb. Do you want to come watch?'

'Watch?' she asks, arching an eyebrow. 'Maybe we could race. If you're up for it,' she adds, teasing me.

I flashed back to my humiliation of the day before, suddenly lost for words. Luckily, she bails me out.

'Anyway,' she says, 'I actually can't stay; I'm on my way home. I just saw you sitting over here by yourself and thought I'd say hey.'

'Oh,' I say, lamely. 'Hey.'

'Hey,' she repeats.

And then comes an awkward silence, almost like Maddy's nervous too. Her gaze bounces away from me and her mouth screws up, as if she's trying to figure out what to say. I wonder if she plans conversations out in her head too.

When she speaks again, her words are a torrent of nervous energy.

'I saw you yesterday and you were by yourself then too and that's totally cool, if you like working out alone, but I'm new here and it's been sort of hard to meet people, so I figured maybe we could, like, team up and fight solitude together.'

I blink at her. I can't believe my luck.

'Sorry,' she says, rolling her eyes. 'I'm not usually this much of a spaz.'

'You're not a spaz,' I reply.

'Okay, good. I've got you fooled.' She laughs nervously. 'Okay. Shut up, Maddy. Here.' She reaches into her bag and hands me a piece of paper with her name and number scribbled on it.

'If I didn't just totally freak you out, you should call me,' she says, hopping off the bench before my idiot brain can even form a reply.

11

Wind whips around us as we stand on the roof of the John Hancock building, sending the drone that's floating above me and Sandor listing momentarily downward. We're trying out his newest creation, a hollowed-out toaster with steel glider wings protruding where the bread slots should be. I brush my gloved fingers across the drone controls, correcting its course against the wind. Its tiny motor hums sharply in response. We always take Sandor's new creations for test runs, knowing they might one day be our only allies against a horde of Mogadorians. In the meantime, I'll most likely end up staring down this latest buzzing contraption in the Lecture Hall.

'So,' says Sandor, 'how long has it been since you got her number?'

I keep my eyes on the drone.

'Five days,' I reply.

'The humans have a rule about calling girls,' muses Sandor. 'Something like waiting three days unless you want to look desperate.'

I grunt.

'You're in the clear as far as that goes,' he concludes. 'What are you waiting for?'

'What's the point?' I ask, trying not to sound as sullen as I feel. I don't think I pull it off.

Ever since our meeting in the park, I've done little but train and think about Maddy. We only spoke for a couple of minutes, but I could tell that she's lonely like me. She's new in Chicago and, even though I've been here for five years, for all the socializing I've done I might as well be new too. Admittedly, I've fantasized about having a social life that's more than playing robots with my Cêpan, but I never dreamed that a beautiful girl would come along, much less actually be interested in me.

Now that it's actually happening, what can I even do about it? Maddy doesn't have any scars on her ankle. She hasn't been conscripted into an intergalactic war. She'll make friends in the city eventually, go off to college, live a normal life. Me? I've got to make a race of warmongering monsters accountable for the genocide of my people. It's nice to think about escaping all that, to daydream about having a girl-friend and going on dates. Except one day the daydream ends and I go to war. How does getting to know a human fit into that – let alone having a girlfriend?

It doesn't.

Sensing that my mind is elsewhere, Sandor eases the controls out of my hands and brings the drone back to the roof. His puts his hand on my back and we walk over to the edge of the roof and peer down at the city below us.

'You can never escape who you are,' he begins.

'I know that,' I say, wanting to cut short whatever kind of

exasperating pep talk he has in mind. I don't know what's gotten into him lately.

'Listen,' he continues. 'Just because you've got a destiny doesn't mean you don't also have a life to live.'

'That's not what it feels like.'

He sighs. 'Maybe I've made a mistake with you, keeping you so isolated. If that's the case, I'm sorry. I guess I forgot what it's like to be young.'

Sandor rubs his beard, searching for words.

'I've had some, uh, friends since we've been on Earth.'

'Friends.' I snort. 'Is that what those girls are?'

'Whatever,' Sandor says with a nervous cough before elbowing me. 'The humans can be a welcome distraction, that's all I'm saying.'

'I don't need a *distraction*,' I say sarcastically and kick the drone. 'I have video games. And toy robots.'

'That's not the point,' Sandor continues. 'Distraction, that's the wrong word. They can be a reminder too. A reminder that what we're doing, why we're here and fighting, that it's worth something. We can have lives, Nine. When we win this war – and we will win – you can be Stanley, for real. Or someone else, even. You can be whoever you want.'

My eyes sweep across the city. Out there, somewhere, are the Mogadorians. Even if the one from the lakefront was the only one in Chicago, there are others. Hunting me.

'You can't escape what you are, but you also should know what you could be. Why you're fighting.'

Also out there, probably doing homework in her parents'

apartment, is Maddy. I'd much rather think about her than the Mogs.

'Call her,' Sandor says. 'Be Stanley, even if it's only for a little while.'

I glance over at him. I can see how hard he's trying to reach me. I want to believe that he's right.

'Thanks, Sandor.'

He pats me hard on the back. 'Just don't screw it up.'

Later, I sit on my bed with the door closed, holding the phone. This time I don't bother rehearsing – not after how badly that went for me last time. I just take a few deep breaths and dial Maddy's number.

She answers on the first ring.

'Hi,' I say, trying out the words. 'It's Stanley.'

There's a sigh of relief on the other end. Maybe she's been thinking about this moment too, hoping I would call.

'I was beginning to think you weren't going to call,' she says. I can almost hear the smile in her voice and I instantly feel better.

Maddy picks the planetarium for what sandor has annoyingly started to call our 'first date.'

I try to downplay it to him, explaining to him that Maddy and I are just hanging out, but he can tell how excited I am and that only encourages his teasing. The couple of days before the date are filled with equal parts training and unsolicited girl advice.

'Tell her how pretty she looks.'

I stop a heavy bag from careening into me with my telekinesis.

'Ask her questions about herself.'

I duck under a swarm of projectiles.

'Make sure you look interested in what she's saying, even if you're not.'

I pivot around a drone, hitting it with a backhand swipe of my pipe-staff.

'Are you listening to me?'

I wipe sweat from my face and glare at Sandor. 'Not really.'

'Good.' He claps his hands, powering down the Lecture Hall. 'Then you're ready.'

*

Maddy's waiting for me outside the planetarium. Her smile is small and nervous as I approach. She's wearing a light sweater and jeans, which makes me glad I didn't take Sandor's advice to dress up like we were going to the opera or something, opting instead for my usual hooded sweatshirt and jeans.

'I hope you don't think this is nerdy,' she says as we buy tickets.

'No, not at all.'

Nerdy isn't the word I'd choose. Ironic, maybe? I can't explain to her how quaint I find the humans' understanding of the known cosmos. I wonder if other aliens in hiding have had first dates at the planetarium. I doubt it.

'My dad used to take me to the planetarium all the time when I was a kid. I got pretty into it.'

As we take our seats in the domed auditorium and wait for the show to start, she tells me more about her family. Her father is some kind of renowned astronomer, her mother a professor of philosophy. They moved to Chicago so her mother could take a position at the university, but they still travel frequently, since her dad's in high demand on the space-nerd lecture circuit. Maddy sounds sad when she talks about them, like they're never around. Our situations are so different, yet somehow I feel like I know exactly where she's coming from.

'I miss them,' she says, then waves her hands apologetically. 'I mean, they're not gone forever, but it's like I hardly see them since we moved here.'

'Isn't that weird? Being on your own?'

She shrugs. 'It can be cool. No one to yell at me for staying up late on a school night.' She shoots me a playful glance. 'Or to wonder why I'm bringing strange boys to the planetarium.'

I laugh, but I also wonder if she really thinks I'm strange. I hope not. I think I'm doing a pretty good job being regular Stanley.

'Ugh, I'm going on and on. I just unloaded all that on you and I don't know anything about you.'

I'm disappointed that she's done talking. Contrary to what Sandor thought, I didn't have to feign interest. But now comes the part where I have to lie to her.

'What do you want to know?'

Maddy thinks this over. Around us, other people are taking seats. I notice that our shoulders are touching, sharing an armrest.

'Let's start with where you go to school?'

I flash an embarrassed smile. 'I'm homeschooled.'

She gives me a look that makes me think I might as well have told her I'm an alien from the planet Lorien. I remember the weird looks that the Mikes gave me at the rec center, like I was some kind of creepy shut-in. I could've come up with a cover story, I guess, but it feels better to tell her the truth.

'Huh,' she says, her eyebrow arched jokingly, 'and here you seemed so normal.'

'It's really not that weird,' I tell her. 'My uncle, he, uh, keeps things interesting. Actually, maybe it is sort of weird, come to think of it. My uncle's not exactly what you'd call normal.'

'So you live with him?'

'Yeah.'

'Where are your parents?'

I should have a convincing lie ready for that question. Sandor and I used to drill backstory when we were on the road, but it's been a long time. Sandor would tell people that I was his nephew, and that he was taking me on a trip to show me the world, or so that my parents could have a second honeymoon, or that my parents would be joining us eventually. Sometimes he got closer to the truth, telling sympathetic diner waitresses that he was raising me after both my parents had died in an accident. That usually resulted in a bigger than normal slice of dessert. I want the Stanley that Maddy gets to know to be as close to the real me as possible.

'They died when I was young,' I tell her. 'I never really knew them.'

'Oh,' she replies, clearly not sure what to say next.

Thankfully, the lights dim before the conversation gets any more depressing. We recline into our seats as the Milky Way comes alive above us.

A tinny recording begins describing the origin of the cosmos and running down the roster of planets in relation to

Earth. I'm not listening. Lounging in the near darkness with Maddy is pretty much all my brain is capable of processing. I want to remember these details. Her hair smells like vanilla, or coconut, or some other girly thing. Whatever it is, it's great. I concentrate on the space on the arm rest where our shoulders meet, imagining that her every shift in position is some coded message for me.

I glance over at her. Maddy notices and gives me a quick smile, her face bathed in whites and pale blues of the light presentation overhead. I'd spend the rest of this boring lecture staring at her if that wouldn't make her think I was a freak. Instead, I tune out the planetarium soundtrack and listen to her. Her breathing is slow and steady, but using my enhanced hearing I can tell her heart is pounding.

Or wait. Maybe that's my heart.

I close my eyes and spend the rest of the show like that. Afterward, the planetarium stays dimmed, the stars still on display. The rest of the people begin filing out while we stay in our seats. Eventually it's just the two of us and the stars.

Maddy leans close to me and begins to whisper, even though we're alone. She tells me about constellations that weren't covered in the recording, guiding my eyes from Orion's Belt to Aquarius. She laughs softly and corrects me when I mistake the tail of Pisces for one of Pegasus's legs. I already know everything that she's telling me, but it's all so much more interesting with her narrating.

At some point, without even realizing I'm doing it, I take her hand.

It's only for a moment. Her hand is warm and a little damp from sweat. She quickly slips away and stands up.

'I'm sorry,' I start, realizing I overdid it, 'I mean – I didn't mean . . .'

'It's okay,' she says, shaking her head, looking flustered but not mad or weirded out. 'Come on. You can walk me home.'

13

Sandor isn't in the penthouse when I get home, which gives me a couple of hours of alone time to endlessly replay in my head what I've started thinking of as the hand-holding incident. I don't think I even put this much thought into suckering in that Mog. Did I misread Maddy's interest? When Sandor comes home with a soggy bag of takeout, he doesn't even ask me about my date. Instead, he wants to talk about his day prowling the city.

'I drove all over the city with this thing,' he says, holding up his heavy-duty version of my iMog. 'Nothing. Not a single blip. If that Mog had any friends looking for him, they've moved on. I think we're in the clear.'

'That's great,' I reply distractedly.

'To hiding in plain sight,' he toasts, raising a freshly mixed drink.

Over burgers, Sandor finally gets around to asking about Maddy. I tell him everything, not leaving out a single detail, even trying to recreate Maddy's body language for him. For the first time since we've been in Chicago, I feel like I could really use my Cêpan's guidance.

'Huh,' he says when I finish.

' "*Huh.*" That's it?'

He shrugs. 'Women are mysterious creatures.' As he says this, he gives me a strange look, half smirking and half apprehensive, like I'm some kind of weird animal he's afraid will bite him.

'What?' I ask.

'I just can't remember the last time you talked this much. It's nice.'

I wave him away. 'You're no help.'

Just then, my back pocket vibrates.

Immediately, my heart is in my throat. My iMog is signaling a warning. I practically tear the device out of my pocket, staring down at the screen.

But it's blank. Just a solitary white dot in the center.

My cell phone, I realize. It was my cell phone. I carry my phone mostly out of habit; it hardly ever vibrates, unless Sandor wants me to pick him up a bagel on the way home from my run.

The screen blinks with a new text message.

'It's her,' I announce, almost too nervous to open the message.

'What's it say?'

'Had fun today,' I read. 'For the next date, you're picking the place.'

Sandor whoops and mimes a high five from across the table. So, she thought it was a date too. And if she had fun that means I didn't screw up too badly with the hand holding. I don't have long to savor these facts as a fresh wave of anxiety washes over me.

She wants me to plan a date.

'What's wrong?' Sandor asks, reading distress in my expression.

'I have no idea where to take a girl on a date.'

Sandor cuts short a laugh. We sit in silence, both of us pondering.

'I could take her back to the Windy City Wall,' I suggest. 'I could definitely kill that wall now.'

Sandor makes a face.

'You want to spend a date climbing rocks instead of talking to her?'

He has a point.

'You know,' Sandor muses, 'if you really want to impress her, I have an idea.'

14

I make plans with Maddy for the following weekend, which makes the weekdays in between a slog through endless anticipation. I'm filled with nervous energy, but not the kind that I can channel into my training sessions with Sandor. The drones score more hits on me than they should, my mind occupied with cycling through wardrobe choices and practicing imaginary conversations. I can tell Sandor is annoyed as he powers down the Lecture Hall.

'Do you think the Mogadorians will care that you've got a girl on your mind?' he snaps.

I offer my best contrite headshake, knowing he's right.

Later, Sandor summons me to his workshop. He's got his feet up on his desk, crumpling a stack of old blueprints. He has a distant look in his eyes and for a second I think I'm interrupting some pleasant daydream. He looks me over with a wistful smile.

'You know, I wasn't much older than you are now when I was assigned to be your Cêpan,' he says. 'That's young for a Cêpan to be assigned to a Garde. I was good, though. I'd helped the engineers – much older, more experienced – with some tech projects. I think they wanted to get me in the field as soon as possible.'

I'd been expecting a lecture from Sandor. That's something I'm used to. Annoyed Sandor was a familiar entity. Nostalgic Sandor, on the other hand, I've got no idea how to deal with. It's so rare for him to talk about Lorien, I'm afraid to interrupt.

'I liked to think I was ready,' he continues. 'It was a big honor, that's for sure. Even if you were an unruly little piece of work.' He winks at me and I can't help but smile.

'Bonding with a Garde, that's a full-time responsibility. As ready as I wanted to be, I had other things on my mind too. I had a girlfriend. Things were getting kind of serious, you know? I was trying hard to balance it all.'

'What happened?' I ask, before realizing what a stupid question that is.

A shadow crosses Sandor's face, although he's quick to hide it. 'You know what happened.'

Sandor sits up and tears a piece of paper out of a legal pad. He hands it to me, the lines filled with his precise writing. A shopping list.

'Since you're no good to me in the Lecture Hall, you might as well go run some errands,' he says, stern Sandor resurfacing.

I take the list and head for the door, but Sandor stops me.

'I never figured out that balance,' he says. 'Maybe you can. Until you do, just remember what your real responsibilities are. All right, man?'

This isn't the first time I've run errands for Sandor. It isn't groceries he sends me out into the world for; that'd be too easy. I'm after spare parts. It's not like we couldn't just order whatever high-tech items Sandor needs for his drones off the internet, but I think he enjoys the challenge of taking broken-down Earth junk and making it work again. He's tried to get me more involved in his salvage projects, but it's never really worked. I'm way more interested in smashing his inventions than putting them together.

I spend the afternoon dutifully patrolling downtown's pawn shops and thrift stores. I find a few things on Sandor's list – an ancient compact disc player and an automatic vegetable slicer with curving blades that I dread to see flying at me in the Lecture Hall. I also pick up some stuff I know he's always on the prowl for, a fried circuit board here, an orphaned length of cable there.

It isn't until the last thrift store on my route that I get the tingly feeling that someone is watching me.

Instinctively I make a discreet check of my iMog. There's no sign of danger nearby. As I slip the device back into my pocket, I notice her. Standing two aisles over, next to a rack of vintage T-shirts, is Maddy.

At first, I think it must be my eyes playing tricks on me. She's been on my mind so much that I'm starting to hallucinate. Then Maddy holds up her hand in a shy wave and I practically bound over to her.

'Hey,' I exclaim, trying not to sound too excited and probably failing. 'What're you doing here?'

'Hey,' she replies, glancing around like she's as surprised to be in a musty thrift store as I am to find her here. 'I'm, uh, stalking you.'

I grin like an idiot. 'Seriously?'

'No!' She rolls her eyes. 'My dad, he's really into antique telescopes and stuff like that. I'm just looking around.'

'Oh,' I say, playing crestfallen. 'I was actually hoping you were stalking me.'

Maddy glances at the bags I'm holding from other stores, each of them bulging with weird shapes. 'What's all that?'

'Science project stuff,' I say, thinking quickly.

'For homeschool?'

I shrug. 'My uncle is weird.'

Together we wander the aisles of the thrift store. Maddy pulls a maroon leisure suit off a rack and holds it up to me.

'Maybe you should wear this on our date this weekend,' she says, cocking her head, trying to imagine me in the suit.

Sandor would probably burn this suit if I dared desecrate the penthouse with its presence.

'Would you even come outside if I showed up in this?'

'Probably not. Here, hold it up,' she orders, and I take the suit with my free hand.

Before I realize what she's doing, Maddy's held up her phone and snapped my picture. She laughs, looking at what I'm sure is my startled expression above the most hideous suit in history.

'Perfect,' she says. 'Hello, new wallpaper.'

'Now I definitely have to buy it. You've talked me into it.'

When I jokingly check the price tag, a moth flutters out from the sleeve. I drop the suit, grossed out, and Maddy laughs again. We dart out of the store, the old man behind the cash register glaring at us.

'I hope I don't have fleas,' I say once we're out on the sidewalk.

'Actually, I think I see one,' she says. She leans close, inspecting, and then gives me a quick peck on the cheek.

She leans back and laughs again, this time at what must be the dumbfounded expression on my face.

'See ya Friday, Stanley,' she says playfully, adding, 'Take a bath.'

15

It's the big night.

Sandor and I stand in the subbasement garage of the John Hancock building. Arrayed before us, each neatly tucked beneath a tarp, is Sandor's collection of getaway vehicles.

Really, I've never thought we needed more than one car. Sandor, however, has taken to collecting the things since we've been in Chicago, outfitting each with his various improvements. I guess Cêpans need hobbies too. He's lucky that being a Cêpan comes with unlimited funds; I'd hate to imagine him driving a beat-up old clunker.

Sandor pulls the tarp away from a sleek, dark red convertible. He runs a hand lovingly across the hood. Then he gives me a deathly serious look.

'Please don't make me regret this.'

I grin at him, eager to get behind the wheel.

'That smile doesn't exactly inspire confidence.'

Still, he opens the driver side door for me and I hop in. Sandor leans in the window as I adjust the seat and mirrors.

'How fast are you going to go?' he asks.

'Five miles under the speed limit at all times,' I recite. We've had this conversation all week, ever since Sandor suggested I take one of the cars. 'Always signal; no racing to catch yellows; keep the top up. I get it.'

'You better,' replies Sandor, his tone more parental than ever. He looks a bit anxious about the way I'm excitedly drumming my hands on the wheel, but he steps back.

'Have a good time,' he says.

I carefully pull out of the parking garage. Sandor, watching me and nervously rubbing his beard, disappears in my rearview mirror.

When I'm a few blocks away from the John Hancock building, I hit the button to roll the top down. What Sandor doesn't know won't hurt him.

I pick Maddy up at the park across the street from the rec center. The convertible handles like a dream and I cruise over to her place following all of Sandor's rules. Except for the top, of course. The cool night air swirls around me and I feel energized.

This is as free as I've ever felt.

Maddy is sitting on the bench when I pull up, and does a double take when she sees me behind the wheel. I wave her over.

'Want to go for a ride?' I ask.

'Oh, wow, is this yours?'

'My uncle's,' I tell her, shrugging nonchalantly. 'He's cool with it.'

Maddy glances up and down the street, a bit apprehensive.

'You're a good driver? I can trust you?'

Okay, I don't *technically* have a license. But I do have an extremely convincing fake that Sandor forged in his workroom. I've also got plenty of experience behind the wheel. Back when we were nomads, Sandor had me practice driving as soon as my feet could reach the pedals, mostly to relieve him when he got tired.

'Of course,' I reply.

We engage in a mini staring contest, her jokingly sizing up my trustworthiness, me trying my hardest to look innocent. I can't help the devilish smile that creeps across my face.

'Aha!' she says, pointing. 'The look of a speed demon.'

Before I can defend myself, Maddy vaults over the passenger door and flops down in the seat beside me. She flashes me a lopsided grin.

'I've always wanted to do that.'

I can't take my eyes off her. Right then, Maddy looks more beautiful than I've ever seen her. I watch as she pulls her hair back into a ponytail, not wanting to get it tangled in the wind. I'm immediately swept into a vision of just driving forever, out of Chicago; it doesn't matter where as long as Maddy's next to me. Still, something nags at me, a sensation that I can't quite place, adding a dark edge to what is an otherwise perfect moment.

I ignore the feeling.

'Ready?' I ask her.

'Ready,' she answers.

I don't take my eyes off her as I pull away from the curb with a flourish.

Immediately, I rear-end a conversion van that's double-parked a few feet away. That definitely wasn't there a few minutes ago.

'Oof,' groans Maddy as we're both jerked forward.

'Are you all right?' I ask, my hands shaking uncontrollably on the wheel. I'm simultaneously terrified that I've hurt her and mortified that I've made such an unbelievable asshole of myself.

'I – I think so,' she stammers.

In front of us, the doors of the conversion van swing open and three men jump out. They're all dressed in dark clothes, matching fedoras pulled low over pale faces.

I realize that in my back pocket, my iMog is vibrating like crazy.

16

I don't need the incessant vibrating from my pocket to tell me that the three men standing in front of my car are Mogs. I know my enemy.

'They probably want your insurance info,' says Maddy as she begins rifling through the glove box.

For a second I try to convince myself that this could just be a coincidence, that they don't know exactly who – or what – I am. But they're not looking at the damage to their van. I've crumpled their back bumper pretty good and shattered one of their taillights, but they don't seem to care.

All three of them stare at me. Slowly, one of them begins to reach under his coat.

There's no way this is random. Wishful thinking. My date is ruined before it's even started.

'Hell with it,' I growl, and throw the car into reverse.

The Mogs immediately fan out, trying to cut off my escape. As if I won't run them over. I rev the engine and peel out, forcing one of the Mogs to dive out of the way. As I shoot by, I see the others already scrambling into the van.

'What are you doing?!' screams Maddy.

'I think one of them had a gun,' I shout back, weaving around a slow-moving sedan.

'Are you nuts? Stanley, slow down!'

I do the opposite. Flooring it, I blow through a red light. The convertible's tires screech as I jerk the wheel hard left, nearly fishtailing us through a turn. Maddy is thrown against her seat belt and I wince as she cries out in pain.

In the rearview, I see the Mog van cut off by traffic. I realize that I've been holding my breath and let an exhale hiss through my teeth.

'Let me out,' says Maddy. 'Let me out of this car right now.'

I start to slow down, trying to blend into the rest of the traffic. That's not going to be easy considering my flashy car. I hope Sandor's out there somewhere watching this all go down on his network of hacked cameras, that he's sending a drone to bail me out as we speak.

The iMog in my pocket vibrates with renewed vigor.

'Hold on,' I say, punching the gas just as the Mog's van comes barreling out of a side street, nearly clipping the convertible's bumper.

The van is riding hard on our tail, trying to grind us off the road. Other cars let loose whining honks as we speed down the middle of the road. Maddy looks over her shoulder, staring in horror at the van bearing down on us and its stone-faced driver.

'They're right behind us.' Her voice is almost a whisper. Her hand is clutching my arm, nails digging right through my shirt. 'Why is this happening?'

I don't respond; there's no lie I can think of that could possibly explain it.

With sweaty fingers, I flick open a hidden panel on the steering wheel. Sandor planned for this sort of thing.

'Sit back,' I warn. Maddy looks at me, her frightened expression apparently not reserved just for the Mogs.

I hit the button for nitrous oxide.

The convertible's engine roars and then bucks and for a moment I'm worried the car can't handle Sandor's modification. Then, with a gut punch of pressure, it screams forward.

We're going way over the speed limit. I'm too afraid to check the speedometer, keeping my eyes pinned to the road as I weave through traffic. Maddy is glued to her seat, terrified. Seeing us coming, other cars try to move out of the way. Red traffic lights fly by. I hear a siren and, briefly, blue lights flash across my rearview, but any cops are outdistanced before they can even make out my license plate. We're a blur.

I keep driving until my iMog stops vibrating, and then I swing the car into a secluded alley and kill the lights.

My body hums with adrenaline. I can't believe what I just did, evading a pack of Mogs in a high-speed chase like something out of a movie. I'm an action hero. A mixture of euphoria and relief hits me.

And I don't really know where the next part comes from. Maybe it's pure adrenaline or maybe I'm just going totally crazy. But before I even realize I'm doing it, I lean into Maddy and start to kiss her.

I guess it wasn't the right thing to do.

'You bastard!' Maddy cries, pushing me away. She throws open her door, knocking over some nearby trash cans. In the dim light of the alley I can see that her beautiful face is streaked with tears.

Stunned from her reaction, I don't say anything as she runs out of the alley.

Alone in Sandor's banged-up convertible, I'm left to ponder the adventure-filled life of a Loric hero.

17

I abandon the convertible in the alley and head back to the John Hancock building on foot. I stick to side streets and back alleys as much as possible. My iMog never vibrates. Wherever those Mogs came from, they're gone now.

I call Sandor and tell him what happened. I catch him as he was on his way to try and find me – just as I suspected, he was monitoring me the whole time and freaking out.

It's past midnight when I make it back home. Sandor is waiting for me outside the building.

'What the hell?' he asks.

'I don't know,' I say. 'They just appeared.'

'A high-speed chase through the middle of Chicago? What were you thinking?'

'It was the only way.'

Sandor groans, dismissing that with a wave of his hand. 'You're acting like a child.'

'You said there weren't any Mogs in the city,' I protest.

'So stupid,' he says. 'I was so stupid to let you take that car. To even let you out of my sight. All because of some girl.'

'She's fine, by the way,' I snap.

'Who cares?' Sandor hisses, getting right in my face. 'She doesn't matter. *You* matter. Do you understand what you've put at stake? The years of progress you've undone in one night, all for some stupid crush?'

I take a step away from him. 'Don't talk about her that way.' He's being such a hypocrite. He was the one who wanted me to go after Maddy in the first place.

Sandor rubs his hands over his face, exasperated.

'Where did you leave the car?'

I give him the rough address of the alley.

'It needs to be destroyed,' he says, 'our presence here minimized. I'll handle that. You – you go upstairs and pack a bag.'

'What? Why?'

'We're leaving in the morning.'

I was close. So close to having a life that was more than just Sandor, more than just training.

I pace around the penthouse, letting my gaze drift aimlessly across all the luxuries we've amassed over the last five years. Five years living here in peace and comfort – all ruined because I was bored. When I killed that Mog in the elevator, I thought things would change. I thought that I would assume my destiny and begin the war against the Mogadorians. I thought that would make me happy.

Instead, it's only made things worse.

What felt best about killing that Mog wasn't that some small justice was done. It was that I had chosen how and when to do it. It was my choice.

And yet now my options are fewer than ever. Sandor

wants us back on the road, just when I was starting to figure things out. It doesn't seem right that he should get to call all the shots.

Shouldn't I get some say in our next move?

I can't bring myself to pack a bag. I'm still clinging to some hope that Sandor will change his mind.

I try to call Maddy, but her phone goes right to voicemail. Not that I would know what to say if she did answer. What kind of lie could I tell her? I spend the better part of an hour trying to compose an apology for nearly getting her killed, for scaring her, and for not even realizing that I was doing it.

In the end, I settle on texting a simple 'I'm sorry.'

There's going to be no sleep for me tonight.

I pass through Sandor's workshop and into the Lecture Hall. There are automated training modules programmed into the room's interface. I select one at random and stride into the center of the room, holding my pipe-staff.

When the first ball bearing fires out of the Lectern's turret I don't deflect it with my telekinesis or bat it away with my pipe-staff. I let it hit me right in the chest. I suck in my breath as dull pain courses through my sternum.

Gritting my teeth, I clasp my hands behind my back and lean forward. The next ball bearing strikes me a few inches to the left of the first, bruising my ribs.

When the third ball bearing is fired, my instincts take over. I push it aside with my telekinesis and pivot to the side, anticipating the next shot. I spin my pipe-staff over my head as the program really gears up, heavy bags swinging at me from behind, a mechanical tentacle grasping at me from the floor.

My mind turns off. I fight.

I'm not sure how long I keep going like that, dodging and swinging, acting instead of thinking. Eventually I'm dripping with sweat, my shirt completely soaked through. It's then that the Lecture Hall's patterns change; the attacks become less predictable, more coordinated than the auto-program could pull off.

I realize that Sandor has returned and climbed into the Lectern's seat, his fingers dancing across the control panel.

Our eyes meet as I leap over a metal-plated battering ram. His look is one of sadness and disappointment.

'You didn't pack,' he says.

I square my shoulders and glare at him in defiance. *Go ahead,* I want to tell him, *throw everything you can at me. I can take it.*

I'm going to prove to Sandor that I'm not his young ward anymore.

'I suppose one last training session before we leave won't hurt,' Sandor says.

A glimmering tennis ball–sized object floats up from the floor, emitting a disorienting strobe light. It makes the next round of projectiles harder to see, but I manage to catch them in the air, using my mind to hold them inches from my bruised chest.

'That hasn't been decided yet,' I say evenly as I launch one of the projectiles at the flashing ball, exploding it. It clatters to the floor, blinking out.

'What hasn't been decided?' he asks.

'That we're leaving.'

'No?'

A pair of heavy bags career toward me, quickly followed by another volley of ball bearings. I swing the pipe-staff as hard as I can at one of them, my muscles screaming in protest. The pipe-staff shreds through the bag, sending sand spilling onto the floor.

One of the ball bearings strikes me in the hip, but I catch the others and hurl them back the way they came. The turrets in the wall hiss and pop when the ball bearings reenter their barrels the wrong way. There's a short puff of smoke and then they hang dormant.

'I get a vote,' I tell him. 'And I vote we stay.'

'That's impossible,' Sandor replies. 'You don't understand what's at stake. You're not thinking clearly.'

Three drones deploy from the floor. I've never fought that many at once before. One is the propeller-powered toaster that just days ago we were trying out on the roof. The others I haven't seen before. They're the size of soccer balls, metal plated, with scopes attached to the front.

The toaster bobs in front of me, distracting me as the other two flank me. When they're in position, the soccer balls emit two bursts of electricity, jolting me.

I retreat toward the back of the room, the drones zapping

at me. My ears are ringing from the last shock. The drones close in, pursuing me. I'm running out of room.

Before I realize what I'm doing, I run up the wall. My aim was to flip off the wall, to land behind the drones, but something is different. I don't feel gravity pulling at me. I plant my feet.

I'm standing on the wall. Except for a sudden feeling of vertigo, it feels no different than standing on the ground.

My Legacy. I've developed one of my Legacies.

Staring at me, Sandor is too stunned to adjust the course of the drones. The toaster crashes into the wall. From above, I swing my pipe-staff down on the two floating soccer balls, destroying them both.

Sandor lets out a cry of triumph.

'Do you see?' he shouts. 'Do you see what you're capable of? My young ward gets an upgrade!'

'Upgrade?' I growl.

I run up the rest of the wall and onto the ceiling. The room turns upside down. I sprint across the ceiling that's now the floor to me, gathering up a head of steam. When I'm right above Sandor and the Lectern I jump, twist in mid-air, and bring my pipe-staff shearing down on the Lectern.

The control panel explodes in a waterfall of sparks. Sandor dives aside, grunting as he lands hard on his shoulder. My pipe-staff has carved deep into the front of the Lectern, practically cutting it in two. It lets out a series of ear-splitting mechanical squawks, and then the Lecture Hall goes dark.

'I'm not one of your gadgets,' I shout into the darkness. 'You don't get to just control me.'

Starbursts of light flash across my vision as my eyes try to adjust to the darkness. I can't quite see Sandor, but I can hear him shakily climb to his feet.

'I don't – I don't think that,' Sandor says. I'm thankful I can't see his face, the hurt plain enough in his voice. 'Everything I've ever done, all these years –' He stops, searching for words.

As I come back down to earth, the memories of the night come back to me. I realize what I've done.

'Nine . . .' I feel Sandor's hand on my shoulder. 'I –'

I don't want to hear this. I shrug his hand roughly away and run.

18

The sun is beginning to rise. The air is still cool, chilling my skin under my sweat-dampened T-shirt. I fled the John Hancock building with nothing but the clothes on my back – the same clothes I wore on my ruined date the night before – and my cell phone and iMog tucked into my back pockets.

A part of me knows that I'll need to go back to Sandor eventually. But right now, I'm ignoring that part as hard as I can.

I want to know how long I can last out here on my own. The day is just beginning. I can do anything I choose with it.

I feel like Spider-Man, using my newest legacy to stand on the outside of an anonymous Chicago skyscraper, fifty stories up. Beneath my feet, inside the windows, the office building's automatic lights are coming on. I gaze down at the streets below, the city just starting to wake up.

Thanks to my antigravity Legacy, I'm seeing Chicago from angles I never imagined.

I sprint across the skyscraper's windows, then jump across the narrow gap between buildings. On the next building I jog upward, bounding over a stone gargoyle until I'm balancing right on the roof ledge. I walk across the ledge, my arms spread out like a tightrope walker, even though there's no chance of me losing my balance. Hundreds of feet above the ground and it's as if I'm on the sidewalk.

This would have come in handy that first day at the Windy Wall.

Across the street, I catch sight of an executive type settling in behind his desk with his morning coffee. That's my signal to rein it in. I don't need Sandor around to tell me it'd be a bad idea to be seen strolling around on the sides of buildings.

I hop onto the roof. For a while I just sit and watch the sun coming up. I've got no place to be. It's peaceful. When the sun hangs in full view above me, the noise of the city below increasing to rush hour decibels, I decide to check my cell phone.

Three voicemails and four text messages. All of them from Sandor.

I delete them.

Suddenly I'm very tired. I didn't sleep at all last night. It's a nice day and there's a sense of calm on this rooftop. My eyelids start to feel heavy.

I curl up in a shady spot near the edge of the precipice. The roof is hard but my body is too exhausted to do much complaining.

For some reason, my mind drifts to the dream I had of Lorien. I think about the way I flung myself at Sandor, getting us both all muddy, and the way he lifted me into the air afterward, grinning. That was a nice memory. I hope I dream it again.

*

I don't dream at all. It's a deep sleep, and when I finally wake up the sun has almost set. I slept away the entire day. My body aches, both from the exertion of the night before and from passing out on a slab of hard rooftop.

Groaning and stretching, I sit up. I decide to check my cell phone again, even though I know what's waiting for me.

More voicemails and texts from Sandor, the texts increasingly panicked as he begs me to let him know where I am, that I'm all right. My stomach turns over with guilt. I'll let him know eventually, I decide. I just need more time.

And then I see it. A single text from the only other number programmed into my phone.

Maddy.

'Maybe we can try again if you promise no cars.'

I leap to my feet, punching the air in celebration. After everything I put her through last night, even after the whole thing with the kiss, and she still wants to see me again. That has to mean something, right? With one simple text Maddy has reassured me that the connection I felt between us is real.

Even knowing that it can never be simple and easy between us, that eventually this brief freedom I have will be gone and I'll be swept back up in my destiny – even knowing all that, I still have to see her. I know I can set things right between us. And maybe I can have just one perfect, normal moment.

I bound across the rooftops as the sun sets, a shadow above the heads of tired commuters. I chart a course across walls and windows and power lines, heading for Maddy's house.

I'm cautious during my approach. The Mogs were following me last night, so they're obviously onto me. I need to make sure they're not still lurking around. They could be anywhere. I prowl the surrounding blocks, sticking to the rooftops, one eye always on my iMog.

There's no sign of any danger.

From across the street I scope out Maddy's house. I feel sort of like a stalker. The sight of parents would be almost as bad as the sight of Mogs. Showing up unannounced might not go over too well with Maddy's folks. I don't want to have to throw pebbles at her window.

I climb up the building opposite Maddy's, careful to stay hidden, and watch her windows. She told me that her parents travel a lot. It looks like I've lucked out and that's the case tonight. The only movement I see in the apartment is Maddy, lounging on a couch with her laptop.

It feels gross to spy on her longer than necessary, so I walk back down to the street and approach her building the normal way.

A few seconds after I buzz her, Maddy's voice pipes uncertainly out of the intercom.

'Hello?'

'Hi,' I say into the mic. 'It's Stanley.'

There's a lengthy pause, long enough for me to consider that this was a stupid idea. She could be peering down at me right now, hoping that I'll slink off into the night and leave her alone. Or, worse yet, she could be calling the cops.

I'm relieved when the door finally buzzes, letting me in.

Maddy's apartment is on the third floor. I bound up the stairs. She's waiting for me in the hallway, dressed in baggy pajama pants, a tank top, and an unbuttoned cardigan sweater.

'Are you okay?' Maddy asks as soon as she sees me.

I realize how I must look. I'm wearing the same clothes I wore yesterday and in the time since then I've endured my most intense Lecture Hall workout ever and slept on a rooftop. Belatedly, I run a hand through my hair and try to brush some wrinkles out of my T-shirt.

'I've had a really bad twenty-four hours,' I tell her honestly.

'I think I know what you mean.' She gives me a nervous little smile. 'So . . .'

'I'm sorry to just show up,' I explain, in a rush to defuse the awkwardness. 'I just – I'm not sure when I'll be able to see you again and I wanted to apologize in person.'

'Thank you for coming,' Maddy says, a note of relief in her voice. And then she's hugging me, her face pressed into my chest.

I let myself enjoy that moment, trying to commit to memory how her body feels pressed against me, wrapped in my arms.

'Don't take this the wrong way,' she whispers, 'but you kind of smell.'

*

165

Just as I thought, Maddy's parents are out of town. She invites me in, joking that breaking their rule about having boys over while they're away is nothing after flagrantly violating their stance against high-speed car chases. I laugh, but I also notice the bruise peeking out from under Maddy's sweater where the seat belt dug into her shoulder and I feel guilty all over again.

Maddy insists that I take a shower. She gives me a pair of her Dad's sweatpants and a faded NASA T-shirt and sends me into the bathroom to get cleaned up.

I linger in the shower. The water is hot and feels good on my sore muscles. For a while I let myself imagine that I'm just another teenager grabbing a shower after sneaking over to his girlfriend's house while her parents are out of town. Not that Maddy is my girlfriend, but she could be.

It's strange to be in a house like this. Obviously it doesn't match the John Hancock penthouse in opulence, but it makes up for that in coziness. Unlike where Sandor and I have been staying, Maddy's house actually feels lived in. The furniture is broken in. There are pictures of Maddy and her parents everywhere. Knickknacks and trinkets clutter bookshelves, mementos from trips taken as a family. There is an entire history here. I'm envious.

Maddy is waiting for me in her bedroom when I get out of the shower. I realize it's the first time I've ever been in a normal kid's bedroom. There are pictures of Maddy and her friends, school trophies, posters of movie stars on the walls.

It's so different from my utilitarian room, filled with just video game systems and dirty laundry.

She pats the bed and I sit down next to her. I can tell she's been trying to work out what I'm doing here, why I arrived in such a state.

'Tell me the truth,' she begins. 'Did you run away from home?'

'Kind of,' I reply, a little embarrassed. I lay back on the bed, draping an arm over my face. Maddy lies down next to me, trying to look at me.

'Do you want to talk about it?'

I do. But how much can I tell her?

'I got in a fight with my uncle.'

'Because of the car?'

'Yeah. Well, not really. That was like the straw that broke the camel's back. It's been building up for a while.'

Maddy makes an encouraging noise, and I realize that she's holding my hand.

Then it all comes pouring out of me.

'I feel like my uncle has my entire life mapped out. Like every decision that affects me I just have no control over. And then when I do try to act on my own, something horrible happens. Like last night.'

I think about the bruises on Maddy's shoulder. As if sensing my guilt, she gives my hand an encouraging squeeze.

'I want to get away from everything. From my entire life. But I feel like any decision I make, I'll just end up regretting.'

I lift my arm from my face and squint at her in the darkness.

'Does that make any sense at all?'

I think I see tears in Maddy's eyes. She nods her head.

'Yes,' she says quietly.

We lie on her bed, holding hands. Eventually, just like it did in the Lecture Hall, my mind shuts off. I don't want anything more than this. I have to figure things out with Sandor tomorrow, but for tonight, this is perfect. Normal.

We fall asleep.

19

At some point, I feel Maddy get out of bed and leave the room.

I linger in that space between being asleep and awake, vaguely aware that it is morning. Maddy's bed is insanely comfortable and I don't want to get up. In my dreamy state, I let myself wonder how many days Maddy's parents will be out of town. Maybe I can stretch this vacation from responsibility out a little further.

There is a shuffling next to the bed. Probably Maddy returning.

A set of fingers touch my arm. They are strangely cold.

My eyes snap open. Two thin, pale men stand over me, both of them with their jet-black hair shorn close to their skulls.

The Mogadorians have found me.

Almost more frightening than the pair of ugly faces glaring down at me is the empty spot in the bed next to me.

Maddy. What have they done to her?

A surge of fear breaks over me. These Mogs might be able to capture me, but they can't actually hurt me. Not when I'm protected by the Loric charm. Maddy, on the other hand – they could do whatever they want to her. For a moment, I hope this is some really intense nightmare. When they make a grab for my arms and legs, working in tandem to pin me down, I know it's real. I squirm away from the one grabbing my ankles and kick him in the chest with as much strength as my still-groggy body can muster. The Mog goes crashing backward into Maddy's desk, knocking through her things. Her purse goes tumbling to the floor, spilling its contents next to a newly broken swimming trophy. When the Mog tries to regain his feet, he ends up shoving Maddy's laptop to the floor as well.

I've made a mess of her room. I've made a mess of her life.

The other one's gotten hold of my wrists and is pinning me to the bed. He grunts as I thrash against his grip, his face close enough that I can smell his sour breath. His face is close enough, in fact, that I can head-butt him.

The blow caves in the Mog's nose. His grip on my wrists loosens and I'm able to wriggle free. I bring my legs up, doing a backward somersault. My feet hit the wall and just like that my perspective shifts, the anti-gravity Legacy kicking in. I'm eye level with one of them even though our bodies are perpendicular, and I punch him in the face.

Both Mogs are taken aback that I'm suddenly running across the ceiling. Good. That should buy me a second or two. I need to find Maddy and get us out of here. I wonder if she keeps an emergency bag hidden somewhere, but then I realize that keeping a bag of road supplies handy isn't at all a human thing to do. I think about grabbing her purse, but when I see the contents spilled out of it onto the floor, dozens of plastic IDs with her photo smiling up at me – why does she have so many IDs, anyway? I wonder – I know there's no time. Sandor will just have to make her a new identity on the fly.

I kick open her bedroom door from the ceiling, leaping over the uppermost part of the doorframe as I go. There's another Mog waiting outside, but he didn't expect me to come from above. The ones behind me shout a warning at their friend. Too late.

With a roar, I grab the surprised Mog under the chin with both my hands. Then I jump from the ceiling, simultaneously pulling back on his head. The physics are impossible. I can hear bones popping inside the scout as I spike his head into the ground, his forehead touching the floor a few inches from his heels.

The Mog disintegrates into a cloud of ash. The pictures of Maddy's family that line the hallway are covered in dust. I feel guilty once again. Maddy's home felt so perfect when I arrived last night, and now, by bringing the fight here, I've roped her and her perfect family into an intergalactic war. Great.

I run back up the wall, onto the ceiling, and sprint toward Maddy's living room, screaming her name. The two Mogs from the bedroom chase after me, one clutching his broken face.

There are three more of them in the living room. Two of

them flank the couch where Maddy sits with her head in her hands. I can't tell if she's hurt or crying or both.

'Maddy!' I shout. 'We have to run!' She flinches at the sound of my voice, but otherwise remains still.

The third Mogadorian stands in front of the apartment's door. He smiles when he sees me. It's a sickening expression; his teeth are gray and rotting, pointing in all the wrong directions. This one is larger than the others. He must be the leader. A wicked-looking sword dangles from his hip, but he makes no move to reach for it. He seems content to just block our only exit.

He doesn't realize that there's always another exit when you can walk on walls.

I stoop down and, with a shout, tear the ceiling fan at my feet from its moorings. I wish I had my pipe-staff, but this will have to do.

With the exception of their leader, the Mogadorians have all converged on me. I jump off the ceiling with the fan in hand, bringing it down on top of the closest Mog's head. The wooden fan blade snaps in half as it splits his skull. His body immediately decomposes into ash, mixing with fan fragments on Maddy's carpet.

Two down, four to go.

I spin in a circle, swinging the remains of the fan around as I do. My assailants are all forced back a step as I gather momentum. I let the fan loose and it goes flying between two Mogs. They smirk, thinking I've missed them, but they were never my intended target. Behind them, the living room window shatters, glass and pieces of wood spraying into the street below.

There's our exit.

One of the Mogs manages to wrap his arms around me from behind. Another – the one whose nose I broke – forgets the rules and hauls off to punch me. A warm sensation spreads across my face as a fresh bruise spreads across his, staggering him. I elbow the other Mog in the gut, breaking free.

'Maddy!' I shout, making a bull rush toward her. One of the Mogadorians tries to cut me off. I drop my shoulder low, like I would to duck under a heavy bag in the Lecture Hall, and drive into his knees. The Mog flips over me and goes smashing through a coffee table.

At the door, I hear the leader quietly chuckle. I'm not sure what's funny about his squad getting their asses handed to them. At least he's a good sport.

I grab Maddy by the shoulders and pull her to her feet. Her hands fall to her sides and I can see that her face is ashen. Her eyes are red-rimmed and distant, totally checked out. I don't even want to imagine what the Mogs did to shut her down like this. She's deadweight in my arms.

'Come on!' I shout, shaking her by the shoulders.

And then something strange happens. I feel energy welling up in my core and rushing out through my limbs, fingertips tingling. Maddy must feel something too – a rush, a burst of energy – because her eyes snap into focus.

'What – what are you doing?' she says in a shaky voice.

I don't know how I know, or even exactly how I did it, but I'm certain that a new Legacy has just presented itself based on the feeling coursing through me. 'Just trust me for now,' I say. 'Go with it, okay?'

Taking Maddy by the hand, I run toward the nearest wall. The Mog with the broken nose tries to cut us off, but I knock an end table into his legs, upending him. When we reach the wall, I feel that rush again, and know instinctively that I've extended my antigravity Legacy to Maddy. That must be what I felt just a second ago – I now have the ability to share my powers with someone else, but I have no idea how long it will last. I kick out, still holding her hand, and feel the axis of the room shift as I run up the wall. At first it feels like Maddy's just going to let me drag her but then she follows, defying gravity a few steps behind me. I smile to myself as she lets out a gasp, not quite believing what she's doing.

'Almost there,' I shout over my shoulder.

I lead us toward the window. Escape is only a few feet away. I realize that we aren't being chased anymore. Are they letting us go?

Suddenly Maddy plants her feet. I jerk to a stop, still holding her hand. I turn to face her, expecting one of the Mogs to have grabbed her.

But she's just standing there.

'Maddy?' The sight of her, eyes downcast, face ghostly pale, doesn't make any sense to me. Something tells me I should run, but I can't bring myself to let go of her hand.

I look down and see a taser in a white-knuckled grip in her free hand. Where did she get that?

'I'm sorry,' she says. And then she tases me. The electric current surges through us both. We fall off the ceiling, both of us spasming, bouncing hard off the floor.

The Mogs descend on us.

20

I come to in the back of a van. I'm seated on a bench, my hands bound behind me, my ankles similarly secured. I can tell that we're traveling fast. My spine bounces uncomfortably against the van's steel wall.

Maddy is seated across from me. The look of shell shock has returned to her face. She keeps her eyes pinned to the van's floor. They haven't even bothered to tie her up. It's starting to dawn on me why that is, but I put it out of my head. I'm not ready to think about it now.

Next to Maddy is the huge Mogadorian from the apartment. He studies a small object, turning it over in his thick hands.

It's my iMog.

The Mog notices that I'm awake and watching him. His lips peel back and I'm forced to endure his sickening smile up close.

'Cute toy,' he says, holding up my iMog. The screen is littered with red dots. 'Too bad it didn't do you any good this time.'

He crushes the device between his hands, dropping it mangled to the van floor.

He watches with amusement as I strain against my bonds. There's no give at all in the metal shackles securing my wrists and ankles. I take a closer look around the back of the van; the benches on either side are bolted to the floor, a chain-link mesh separating us from the driver, nothing else of note.

There's no escape.

I consider throwing myself at him. Maybe I can get close enough to bite him. However, I'm not just shackled, I'm also chained to the bench. They've taken every precaution.

'You're stuck with me,' says the Mog, sensing my resignation.

I grit my teeth and stare at him. He smiles back.

'Tell me. Where is your Cêpan?'

'Rio de Janeiro,' I reply, picking the first place that comes to mind.

He scoffs. 'How stupid do you think we are?'

'Pretty freaking stupid.'

'Hmm. We found you, didn't we? One of my scouts goes missing. His last reported location is the Chicago lakefront, tailing a boy matching your description. For my scout to simply disappear, I figure you brought him someplace. So, you must have a safe house in the area.' He kicks the broken pieces of my iMog. 'You must have a way to get the drop on him.'

I try to keep my expression neutral, but inside I'm screaming. This is my fault.

'Where is your Cêpan?' repeats the Mog. 'Where is your safe house?'

'You don't know?' I ask. 'Tough luck, dude. I guess you're on your own.'

He sighs. 'So much bravado. I wonder if that will hold true once we've killed our way to whatever number you are.'

My mind races. I try to figure out how much the Mogs could know. They had my description, knew that I liked the lakefront, and guessed that we had some way to see them coming. What else could they know? How much did I tell Maddy about my life?

Maddy. I look over at her. It had to be her. She was helping them. But why would she do that? And how long has it been going on? Did they get to her after the car chase? Coerce her somehow? Could she be one of them? I dismiss the last possibility – my iMog would have alerted me.

I remember the mess my fight with the Mogadorians made in Maddy's room, the contents of her purse all over the floor. So many ID cards. Way more than normal. I didn't think anything of it in the heat of battle. Those IDs, just like the one I have for Windy City Wall, but different. I realize they were membership IDs for rec centers all over Chicago.

My stomach turns over as I think back to the way Maddy looked at me on that first day. So interested at first, yet nervous when I noticed her, and then disappearing before I could talk to her.

'You were looking for me,' I say, dumbfounded.

The Mogadorian lounges back, lazily draping an arm

around Maddy's shoulders. She shudders and attempts to shrink away, but he holds her close.

Her just happening to show up at the thrift store. Taking my picture. The way the Mogs appeared in that van on the night of our date. How mad she was at the end of the car chase. None of it was coincidence. As much as I don't want it to, suddenly Maddy's interest in me begins to make sense.

'You Lorien act so high and mighty, yet you're just like the humans. All it takes is a pretty face to cloud your judgment.'

He pinches Maddy's cheek. I make a futile lunge forward, only succeeding in rattling my chains and hurting my wrists. The Mog chortles.

'So chivalrous,' he sneers. 'Are you so dense that you don't realize what's happened? She betrayed you, boy. The girl works for us. We've had her for some time, although we didn't know what to do with her. Humans. So useless, you know? But when we asked her to find you, she did a bang-up job. Didn't you, sweetheart?' He gives Maddy a mockingly affectionate squeeze.

I know all this is true, as true as the electric shock she pumped into my body just a few hours ago, but I don't want to believe it. There has to be an explanation.

I ignore the Mog, trying to catch Maddy's eye.

'Why?' I ask her.

Her mouth tightens, almost as if she has to stop herself from answering. He responds for her.

'Her father the so-called astronomer saw something he

shouldn't have,' he says. 'These primitives and their tele-scopes, sometimes they get lucky. We were forced to detain him and her mother.'

I can see the pain in Maddy's face as the Mog gleefully finishes his explanation.

'She traded you for them.'

21

The Mog spends the next couple of hours trying to wheedle information out of me, alternating between taunting me and trying to frighten me. I adopt a strict policy of silence and eventually he gives up. But I know it's not over. We ride on in silence.

I stare at Maddy. She never once looks up at me.

If what the Mog told me is true – and it must be, or otherwise Maddy would have defended herself – then she's been playing me since I first saw her. The connection I felt between us was just a sham, something I let myself believe because of how desperate and lonely I was. I was so stupid to believe that a girl like Maddy would be interested in me.

And yet the more I study Maddy's face, the more I'm able to convince myself that maybe it wasn't all just some Mog trick. She looks terrified, like she's stuck in a nightmare that refuses to end. But it isn't just terror that keeps her from looking at me. That's guilt.

She wouldn't feel guilty if there had never been anything at all between us. Would she?

Sandor was right. I've been acting like a child.

I know the responsible thing to do is to remain silent, to

keep up my air of detachment until a way to escape presents itself. But I need to know the truth.

'Did you ever like me?' I ask Maddy.

Maddy cringes when I speak. The Mog claps his hands, delighted, but I ignore him. Slowly, Maddy raises her head to look at me.

'I'm s-sorry,' she stammers. 'I'm sorry I didn't get a chance to know you better.'

'How romantic,' quips the Mog, and then he grabs Maddy roughly by the shoulders, shoving a black hood over her head.

'You're next, loverboy,' says the Mog, yanking a hood over my head as well.

I never have a chance to ask Maddy what she meant.

Sitting in the dark, I try to put myself in Maddy's position. What would I do if the Mogs had taken Sandor hostage and forced me to work for them?

I'd kill them all, of course. But, that really wasn't an option for Maddy.

I don't blame Maddy, I realize. How could she have done anything different? She had no idea what was really at stake.

I can still fix this. I can escape, and I'll bring Maddy with me. It doesn't matter what she did. I know she's not the real enemy here.

The van stops and the Mogs pull me and Maddy out. We stumble along in darkness, at first over rough terrain that I take for the woods, and then over metal grates that cause our footsteps to echo loudly. Wherever the Mogs have taken us, it sounds cavernous and busy, activity reverberating around us.

For a while I keep track of Maddy's footsteps as she staggers behind me, but at some point the Mogs yank her in a different direction. They prod me onward, forcing me to shuffle awkwardly with my shackled ankles across narrow catwalks and down endless hallways.

Finally, we stop. The large Mog from the van yanks the hood off my head, ripping out a few strands of my hair in the process. We're in a dark room with no furniture or distinguishing features to speak of, only a single large window cut out of one wall. Some other Mogs have gathered there, most of them leering at me, others excitedly peering out the window.

'I thought you'd like to see this,' says the Mog, dragging me by the elbow over to the window.

The room is some kind of observatory. Outside the window, below us, I see Maddy walking through a large, empty room. Seeing her alone down there, my stomach begins to churn.

A door at the opposite end of the room hisses open and a middle-aged man and woman step slowly into view. They both look thin and dirty. The man is particularly haggard, one sleeve of his yellowed dress shirt actually ripped off and tied around his forehead in a crude bandage. The woman has to partially support him as the pair walk toward Maddy.

'We promised we'd reunite her with her parents when she brought us to you,' muses the Mog. 'A job well done, I'd say.'

Maddy races across the room, nearly bowling over her parents when she reaches them. They hug and I can see even from this distance that they are all crying. I press my forehead to the glass, wishing I could be down there with them.

'However,' says the Mog, 'we never said we'd let them leave.'

I hear the beast before I see it, a ferocious roar rattling the walls around us. The Mogs on either side of me shift in excitement as the creature lumbers into view. Sandor told me about the piken and the role they played in the destruction of Lorien, but I've never seen one in person. The piken is as big as a truck with a body that would resemble an ox if not for the two extra legs and row of twisted spikes that curve down its spine. Its head is snakelike and narrow, its slavering mouth filled with crooked fangs.

Maddy's father sees the piken first. He tries to put himself between his family and the beast, but he's too weak. He collapses onto one knee before the piken has even begun to circle.

Maddy is looking up at the observatory window. I'm not sure if she can see me. She waves her arms and screams. It's hard to hear exactly what she's saying through the thick glass, but I think it's 'You promised!' over and over.

And then, as the piken lunges forward, her words change. This time, I have no problem reading her lips.

'Stanley!' Maddy screams. 'Help us!'

I throw up.

My mouth tastes like bile. I sink down to my knees, humiliated, turning my head away from the gruesome scene below.

The Mogs laugh and cheer. This is like sport to them.

The big one pats my shoulder companionably.

'If it's any consolation,' he says, 'pretty soon that will be you down there.'

22

My life becomes push-ups and silence.

The Mogs have stuck me in a small cell and seem to have forgotten me. There's no night and day here and, as best as I can tell, they only feed me when they feel like it. Keeping track of the time becomes impossible. So I do push-ups. On the floor, on the walls, on the ceiling – wherever I can in my tiny prison.

I think about Sandor. I have faith that he's still out there looking for me. One day he'll find me. We will break out of here and I will kill every Mog that dares stand in my way.

I thought I was in good shape before, but I'm getting bigger and stronger. I can tell by the way the Mogs who bring my food keep a careful distance that I intimidate them.

I'm glad. Let them think about what's coming when I get out of here. I hope they dream about it like I do.

Sometimes the large Mog who captured me, or one of the other important-looking ones, stops by my cell to ask me some vague question. Where have I hidden my transmission device? What do I know about Spain?

I never answer. I haven't spoken since my first day here. I grunt and growl, and show them my teeth. Let them think that I've gone crazy, that captivity has turned me into some kind of animal. Maybe it has.

When I sleep, the nightmares come. They feel as real as the vision I had of Lorien, but offer none of the comfort. In them, an enormous Mogadorian covered in heinous tattoos and scars points a golden weapon shaped like a giant hammer in my direction. On the flat part is painted a black eye that pulses when aimed at me, creating a sensation like having my guts scooped out.

Somehow, I know who this giant monster is. Setrakus Ra. My enemy.

Sleeping is bad, but sometimes being awake is even worse. These are days where I feel like I can't breathe. It feels as if the entire cavernous prison is sitting on top of me. The need to escape becomes primal then, and I throw myself against the glowing blue force field that keeps me in my cell, letting it buffet me across the tiny space until I'm too exhausted to do it again.

The nausea sets in then. I learn to fight through it. Each time I hit the force field, it hurts a little less.

I try not to think about Maddy.

One day the Mogs take me out of my cell. If I had to guess, I'd say that it has been months since I came here.

They lead me to a different cell, where they place me behind another blue force field. The large Mog from the van is in the room, seated on what I immediately recognize as a Loric Chest.

My Loric Chest.

'We found him in Ohio,' says the Mog matter-of-factly. 'Snooping around the office of a little newsletter we've been keeping under surveillance. Looking for you.' He presses a button and a panel in the back of the cell raises.

My heart stops when I see what's behind it.

It's Sandor. My Cêpan hangs upside down from the ceiling. He's been badly beaten – both of his eyes are blackened, his lips swollen, his torso marred by grisly slashes. Perhaps worst of all, they have torn out chunks of his usually perfectly maintained hair and left his finely tailored suit in tatters.

He is not at all the man I remember. They've destroyed him. My eyes fill with tears, but I fight them back.

Sandor sucks in a breath when he sees me. I wonder how different I must look to him after these months of captivity. It's hard to say with his face so swollen and covered in bruises, but Sandor looks almost happy.

I'm ashamed of myself – both because it's my fault we've been captured, and because I'm so powerless.

'My young ward,' he whispers.

The Mog turns to me. He's holding a wicked-looking dagger.

'Your little vow of silence routine has been fun,' the Mog says to me. 'But it ends today.'

He walks over to Sandor and lightly drags the dagger down his sternum.

'I don't think you know anything,' muses my captor. 'Nothing that we don't know already, at least.' He shrugs.

'But I'm going to torture your Cêpan anyway. Until you ask me to stop.'

He wants to break me. I say nothing. I remember Sandor's lectures on what to do if the unthinkable should happen and I'm captured. Don't give them anything, he told me. Even the slightest bit of information could hurt the other Garde who are still in hiding. Don't let them make you weak.

I hope it's not too late to make Sandor proud.

I stare into Sandor's eyes. He stares back until the Mog begins making his cuts; precise, surgical slices that must hurt like hell but aren't deep enough to kill. My Cêpan clenches his eyes shut, screaming into his gag.

When the Mog is finished, Sandor has passed out from the pain and a pool of blood has collected on the cell floor beneath him.

I keep my silence.

The next day, it starts over.

I keep my body rigid and my mouth shut. When Sandor can manage to focus on me, I think that I see pride in his eyes.

This continues for days. After every session, the Mogs return me to my cell, where I shake uncontrollably until the routine starts over again.

When they take Sandor's fingers off, I have to turn away.

At the next session, the Mog hums tunelessly while he cuts away at Sandor. My Cêpan flits in and out of consciousness. I wait for him to make eye contact with me before I finally speak.

'I'm sorry for everything,' I croak, my voice like gravel after months of disuse.

The Mog spins to face me, stunned. 'What did you say?'

Barely able to move, Sandor can manage only a subtle shake of his head, as if to absolve me of all the mistakes that led us here. I don't find any peace in forgiveness, but maybe Sandor does in the forgiving.

Sandor closes his eyes.

And something in me snaps. Mustering every bit of strength I have, I hurl myself against the force field, ignoring the pain. There's a buzz and a crackle and then the sound of a small explosion and I find myself sprawled on the floor of the room, looking up at the Mogadorians, whose monstrous faces betray their shock at what I've managed to do. I've disabled the force field. I'm through.

I know I only have a second to act before the element of surprise wears off. I push through overwhelming dizziness and nausea and try to use my telekinesis to wrest the dagger from the Mog's hand, but nothing happens. The field must have somehow zapped my Legacies. For now, I'll have to rely on the part of me that's human. Normal.

The Mogs lunge for me, but I'm ready for them. I kick the first one in the stomach, knocking the wind out of him and sending him flying, and yank the other one's ankles, pulling his legs out from under him. His head makes a loud crack against the floor and I jump to my feet. They're both knocked out, but not for long.

I grab the dagger from the floor where the Mogadorian

from the van dropped it, and I'm contemplating which one to kill first when I hear a grunt from behind me. It's Sandor.

'No,' he mutters. I spin around to face him. His eyes are open again, and it seems like he's using every bit of energy he has to speak.

'Not them,' he says. 'It won't do any good. There will just be more.'

'Then what?' I ask. My voice catches in my throat. This isn't fair. It wasn't how it was supposed to be. 'What should I do?'

'You know what you have to do,' he says.

'I can't. I won't.'

'You've always known I would die for you. That I would die for Lorien.'

I almost argue with him, but there's not time. The Mogs behind me are beginning to come to. I know he's right. And I know what I must do.

I take the dagger and plunge it deep into Sandor's heart.

My Cêpan is dead.

I barely know what's happening as they pull me off him and drag me back to my cell. They're yelling at me – screaming really, madder than I've ever seen them – but it's like they're speaking another language. I have no idea what they're saying, and I don't care.

It was mercy, what I did. The last bit of mercy left in me. There will be none left when I get my chance again.

23

The Mogs leave me to rot in my cell; the only contact comes in the form of the occasional tray of slop under my door. I try to bust through the force field again and again, but it doesn't work this time. They must have increased its strength. They're afraid of me.

I don't blame them. Sometimes I'm a little afraid of me too.

I cling to the memories of Sandor and Maddy, reliving their last moments. I feel the rage bubble up inside me and my mind shuts off. When I return to myself, I'm sweating, my knuckles bloodied, chips of stone hacked out of the walls of my cell. I've forgiven Maddy but I haven't forgiven myself.

There is nothing else to do but wait, remember, and get stronger.

And then one day it happens.

I can tell something is going wrong. There's a rumbling from below that causes dust to fall from the ceiling. I can hear large groups of Mogs running by my door, voices raised in panic. Wrong for the Mogs could mean right for me.

I feel a rush of energy like I haven't felt since the first time Sandor let me loose in the Lecture Hall. I can't keep my fists from clenching and unclenching.

I walk as close to the door as I can without triggering the bubbling force field. I feel like those bulls at the rodeos right before they're let free from their pens.

When the force field flickers and disappears, I almost can't believe it. The sickly blue light has been a fixture of my world for so long that it takes my mind a moment to adjust to its absence.

There is a voice on the other side of my door. It's not a Mogadorian voice; it's a teenage one. I don't know what he's asking and I don't care.

'Shut up and stand back, kid.'

I tear the door loose and throw it into the hall. I'm stronger than I remember being. Part of the ceiling collapses with its impact and I can see the larger of the two boys in the hall focus, using his own telekinesis to shield himself and his friend from the rubble.

A Garde. It's about time.

A dorky-looking runt is pointing a gun at me. His hands are shaking badly. The Garde gets a good look at me and drops the two Chests that he's carrying. One of them is mine.

'What number are you?' he asks. 'I'm Four.'

I study him. For some reason, I expected the other Garde to be bigger. Four has to be about my age, yet he seems so much younger. Younger and softer.

I shake his hand. 'I'm Nine. Good job staying alive, Number Four.'

Four and the other boy, a human named Sam, explain to me

what they're doing here while I rummage through my Chest. I'm not really listening until they get to Sam's story – his father missing, possibly taken by Mogs. I wish I could save him. I wish I could save everyone. But I can't. And who was there to save Maddy? Who was there to save Sandor?

I fish a stone out of my Chest that I remember Sandor using when he was deconstructing a particularly complicated machine. It let him see through parts, into their inner workings. It should allow Sam to see through walls, maybe find his father. All he needs is a little juice.

I press my thumb to Sam's forehead, sharing my power with him. 'You've got about ten minutes. Get to it.' He takes off down the hall.

And that's when the Mogs finally come.

They stream down the corridor. I pluck my pipe-staff out of the Chest and rush to meet them. I spring up the wall, along the ceiling, moving faster than I can remember moving before. They don't even see me coming until I've dropped among them, impaling two of them on the end of the staff.

I've waited so long for this.

I feel giddy as I tear my way through the Mogs – caving in a skull here, crushing a sternum there. I whirl through their ranks, spinning my pipe-staff as I go. Was the Mog that captured me and tortured Sandor in that first group? It doesn't matter; they all die the same. I'll get him now or I'll get him later.

I don't realize that I'm laughing until the bitter taste of Mogadorian ash fills my mouth.

I savor it.

The skirmish is over too soon. I'm sprinting along the wall back to Four and Sam in seconds, trailing a cloud of ash. I want more.

'We have to go,' says Four.

I don't want to go. I want to tear this place apart. Yet something tells me that I should listen to this boy, that we should stick together. It's what Sandor would want.

We have to fight our way out. My mind shuts off as the fighting grows more intense. At some point I realize that Four and I have become separated from Sam. I feel bad for the kid – another piece of human collateral damage.

My sympathy is quickly drowned out by the urge to tear this entire place down.

I drive my pipe-staff into the neck of a piken. I'm straddling its neck as it collapses, its blood spraying me, blending with my coat of Mogadorian ash. I can taste it mixing with the coppery tang of my own blood.

I'm grinning. Four stares at me aghast, like I'm only a little better than the monsters we're killing.

'Are you crazy?' he asks. 'You're enjoying this?'

'I've been locked up for over a year,' I tell him. 'This is the best day of my life!'

It's true. I haven't felt this good in forever. Still, I try to downplay just how much I'm loving this. I don't want to freak Four out.

For all his judgment, Four doesn't hesitate to take my hand when we need to use my antigravity Legacy to escape.

It's a long and brutal fight. When we finally catch a glimpse of daylight, I feel disappointed. I wish they'd never stop coming. I glance at Four. He's pretty beaten up, but he's killed his fair share of Mogs and piken on the way out, even if he lacks my enthusiasm.

Perhaps we'll make a warrior out of him yet.

We escape from the Mogadorian base and I greedily suck in my first breath of free air in more than a year. Immediately, I gag. The smell of dead animals is overwhelming.

Four and I jog for the tree line. He barely makes it there, collapsing against a tree almost immediately. He's in rough shape physically and, if the tears are any indication, equally bad shape mentally. He's beating himself up over leaving Sam behind.

I know a thing or two about guilt, but I don't know what the hell to say to this kid. Buck up, champ, we'll kill them next time? Everything I think of seems hollow, so I keep my mouth shut.

He'll learn to shut off his emotions eventually. Emotions will get you killed. They'll get someone else killed too.

As I press a healing stone to Four's back, the sky overhead begins to writhe with an ominous-looking storm. At first Four thinks it's Number Six coming to help us.

It's not. It's Setrakus Ra.

Despite seeing him in nightly visions, I'm not prepared for his true size. He is bigger than any Mogadorian I've ever seen, utterly repulsive even from this distance. The sight of the three Lorien pendants glowing around his thick neck causes me to clench my fists, fingernails digging into my palms.

Suddenly I understand exactly what Sandor was training me for. This is the battle I was meant to fight. Killing Setrakus Ra is the destiny I've been chasing.

Together with Four, I charge.

24

'Is he okay?' I ask.

He needs rest, the Chimæra's kind voice says inside my mind. Talking to animals, that's new. It's been a day of surprises. So much has happened, I don't even have time to consider my newly discovered Legacy. I'll figure it out later, when things have settled down.

If they ever settle down.

Four stretches across the backseat of his SUV, nearly doubled over. His Chimæra, named for some weak human athlete, lies next to him, gently licking his face. I'm reminded of my dream, of playing with my own Chimæra on Lorien, but I push that memory back down with all the other things I want to forget.

The war has begun. I have only one purpose.

The coward Setrakus Ra fled into the Mogadorian base before we could get to him. With Four getting wrecked by the force field and no way back into the base, I decided to make a strategic retreat.

Ra's day will come. When I told Four that I'd stab him once for every day his people had Sandor tortured, I meant it.

I start the engine. It's the first time I've driven since that fateful night with Maddy. I think about the way she clutched my arm as we screamed through red lights, then discard that memory as well.

'So what's our next move?' I ask Four.

'Head north,' he says. 'I think north would be good.'

'You got it, boss.'

I already knew where we were heading, but it's easier not to have to convince Four.

It will be good to see Chicago again. I'm pretty sure the Mogadorians never found our safe house – they would have bragged about it if they had, used it to demoralize me even more. It should still be there, on the top floor of the John Hancock Center, a safe place for me to plan our next move.

A place filled with painful memories I'll have to ignore.

I drive north, my foot heavy on the gas. It's ironic. At last I have my freedom. But at a price. Now my destiny is mine to choose.

And I've already chosen.

Today will go down as a dark day in the Mogadorian history books. It is the day that they allowed me to get loose. In whatever dismal corner of the universe the Mogadorians that manage to escape me gather, this day will be discussed in hushed tones as when the annihilation of their race became a certainty.

I'm going to kill them all.

I AM NUMBER FOUR
The Lost Files
The Fallen Legacies

I

Sometimes I wonder what they would think if they knew we were here. Right under their noses.

I'm sitting with my best friend, Ivan, on the grassy, crowded National Mall, the stupid stone obelisk of the Washington Monument looming above us. I've put my homework aside for the moment, and as I watch the tourists studying their maps, the lawyers and officials scurrying obliviously down Independence Avenue to their next meeting, I'm almost amused. They're so caught up with silly fears about UV rays and chemicals in their vegetables and meaningless 'terrorist threat levels' and whatever else it is that these people worry about, that it never occurs to them that two kids working on their homework in the grass are the real threat. They have no idea that there's nothing they can do to protect themselves. The true enemy is already here.

'Hey!' I sometimes want to shout, waving my arms. 'I'm your future evil dictator! Tremble before me, jerks!'

Of course I can't do that. Not yet. That time will come. In the meantime, they can all stare right through me as if I'm just another normal face in the crowd. The truth is I'm anything but normal, even if I do my best to look it. On Earth, assimilation protocol demands that I be known as Adam, son of Andrew and Susannah Sutton, citizen of Washington DC. But that's not who I am at all.

I am Adamus Sutekh, son of the great general Andrakkus Sutekh.

I am a Mogadorian. I am who they should be afraid of.

Unfortunately, for now, being an alien conqueror isn't as exciting as it should be. At the moment I'm still stuck doing my homework. My father has promised me that this won't last forever; when the Mogadorians ascend to power on this crappy little planet, I will control the capital city of the United States. Trust me, after spending the last four years in this place, I've got a pretty good idea of some changes I'll make. The first thing I'll do is rename all the streets. None of this Independence, Constitution stuff – this weak, stupid patriotism. When I'm in charge, no one will even be able to remember what the Constitution is. When I'm in charge, my avenues will carry titles of appropriate menace.

'Blood of Warriors Boulevard,' I murmur to myself, trying to decide if it has a good ring to it. Hard to say. 'Broken Sword Way . . .'

'Huh?' Ivan asks, glancing up from his spot on the grass next to me. He's lying on his stomach, a pencil held across his index finger like a makeshift blaster. While I dream of the day I'll be the ruler of all I survey, Ivan imagines himself as a sniper, picking off Loric enemies as they leave the Lincoln Memorial. 'What did you say?'

'Nothing,' I reply.

Ivanick Shu-Ra, son of the great warrior Bolog Shu-Ra,

shrugs his shoulders. Ivan has never been much for fantasies that don't include some kind of bloody combat. His family claims a distant relation to our Beloved Leader, Setrákus Ra, and if Ivan's size is any indication, I'm inclined to believe them. Ivan's two years younger than me but is already bigger, broad shouldered and thick while I am lithe and agile. He already looks like a warrior and keeps his coarse black hair cropped close, eager for the day when he'll be able to shave it off entirely and take on the ceremonial Mogadorian tattoos.

I still remember the night of the First Great Expansion, when my people conquered Lorien. I was eight years old that night, too old to be crying, but I cried anyway when I was told I'd be staying in orbit above Lorien with the women and children. My tears only lasted a few seconds until the General slapped some sense into me. Ivan watched my tantrum, dumbly sucking his thumb, maybe too young to realize what was happening. We watched the battle from our ship's observatory with my mother and infant sister. We clapped as flames spread across the planet below us. After the fight was won and the Loric people were destroyed, the General returned to our ship covered in blood. Despite the triumph, his face was serious. Before saying anything to my mother or me, he knelt before Ivan and explained that his father had died in service to our race. A glorious death, befitting a true Mogadorian hero. He rubbed his thumb across Ivan's forehead, leaving a trail of blood. A blessing.

As an afterthought, the General did the same to me.

After that, Ivan, whose mother had died during childbirth,

came to live with us and was raised as my brother. My parents are considered lucky to have three trueborn children.

I'm not always sure that my father feels lucky to have me, though. Whenever my test scores or physical evaluations are less than satisfactory, the General jokes that he might have to transfer my inheritance to Ivan.

I'm mostly sure he's joking.

My gaze drifts towards a family of sightseers as they cross the lawn, each of them taking in the world through digital cameras. The father pauses to snap a series of photos of the Monument, and I briefly reconsider my plans to demolish it. Instead, perhaps I could make it taller; maybe install a penthouse for myself in the uppermost floor. Ivan could have the room below mine.

The daughter of the tourist family is probably about thirteen, like me, and she's cute in a shy way, with a mouth full of braces. I catch her looking at me and find myself unconsciously shifting into a more presentable position, sitting up straighter, tilting my chin down to hide the severe angle of my too-large nose. When the girl smiles at me, I look away. Why should I care what some human thinks of me?

We must always remember why we are here.

'Does it ever amaze you how easily they accept us as their own?' I ask Ivan.

'Never underestimate human stupidity,' he says, reaching over to tap the blank page of homework sitting next to me. 'Are you going to finish this shit or what?'

The homework lying next to me isn't mine – it's Ivan's.

He's waiting for me to do it for him. Written assignments have always given him problems, whereas the right answers come easily to me.

I glance down at the assignment. Ivan is supposed to write a short essay on a quote from the Great Book – the book of Mogadorian wisdom and ethics that all of our people must learn and live by – interpreting what Setrákus Ra's writing means to him personally.

'"We do not begrudge the beast for hunting,"' I read aloud, although like most of my people I know the passage by heart. '"It is in the beast's nature to hunt, just as it is in the Mogadorian's nature to expand. Those that would resist the expansion of the Mogadorian Empire, therefore, stand in opposition to nature itself."'

I look over at Ivan. He's taken aim on the family I was watching before, making high-pitched laser beam noises through gritted teeth. The girl with the braces frowns at him and turns away.

'What does that mean to you?' I ask.

'I don't know,' he grunts. 'That our race is the most badass, and everyone else should deal with it. Right?'

I shrug my shoulders, sighing. 'Close enough.'

I pick up my pen and start to scribble something down, but am interrupted by the chime of my cell phone. I figure it's a text message from my mother, asking me to pick up something from the store on my way home. She's really taken to cooking over the last couple of years, and, I'll admit it, the food here on Earth blows away what we used to get on

Mogadore. What they consider 'processed' here would be treasured on my home planet, where food – among other things – is grown in subterranean vats.

The text isn't from Mom, though. The message is from the General.

'Shit,' I say, dropping my pen as if the General had just caught me helping Ivan cheat.

My father never sends text messages. The act is beneath him. If the General wants something, we're supposed to anticipate what it is before he even has to ask. Something really important must have happened.

'What is it?' asks Ivan.

The message reads simply: HOME NOW.

'We have to go.'

2

Ivan and I take the metro out of DC, pick up our bikes at the train station and pedal into the suburbs as fast as we can. When we finally zip through the gated entrance of Ashwood Estates, I've fallen at least thirty yards behind him. I blame my sweat-dampened T-shirt on the unseasonable warmth and my feeling of nausea on the ominous text message from my father.

Ashwood Estates is identical to many of the wealthy gated communities outside of Washington – or at least it *looks* identical. But instead of being owned by politicians and their families, the mansions and immaculately maintained lawns behind the front gates are owned by my people, the Mogadorians, Earth's soon-to-be conquerors. And the homes themselves are only a tiny part of the *real* Ashwood Estates. Underneath the houses is a huge maze of tunnels that connect the many Mogadorian facilities that are the true purpose of this place.

I've only been granted access to small parts of our underground headquarters. I have no idea how far they extend or how deep below the Earth they reach. But I know that this sprawling underground network houses many laboratories, weapons stores, training facilities and probably more secrets that I can't yet begin to guess at. It's also down there that the vat-born live.

If it wasn't for our Beloved Leader, Setrákus Ra, the Mogadorian race would have never survived long enough to begin the Great Expansion. Over the last hundred years, for reasons that are still mostly unknown, it has become more and more difficult for Mogadorians to bear children. By the time Kelly was born, natural Mogadorian births were so rare that our ancient, proud species was in grave danger of dying out entirely. When children *were* able to be conceived, Mogadorian women, like Ivan's mother, often died during childbirth. Because of this, Setrákus Ra and a team of scientists had been working to artificially breed a new generation of Mogadorians. Rather than being birthed in the usual way, our vat-born Mogadorian brothers and sisters are grown in giant chemical vats, from which they eventually emerge, fully grown and ready for battle. These vat-born not only ensure the continued existence of Mogadorian life but, with their heightened strength, speed and stamina, are also the backbone of our army.

Besides their increased physical prowess, the vat-born are different from trueborn Mogadorians like me in other ways too. They've been engineered to be physically suited for war, but to be soldiers rather than officers. In his wisdom, Setrákus Ra has created them to be more single-minded than trueborn Mogadorians – almost machine-like in their adherence to the tasks they're assigned – and as natural warriors, what they have in the way of rational thought often gives way to rage and bloodlust. But the most important difference between the vat-born and the trueborn, at least here on Earth, is the fact that they look different from the rest of us. While the trueborn are able to pass amid humans, the vat-born are not. Their skin is ghostly pale from subterranean living, and their teeth are small and sharp for close combat rather than eating. This is why, until we are able to reveal ourselves, they are only rarely allowed to show their faces in daylight.

So when I see the vat-born openly celebrating on the lawns of Ashwood Estates alongside their trueborn betters, I know something huge is happening.

Ivan knows it too, and gives me a befuddled look as he skids to a stop in our cul-de-sac. I pull up beside him, catching my breath. All of the families of Ashwood Estates are in front of their homes, mingling with each other, raising toasts from freshly opened bottles of champagne. The vat-born, with their jarringly pale skin hidden beneath trench coats and hats, look both excited and disoriented to be out in the open. The air of jubilation is unusual in Mogadorian culture. Normally my people are not given to open displays of joy, especially with the General in the vicinity.

'What the hell is going on?' Ivan asks, as usual looking to me for answers. This time I just shrug back at him.

My mother is sitting on our front steps, watching with a small smile as Kelly dances wildly across the front yard. My sister, spinning maniacally, doesn't even notice when Ivan and I arrive.

My mother looks relieved to see us approach. Though I don't know what the celebration is for, I do know why she wouldn't have joined the other revelers out on the lawns and street. Being the wife of the General makes it difficult for her to make friends, even with other trueborns. Their fear of my father extends to my mother.

'Boys,' she says as Ivan and I roll our bikes up the front walk. 'He's been looking for you. You know he doesn't like to wait.'

'Why does he need to see us?' I ask.

Before my mother can answer, the General appears in the doorway behind her. My father is a large man, standing close to seven feet tall, muscular, with a regal posture that demands respect. His face is all sharp angles, a feature I've unfortunately inherited from him. Since coming to Earth, he's grown his black hair out to hide the tattoos on his scalp, and he keeps it neatly slicked back, like some of the politicians I've seen striding across the National Mall.

'Adamus,' he says in a tone that brooks no questioning. 'Come with me. You too, Ivanick.'

'Yes, sir,' Ivan and I reply in unison, exchanging a nervous glance with each other before stepping into the house. When my father uses that tone of voice, it means something serious is happening. As I pass, my mother gives my hand a gentle squeeze.

'Have fun in Malaysia!' shouts Kelly at our backs, having finally noticed us. 'Kill that Garde as hard as you can!'

3

A few hours later, Ivan and I are headed for Malaysia on board a cold and uncomfortable plane that was purchased as surplus from some government that doesn't ask a lot of questions. The passenger area doesn't look all that different from the cargo hold below – just metal benches with worn seat belts, where Ivan and I sit, crammed among the warriors, some of them trueborn, most vat-born. Our ride isn't glamorous, but I'm too nervous to worry about comfort. This is the first time I've been taken on a mission, even if my purpose is only to observe.

My father flies copilot. Whenever the plane's course becomes momentarily shaky, I wonder if it's a change in the atmospheric conditions or if it's just that my father's made the pilot nervous.

For many of the Mogadorians on the plane, this is their first action since the First Great Expansion. Some of them spend the flight reminiscing about the last time they fought, bragging about their many kills. Others, the older ones, stay quiet, completely focused on the mission, staring into space.

'Do you think we'll get to shoot any guns?' Ivan asks me.

'I doubt it,' I reply. We're along for this mission simply

because I'm the General's son and Ivan his ward. We're too young to be of any real use to the strike team, but not too young to watch the execution of this Loric insurgent from a distance. My father wants us to learn from it. As our instructors always tell us, the combat simulations we run in battle preparedness class – where we *do* get to shoot guns – are no substitution for the real thing.

'That sucks,' grumbles Ivan.

'Whatever,' I say, shifting and trying to stretch my legs out. 'I just can't wait to get off this plane.'

Everything next happens in a blur. We land. We find the Garde and her Cêpan. As instructed, Ivan and I hang back, watching with the General as the Mogadorian warriors go into battle. It's an ugly thing, not at all like the battles described in the Great Book. Two dozen Mogadorians against an old woman and a teenage girl.

At first our goal is simply to capture and interrogate these two. There have been whispers since we came to Earth of some kind of Loric magic that protects the Garde, forcing us to kill them in order. There was talk of a battle in the Alps, where one of our warriors had a Garde cornered, only to have his killing blow somehow turned against him. The General hasn't tolerated talk of this so-called Loric charm, but my people are still careful.

The old woman puts up more resistance than expected, yet she's quickly overwhelmed. The Garde is tougher still – she has powers, the ground quaking beneath the feet of our warriors. I wonder what it would be like to have that kind of power. But if the trade-off is to be part of a dying race forced to cower in crappy huts on the banks of a river, I'll pass.

The strategy to capture them changes once our warriors realize they can hurt the Garde. Either the rumors of the Loric charm are as false as my father believes, or this is Number One. The General might have wanted her taken alive; but when the warriors understand that they can kill her, bringing us closer to our goal, bloodlust overcomes orders.

It ends when one of the warriors puts his sword through Number One's back, impaling her.

'That was awesome!' shouts Ivan. Even my father allows himself a thin smile of approval.

I know I should share in their elation, but my hands won't stop shaking. I feel grateful that I only had to watch from a distance, that I wasn't one of the Mogadorians now reduced to ash on a Malaysian riverbank. I'm also grateful not to be Loric, not to have to spend my life running in fear from impossible odds, only to be stabbed in the back.

It occurs to me that I'm feeling something close to empathy for the Garde. The Great Book warns against that, so I shut it away. I need to get beyond these childish feelings. The battle was less glorious than I expected, but still a great victory for Mogadorian progress. Only eight more loose ends remain and then Ra's vision will be fulfilled; nothing will stand in the way of our expansion to Earth. Nine dead Garde are a small price to pay for my sweet penthouse at the top of the Washington Monument.

They shove Number One into a body bag and dump her

in the plane with the rest of the cargo. The Loric Chest she had with her is taken as well, although even the strongest of our warriors can't pry open the lock. One's pendant is ripped off her body by my father, though I'm not sure what use he has for Loric jewelry.

Her Cêpan's body is left behind. She is of no importance to us now.

On the plane ride back, the benches are a lot less crowded. I stay quiet, but Ivan pesters the warriors from the front line for gory details until the General hisses at him to shut up. If they had been a football team, I'm sure the surviving warriors would be dousing each other with Gatorade the way that human athletes do after a win. But we're not a football team. We're Mogadorians. And my father doesn't even know what Gatorade is. We travel the rest of the way in silence.

During the flight, the General comes to sit beside me.

'When we get back to Ashwood Estates,' he says, 'I have an important task for you.'

I nod. 'Yes. Of course, sir.'

My father looks down at my hands, still shaking no matter how hard I try to steady them.

'Stop that,' he growls before heading back to the cockpit.

4

Although I saw her in the battle, the girl on the metal slab isn't what I was expecting.

Ever since the First Great Expansion, we've been taught that the Garde are the last true threat to our way of life. We've been taught that they are fierce warriors, lying in wait to one day take up arms against the engine of Mogadorian progress. Somehow I thought this threat to my people would look more fearsome.

In death, Number One doesn't look like much at all. She looks to be around my age or just a bit older, and her skin, once tan, is now bloodlessly pale. Her lips are blue. Streaks of dried blood run through her blond hair. Her body is covered with a white sheet, but under the bright lights of the laboratory I can see the grisly shadow of the wound that blossoms across her midsection.

We are beneath Ashwood Estates, in the underground laboratory of Dr Lockam Anu. I've never been allowed down here before, so I try to take in as many of the strange, blinking machines as possible without openly gawking. The General would not be kind if he thought I was distracted.

I stand next to my father, both of us silent, watching as Anu gently eases One's head into a strange mechanical helmet. Anu is an old man, his spine hunched, his tattooed scalp disgustingly wrinkled. He circles around One, connecting loose wires to the open diodes that clutter the helmet.

'Should be ready,' mutters Anu, stepping back.

'Finally,' grunts my father.

Anu pauses over One's left ankle, tracing the Loric charm scarred there. What the Loric charm looks like is one of the first things we were taught when we came to Earth. Scrutinizing every bare ankle for its presence became second nature for me long ago.

'Four years of searching for a child with this symbol,' muses Anu. 'You certainly take your time, General.'

I can practically feel my father clench his fists. It's like standing next to a gathering storm. Yet he makes no reply. Dr Anu heads up the research and science team at Ashwood Estates and is entitled to certain benefits, like making a dig at the General without being immediately beaten.

Anu looks in my direction, his left eye involuntarily drooping and half lidded.

'Did your esteemed father explain why you are here, boy?'

I glance at the General. He nods, granting me permission to speak.

'No, sir.'

'Ah. "Sir." What a polite young man you've raised, General.' Anu gestures to a nearby metal chair, over which hangs an imposing piece of complicated technology. 'Come, have a seat.'

I glance again at my father, but his face gives nothing away.

'You will do our family proud today, Adamus,' rumbles the General. I'm relieved that my hands have finally stopped shaking.

I sit down. Anu crouches before me, his old bones creaking in protest. He binds my wrists and ankles to the chair with rubber straps. I know that I should trust my father. I'm too important for him to let anything bad happen to me. Still, I can't help but squirm a bit as I'm buckled in.

'Comfortable?' asks Dr Anu, smirking at me.

'What is this?' I reply, forgetting the General's rule against asking questions.

My father gazes at me with surprising patience. Maybe he's as uncomfortable seeing his only son being strapped down as I am being strapped.

'Dr Anu believes this machine will let us access the Loric girl's memories,' explains my father.

'I *know* that it will,' corrects Anu. He rubs a warm liquid on my temples before connecting a pair of rubber electrodes. The electrode wires run to a monitor positioned next to Number One, which suddenly hums to life.

'Would you stake your life on this untested creation, Dr Anu?' growls my father.

'Untested?' I start, jerking against my bonds. I immediately regret the note of panic in my voice; it causes the General to grimace. Dr Anu flashes me a placating smile.

'We never had one of the Garde to experiment on before, so yes, untested.' He shrugs merrily, excited to test this contraption. 'But the theory behind it is very strong. Of the trueborns here in Washington, you are closest in age to the girl, which should make the memory download go more smoothly. Your mind will interpret the Garde's memories as visions rather than through her eyes. I'm sure your father wouldn't suddenly want his only son in the body of a little girl, hmm?'

My father bristles. Dr Anu glances over his shoulder. 'Just kidding, General. You have a good, strong son here. Very brave.'

At the moment, I don't feel very brave. I'd watched Number One get struck down – she was barely capable of defending herself in life; she is certainly harmless in death – yet being connected to her, it renews the feeling of unease I felt on the plane ride back from Malaysia. I almost start to volunteer Ivan to be Anu's guinea pig but clamp my mouth shut just in time.

Ivan enjoyed watching One die; it's all he's been able to talk about. For me, even thinking about it makes my hands start to shake again. I steady myself – *stop being such a coward, Adamus* – this is a great honor, something I should be proud of.

I try not to look at the dead girl as Anu reaches above the chair and lowers a metal cylinder down from the ceiling, covered with circuitry that wouldn't look out of place on the inside of a rocket. The vast majority of the wires connected to Number One connect to the cylinder. Anu pauses before the cylinder is in place over my head and peers down at me.

'You'll feel a little shock,' he muses. 'Maybe go to sleep for a few minutes. When you wake up, you'll be able to tell us what this one knew about the other Garde.'

I realize Anu's free hand is on my shoulder. His grip is tight.

A few days ago my biggest worry was dumbing down essay answers enough to pass my work off as Ivan's. Since then I've seen firsthand the Mogadorian warrior I'm expected to grow into, and I'm not sure I'm up for it. Now I'm being ordered to temporarily share a brain with my mortal enemy. I know it's my father's will, and that if the machine works it will help our cause and bring honor to my family. Still. I don't want to admit it, but I'm scared.

Anu lowers the cylinder over my head until it covers my face. He and my father disappear from view.

I hear Anu shuffle across the laboratory. His fingers click across a series of buttons, and the cylinder begins to vibrate.

'Here we go,' announces Anu.

The inside of the cylinder explodes with light – searing white light that burns my eyes, all the way through to the back of my head. I shut my eyes, but somehow the light still penetrates. I feel as if I'm coming apart, the light tearing through me, breaking me into tiny particles. This is what death must feel like.

I think I scream.

And then, everything is darkness.

5

It's like I'm falling.

Bursts of color flash across my vision. There are shapes – indistinct faces, blurry scenery – but I can't make any of it out. It's like being stuck inside my TV while Kelly plays with the remote. Nothing makes any sense, and I start to get this panicky feeling, like sensory overload. I try to squeeze my eyes shut, but that's useless; this is all happening inside my mind.

Just when I feel like my brain is about to be fried to a crisp by the bombardment of colors, everything snaps into focus.

Suddenly, I'm standing in a sunlit banquet hall. Light pours into the room via a skylight through which I can see trees unlike any I've ever seen before, red and orange flowered vines hanging off tangled branches.

Although I've never been there – have only looked down on it from orbit – somehow I know that this is Lorien. And then I realize that I know where I am because Number One knows.

This is one of her memories.

In the center of the room is a large table covered with strange yet delicious-looking foods. Seated all around the table are Loric, all of them wearing fancy dresses and suits.

I flinch when I see them – I'm outnumbered and my first instinct is to run, yet I'm pinned to this spot. I couldn't move if I tried, stuck in this memory.

The Loric are all smiling, singing. They don't seem at all alarmed that a Mogadorian has just appeared at their party. That's when I realize they can't see me. Of course not, I'm just a tourist in Number One's mind.

And there she is, seated at the head of the table. She's so young, maybe five or six, her blond hair pulled into two braids that dangle down her back. When the adults finish singing, she claps her hands in excitement, and I realize this is her birthday celebration. We don't celebrate such foolish occasions on Mogadore, although some great warriors are known to mark the anniversary of their first kill with a feast.

What a useless memory. The General won't be impressed if all I come back with is intel on Loric birthday parties.

Just like that the world goes blurry again and I'm falling. Time passes in a rush and I'm swept along, feeling sickeningly out of control.

Another memory takes shape.

Number One wanders through an open field, her hands extended so that the tall grasses tickle her outstretched palms. She's maybe a year older than at the birthday party, still just a child, happily wandering around her undestroyed planet.

Boring.

One bends down and picks some flowers, twining the stalks together, then wrapping the flower chain around her wrist like a bracelet. How much of this am I going to have to sift through?

Maybe if I focus I can get some control of these memories. I need to see the other Garde, not this girly, happy Loric crap. I try to think about what I want to see – the faces of the Garde, their Cêpans – and then the memory in the field flashes away and I am somewhere else.

It's nighttime, although the darkness is lit by dozens of fires raging nearby. The two Loric moons hang on opposite sides of the horizon. The ground shakes beneath my feet, an explosion nearby.

Number One and eight other children rush across a secluded airstrip, headed for a ship. Their Cêpans hurry them along, shouting orders. Some of the children are crying as their feet slap against the pavement. Number One is not; she stares over her shoulder as a Loric in a sleek bodysuit fires a cone of freezing cobalt energy into the face of a snarling piken. Number One's eyes widen in admiration and fear.

This is it. The First Great Expansion. Exactly the memory I need to see.

'Run!' the Loric in the bodysuit shouts at the fleeing group of young Garde. His Legacies are fully developed and powerful. Still, he'll die on this night, just like all the others.

I sweep my eyes over the children, trying to take in as many details as I can. There's a feral-looking boy with long black hair and another blond girl, younger than Number One, being carried by her Cêpan. Number One is older than most of the other kids, a detail that I know will help my father construct profiles of the remaining Garde. I count how many of them are boys and how many are girls, and try to memorize their most distinguishing features.

'Who the fuck are you?'

The voice is clearer than the thunderous sounds of war from the memory, as if it's being piped right into my brain.

I turn my head and realize Number One is standing right next to me. Not the child Number One of the memory – no, this is Number One as I last saw her: blond hair flowing down her back, shoulders squared defiantly. A ghost. She's looking right at me, expecting an answer.

She can't be here; that doesn't make sense. I wave my hand in front of her face, figuring that this must be some kind of glitch in Anu's machine. There's no way she's really seeing me.

Number One slaps my hand away. I'm surprised that she can touch me, but then I remember that we're *both* ghosts here.

'Well?' she asks. 'Who are you? You don't belong here.'

'You're dead,' are the only words I can muster.

One looks down at herself. For a moment, the massive wound on her abdomen flickers into being. Just as quickly, it's gone.

'Not in here.' She shrugs. 'These are my memories. So in here I guess you're stuck with me.'

I shake my head. 'It's impossible. You can't be talking to me.'

One squints at me, thinking. 'Your name is Adam, right?'

'How do you know that?'

She smirks. 'We're sharing a brain, Mog-boy. Guess that means I know a thing or two about you, too.'

Around us, the fleeing Garde have all boarded their ship, the engines now rumbling to life. I should be scanning the ship for any helpful details, but I'm too distracted by the dead girl sneering at me.

'Your scary-ass pops is going to be so disappointed when you wake up with nothing juicy to tell him.' She grabs me by the elbow, and the feeling is so real that I have to remind myself that this is basically just a dream.

A dream that Number One is suddenly in control of.

'You want my memories?' she asks. 'Come on. I'll give you a guided tour.'

As the scene changes again, I start to understand what's happened.

I'm trapped in here with my sworn enemy. And she seems to be in charge.

6

This time the memory shift is different. Before, I was falling through time, falling through memory. Now I feel still, and suddenly I'm standing outside a secluded ranch in Coahuila, Mexico. In this memory, One and her Cêpan are carrying boxes into the house. It's moving day. This is the first place One and her Cêpan – Hilde, her Cêpan's name was Hilde – settled after the Garde landed on Earth and parted ways.

Wait – how do I know all this?

It's strange. In addition to finding myself existing here, observing this particular moment in One's life, I also have a general sense of her memories of the time. I know the things that she knows and remember what she remembers. The memories are so vivid, it's like they're my own.

It's like I'm her.

Ghost-One appears next to me, watching with me as the younger version of herself and Hilde unpack dishes in the kitchen. It's creepy to have her here, gives me a feeling like vertigo. I try to ignore her, but she just keeps talking to me.

'We stayed here for a while,' she says, sounding almost wistful. 'Then Hilde thought she saw some of your peeps snooping around the city, so we had to leave.'

The Garde move a lot, city to city, country to country,

their movements unpredictable. My father will want to know this. It's completely the opposite of the way we Mogadorians have done it, consolidating our power in bases across the globe. That's why they're so difficult to track.

'She was sort of a drag sometimes,' says One, watching her Cêpan. 'Probably a lot like your dickbag dad. Except, you know, not eeee-vil.' She rubs her fingers together and cackles an eeee-vil cackle in punctuation.

'Shut up,' I spit, sounding angrier than I even realized I was. 'You don't know him.'

I find myself studying Hilde in spite of myself. She's in her late fifties, and her face is wrinkled, both with the natural lines of age and the premature weathering of stress. Her gray hair is tightly bound in a stern braid. Her eyes have a hardness to them; her voice is steely and measured, even when just telling One – the 'real' One – which cupboard the plates belong in. Truth be told, she does remind me of the General.

'I loved her like a mom, though,' says ghost-One, sadness breaking her voice. My mind drifts to the dead old woman we left to rot in Malaysia, and I feel something like guilt but quickly push it away. She's messing with your head, Adamus.

'I wish you'd stop talking to me,' I tell her.

'Yeah? Well I wish your people hadn't killed me.'

After Mexico, One and Hilde move to Austin, Texas. I try to push my way out of these memories, to get back to that night on the Loric airstrip where I can actually find out something useful, but One won't let me. Somehow she's blocking me.

I may be an uninvited guest in her mind, but it's still hers. She can't kick me out entirely, but she does have some control over which rooms I'm allowed to visit.

Most of the time when I try to force my way through her memory, One makes me sit through one of her and Hilde's training sessions.

'I used to hate these,' One says, grinning. 'Hope you feel the same.'

Hilde is a master martial artist, though it's a fighting style that would never make it into Mogadorian training, where brute force is prized above all else. Hilde's is a defensive martial art, one that uses an attacker's own momentum, focusing strikes on nerve centers that will temporarily incapacitate the enemy.

Stuck in these memories, when boredom sets in, I find myself aping Hilde's movements, practicing alongside young One. I know that none of this is real, that it's all in my mind. Or One's mind. I'm not so sure there's a difference.

My slight frame has never served me well in Mogadorian combat training, much to the disappointment of my father and the amusement of Ivan. But in One's memories, I never get tired. Even if this training is basically imaginary, it feels good to finally move in a way that suits me.

Besides, I'm supposed to be gathering intelligence. How the Garde fight is essential information.

In the earlier training memories, One is an eager pupil. She practices with Hilde from dawn until sunset, listening rapt as Hilde tells stories of the Loric heroes she's helped train. Hilde is full of tales of honorable competition, of noble battles fought on Lorien. They're meant to inspire, to demonstrate to One the Loric spirit of perseverance. Compared to the stories in the Great Book, there is a surprising lack of bloody violence and decimation in them.

'One day,' says Hilde, 'you will take your place among them as a great hero to our people. You will be known as the One who protected the Eight.'

I can feel the pride Number One takes in Hilde's words, but also the doubt. There's a part of her that wonders how she can possibly stand alone in opposition to the Mogadorians that conquered her entire planet in a single night.

'I always wondered why I couldn't have gotten lucky and been number *nine*,' muses One as I practice forms next to her younger self. 'But *nooo*. I have to go and be the *first*. Otherwise known as the most doomed of nine doomed assholes. The Elders really screwed me over.'

In Austin, Hilde lets One start attending school, all the better to fit in. I'm dragged along on these memories of her classes. School seems so pointless. The General would never even consider letting us freely socialize with the humans.

And yet, as the memories go by, I find myself being drawn into One's life. She makes some friends, takes up skateboarding. It all starts to feel like something approaching a normal life. At the same time, her training slips. She starts blowing off sessions, even after her telekinesis develops, which is when she should've been working extra hard. For all her rigidity, Hilde couldn't really do anything to One if she slipped out a window to go hang out with her friends. How do you ground the last hope for a dying race?

I don't really care about One's freaking social life. This girl is the enemy of my people. Her death is inevitable, has already happened. And yet . . . drifting through her memories, I can't help but put myself in her situation. Even though she travels the Earth under the constant threat of execution, I realize that One has gotten to see more of this planet than I have. The General has never allowed us to travel out of Washington. Hilde might be a tough Cêpan, but she still allows One to go to school, to make friends, to live a life not entirely dedicated to war.

I wonder what that's like. I wonder what my life would be like without the need to serve Mogadorian expansion, without the drills and training, the supervised readings from Ra's Great Book.

'This is, like, one of my all-time favorites,' says ghost-One, introducing the memory of her punching a cheerleader in the face. The cheerleader started it; she'd been picking on One since she started school in Austin. It's weird, but I feel some of One's sense of satisfaction.

Of course, the punch gets her kicked out of school, which is all the reason Hilde needs to relocate them again. They leave

Austin in a beat-up station wagon, heading for California. One sulks in the passenger seat the whole ride, reclined all the way back, ignoring Hilde in favor of the three seashells she keeps levitated above her with her telekinesis.

We Mogadorians have been warned of the Garde's deadly telekinesis. Watching One juggle the seashells, scrunching up her nose in concentration, it doesn't seem all that deadly. More like mesmerizing. And it's not just the telekinesis either. The way her blond hair is fanned beneath her . . .

I turn away. Was I just checking out the dead Garde whose memories I've stolen? I tell myself it was for research purposes, although a description of how the sun brings out the blonder streaks in One's nice hair is likely not the intel my father expects of me.

When they arrive in California, Hilde tries to inspire One with some kind of Loric magic so that she'll start taking her training more seriously.

'You'll want to see this,' ghost-One tells me, appearing at my side to watch.

Using what appear at first to be plain glass orbs, Hilde creates a floating map of the Loric galaxy. The swirling cosmos, the bright orange sun, and the dead, gray planet Lorien.

'Do you see what the Mogadorians have done?' Hilde asks young Number One.

One nods, staring at the ruined planet. Hilde steps close to the floating Lorien orb and gently blows across its surface. When she does, the smog and fire clear from the planet's surface. Lorien looks like it must have before the First Great Expansion: rich and lush, thriving. The change fades quickly, the planet going gray again.

'This is why we fight,' says Hilde quietly, her eyes watery. 'Not just to avenge our planet and our people and to one day bring life back to Lorien, but to prevent this fate from befalling Earth. Do you understand why you are so important?'

I don't pay attention to One's muted reply. I'm too distracted by the vision of Lorien. Its surface is a hideously charred black, the planet's ruined atmosphere leaking into the space around it. Seeing the planet like this, my people's greatest victory, it doesn't look like anything to be proud of.

'Is that what you want for the entire universe?' ghost-One asks me, gesturing to her destroyed home.

'I've never seen this before,' I reply, trying to keep my voice neutral. The sight of Lorien disturbs me. To think such thoughts is treason, but if our coming to Earth means even half the destruction brought down on Lorien, would it still be a place worth living in?

'Is that what Mogadorian progress looks like?' ghost-One presses.

'Please,' I say, shaking my head. 'Stop talking to me.'

I just want her to go away. I don't want her to see my doubt.

7

I'm standing on the beach. I can't feel anything here in One's memories, but if I concentrate hard, I can almost imagine what it must be like to have the Pacific Ocean lapping at my ankles and the wet sand squishing between my toes. I've never been in the ocean before. When I'm finally awake again, I'd like to try the real thing.

I take a second to imagine a trip to the ocean with the General. My father out of uniform, in a pair of flower-print swim trunks, pulling a cooler filled with cookout supplies out of the trunk of our family's convertible. My mom and Kelly build a sand castle while Ivan and I see which one of us can swim out the farthest. He wins because even in my fantasy I'm a realist. I swim back to shore, and the General is waiting with a hamburger.

'Seriously?' asks ghost-One, standing on the beach beside me, and I realize I have a ridiculous, goofy grin on my face. I quickly let it fade. 'You killed my entire race so you could enjoy a beach barbecue?'

'Stay out of my thoughts,' I say weakly, aware of the hypocrisy.

'Psh,' snorts One, rolling her eyes at me. 'I wish that I could, dude.'

Arguing with One's ghost certainly isn't what my father would describe as productive reconnaissance, so I turn away, trying to ignore her.

In this memory, the real Number One has just finished up a day of surfing. Turns out she's a natural, the only one of her crew of surfer buddies not to wipe out today. Between this and the skateboarding, she's started to wonder if maybe enhanced balance isn't going to be one of her Legacies. I'd never tell One this, but I've enjoyed the surfer memory. In fact, I'd never tell anyone that.

'Please stop checking out my past self,' ghost-One says at my side.

'I'm not,' I protest.

The memory keeps moving. One bounds out of the water, her surfboard passing right through me as she leaps into the waiting arms of a tanned and muscular young human.

Wade.

One had rededicated herself to training after Hilde's display of the solar system. At least, until she met Wade.

Wade is sixteen years old. He has shoulder-length brown hair, strands of which he keeps in grungy little braids. He owns a beat-up Volkswagen van that he sleeps in even though his wallet contains a couple of credit cards paid for by his parents – a fact One discovered while she was snooping through Wade's things to make sure he wasn't a secret Mogadorian.

As if.

'I felt like my parents had my whole life planned out,'

explained Wade on the night he and One first met, his arm slung around her shoulders, the two of them huddled in front of a bonfire on the beach. 'Go to college, get my law degree, join Dad at his practice. Such a bourgeois life plan. It just wasn't for me, you know?'

'I get it,' replied One, way more interested in Wade's muscular arm than in whatever he was saying. I guess she liked him, or at least liked the rush of being with him, an added bonus being that it pissed off Hilde. I didn't get the attraction. 'So I left that whole scene behind, hopped in my van and decided to surf my way down the coast. No plan at all. I'm just going to, like, *be* for a while.' Wade paused. 'Hey, has anyone ever told you how soulful your eyes are?'

One swoons.

Oh, come *on,* I think, and ghost-One appears at my side.

'Cut me some slack,' she says. 'He's hot, and I was stupid. I mean, I wasn't *that* stupid. I knew he was full of it, obviously. But, look at him. He's hot.'

'I wouldn't know,' I say self-consciously.

That memory was a couple of months before the one I slip into next. We're still at the beach, and One wriggles out of her wet suit and settles on the sand next to Wade. She's been regularly skipping training to come surfing with Wade. One and Hilde are barely speaking, except for when Hilde tries to chastise her.

I haven't been enjoying these Wade memories. They're of

no relevance to the Mogadorian cause. Besides . . . I feel like One could be doing so much better.

'I was having *fun*,' says One, popping up to defend herself again. 'I liked pretending I was normal.'

I don't say anything.

'Didn't you ever want to get away from it all?' asks One. She knows that I do. She's been rummaging through my thoughts too. 'You and that douche you hang out with spend a lot of time in DC, but you never talk to any other kids.'

'It's forbidden.'

'Why?'

'To interact directly could compromise operational integrity,' I reply, quoting from the Great Book.

'You sound like a robot,' she says. 'They don't want you to know the humans because then it'd be harder for you to kill them. Just like with me.'

'What do you mean, *just like with you*?'

'I mean that you kind of like me,' she says, looking at me in a way that makes me feel uncomfortable. 'They didn't know what they were doing sending you in here. If you knew all this about me before, would you still want to kill me?'

My head hurts thinking about it, and I wave One away. I am not ready to go back to the memory of the riverbank in Malaysia. Then I remind myself that Malaysia is in the future, not the past.

'Don't feel too bad,' she says. 'I don't know if I'd want to kill you either.'

8

This is how my people find her. The General didn't share these details with me, but I know them now:

Wade believes in taking a stand against capitalism. He does this by shoplifting at every opportunity he gets. He also talks, sometimes endlessly, about the amazing record collection he was forced to leave behind when he left his parents' mansion.

This puts an idea in One's head. She's going to shoplift some records from a store by the beach for him. Part of her wants to impress Wade, another part of her just wants to experience the thrill that he's talked about.

But One gets caught coasting out of the store with a backpack full of merchandise. The owner of the store is a take-no-prisoners type. He calls the cops.

'How was Wade even going to listen to those?' I ask. 'Does his van have a record player?'

One laughs as we watch her former self being slapped into handcuffs. 'I didn't even think of that.'

Number One is taken to the police station. Her 'grandmother' is contacted. The police are going to let her off with a warning, but a particularly overzealous detective notices the

Loric charm on One's ankle. He mistakes the charm for a brand and starts asking One about gang affiliation.

'Yeah,' sneers One, 'I'm in a gang called the Space Invaders. We do surf-by shootings. No lifeguard can stop us.'

The detective doesn't seem to think it's a very funny joke.

He takes a picture of One. He takes a picture of the Loric charm. He uploads both images to a statewide database. As soon as the flash on the camera goes off, I know that this is how it happened.

My people have teams working around the clock patrolling the internet, even the internal government sites, for tips just like this. We have artificial intelligences set up that do nothing but scan image feeds for anything resembling the Loric charm.

After four years of searching, One is on our radar.

Hilde doesn't lecture One when she picks her up from the police station. She doesn't need words to express her disappointment. One knows what it means to have had her picture taken by the police.

For the first time, One's rebellious streak gives way to fear. She packs a bag with shaking hands before Hilde even tells her to. I'm reminded of the way my hands shook after I saw her killed. It wasn't until then that the war we're fighting began to feel real. One must be feeling the same way now.

This time they travel light. Hilde thinks they need to get out of America. They rush to the airport and board the first international flight they can. Their destination is Malaysia.

One notices the two pale men in trench coats at the airport, but she doesn't realize what they are. I do. I recognize my own.

For all their precautions, all their training, all their knowledge of their enemies, what's so clear to me is completely unrecognized by Hilde and One. A Mogadorian scout team is on to them. I know the protocol in a situation like this. When my people have a lead on a Loric, vat-born scouts are dispatched to every conceivable place of departure. We cover them all: airports, train and bus stations, rental car huts. Their objective isn't to engage. Their job is just to keep an eye on Number One.

'You need to lose them,' I find myself muttering. 'You need to lose the scouts before you flee.'

'Oh, thanks for telling me, dude,' the One standing next to me says. She has a sad, rueful look on her face.

For some reason I'm positioning myself between the scouts and One. It makes no sense. I'm a ghost here; they see right through me. And besides, this has already happened. Nothing I can do can change it.

My stomach still drops when they board the flight to Malaysia. I can't see the scouts anymore; they've disappeared into the crowd. I know what they're doing, though. They're radioing back to my father or some other superior, arranging to have a scout team waiting across the ocean when One's flight touches down. My team.

I dread seeing what comes next.

9

Hilde and One hide out in an abandoned stilt house on the Rajang River, their closest neighbors the endlessly screeching monkeys that populate the jungle. Hilde is planning a trip into Kuala Lumpur, where she'll take some money out of their bank account, enough to finance their next move. It's peaceful, without any of the distractions of America. When the river is clear, One practices her telekinesis on its bank.

By the time our team arrives – after an endless flight through who knows how many time zones – I've completely lost track of what day it is. All I know is that the sun is beginning to rise.

Hilde hears the first wave coming. Our soldiers don't make any effort to hide their approach; they have the house surrounded. Hilde shakes Number One awake just as the warriors kick in the door.

The Cêpan moves fast for an old woman. It's easy to see her as the great martial artist, trainer of young Garde, that she was on Lorien. She ducks effortlessly under a dagger strike, burying her fist in the throat of an off-balance warrior. Before the first Mogadorian even hits the ground, Hilde has wrapped her arms around the head of a second, snapping his neck. I catch myself cheering her on, then stop myself.

The next Mogadorian through the door dives for Hilde and places her in a headlock; but Hilde, in a movement so subtle I barely even see it, manages to turn his hold against him, flipping him onto his back even though he's twice her size.

That's when he whips his blaster from his holster, and – orders not to harm her suddenly forgotten in his humiliation – fires it right at her chest.

When Hilde hits the ground, One screams. The entire house wobbles, its stilts suddenly vibrating. Screaming out in grief and agony, One stomps the floor. A seismic wave erupts from her foot, tearing up the floorboards and sending the Mogadorians flying through the tightly woven sticks of the stilt house's walls.

Her first Legacy has developed. Too late.

The little that's left of the house is listing on its stilts. With the Mogadorians regrouping outside, One cradles Hilde in her arms. The wound is fatal. Hilde spits a bubble of blood when she tries to speak.

'It's not too late for you,' Hilde manages to say. 'You have to run.'

One is crying. She feels responsible; she feels helpless.

'I failed you,' sobs One.

'Not yet you haven't,' replies Hilde. 'Go. Now.'

I'm standing right next to her, willing her to move, even though I know what's waiting for her on the riverbank. The ghost-One, the dead girl who's been my companion through all of these memories, has abandoned me now. She's been gone since the airport.

One hesitates for an instant at Hilde's order, and then, knowing it's her only choice, flings herself through one of the windows just as the stilts buckle and the house finally collapses into the river. The Mogadorians meet her on the riverbank.

The house's falling ceiling passes harmlessly through me. I watch as One produces another seismic burst, experimenting with her newfound power, and the wet ground of the riverbank opens up to swallow a pair of advancing Mogadorians.

I remember this. I peer down the riverbank, wondering if she could have seen me where I stood watching with Ivan and my father. No. I was too far away, her attention too focused on the battle around her.

I should be enjoying this, a chance to replay this great victory up close and personal. There's nothing someone like Ivan wouldn't give to be able to witness this again. It's like a highlight reel of Mogadorian dominance. Yet I want to turn away. I was ashamed to admit it the first time, but not now. This battle – one unarmed teenager against two dozen highly trained Mogadorians – repulses me.

Of course, One isn't completely defenseless. The ground around her continues to shake, leaving the Mogadorians stumbling and off balance. She picks up some sharp sections of the broken house with her telekinesis and lances them through the nearest Mogadorians. The hit warriors disintegrate into ash and are lost in the muddy river water.

I feel nothing for the dead soldiers. We are taught about acceptable losses. These strike teams are expendable.

One is pushing herself too hard. Her newly discovered Legacy is barely under control, her telekinesis sloppy from months of blowing off training. She is already close to exhaustion, and the Mogadorians just keep coming. Finally one of the largest vat-born warriors manages to evade her defensive attacks and grab her from behind, yanking both of her arms behind her back to restrain her. As he does it, One yelps in pain just before she manages to slip from his grasp.

It wasn't a loud scream – probably more a cry of surprise than one of injury – but it's enough for the Mogadorians to understand. They've hurt her. *She can be hurt.*

And then things change. I know the Mogadorian training well enough to see the soldiers' strategy shift instantly. They know it's her. The First. Number One. She can be killed. And every single one of them wants to be the one to do it.

One's in such a panic, fighting blindly, that she never even notices the Mogadorian warrior who manages to grab that particular glory. I don't know the warrior's name; he's just another faceless trooper under my father's command. He approaches her from behind, his glowing sword drawn. He takes his time, plotting his steps carefully across the vibrating ground.

When he's close enough, the warrior lunges, burying his sword in One's back, the blade emerging from her abdomen. From this moment on, he will be a hero to my people.

Maybe the only good thing about death is that you never have to relive it. You never have to remember the pain. Except, One does. Though she'd been gone since the airport,

244

ghost-One is suddenly next to me again. She's hunched and sobbing, her mind crying out to mine through the link we share. She can feel herself dying.

Her mind throbs with pain and fear. As it does, I feel the mental block she'd been maintaining crumble and fall, just like the walls of the stilt house. She's lost control over her memories.

Now is my chance to return to the Loric airstrip, to see the identities of the other Garde.

As Number One's body slips lifeless to the ground, everything begins to blur again, like it did when I first entered One's memories. Only now, I'm in control. I cycle backward through her memories, knowing exactly what I want to see.

10

I sit on the beach, waiting for One to emerge from the water. When she does, her wet suit dripping, surfboard slung under her arm, I stop the memory. Then I loop backward a bit further, watching her surf a wave and then return to the beach again.

This is the memory I chose to return to. I replay the scene over and over, unsure how many times I watch her come out of the water, until eventually ghost-One appears beside me. She looks surprised to see me here but sits down on the beach next to me. For a while, we don't say anything; we just stare out at the ocean, watching Number One surf through one of her last happy days. Part of me wishes I could grab a board and go out there with her, but that's not the way this works. This moment will have to do.

'I'm sorry you died,' I blurt out, meaning it.

'Yeah,' answers One. 'That sucked.'

I think back to the floating vision of the solar system. What will happen when my people commence their invasion on Earth? Will this beach look like the ones on Lorien must now?

'I don't understand why any of this has to happen,' I say.

'Maybe you should ask your pops. He's got all the answers, right?'

I nod my head slowly, even though the thought of bringing these feelings to the General makes me feel nauseous. One is watching me, a small smile forming at the edges of her mouth.

'I'm going to,' I say, feeling suddenly resolute. 'I want to know why.'

'Good,' replies One, and she squeezes my hand, even though I can sense that part of her is still sort of repulsed by me.

A shiver goes down my spine, and without quite knowing why, I quickly pull my hand away.

'What happens now?' I ask One.

'Now,' she says, 'you wake up.'

11

I wake up in my bedroom. *My* bedroom, back at Ashwood Estates. I'm not in One's life anymore.

It's morning, and my eyes adjust slowly to the early light. It hurts to open them.

My entire body feels sore and weak. I can't sit up, but I take a few deep breaths and focus on wiggling some feeling back into my toes.

I'm covered by two layers of blankets. One of my arms — pale, paler than usual — rests on top of the blankets, hooked up to a plastic tube that leads to a nutrient drip. Strange.

How long have I been out that they had to hook me up to an IV?

I hear a noise at my bedside and slowly, painfully turn my head. There's a girl kneeling on the floor next to my bed, her back to me. She's narrow and gawky in that almost-a-teenager sort of way. There's something oddly familiar about her, and I struggle to place her from around the neighborhood. What's she doing in my bedroom?

The girl has a Build-a-Piken set spread out on the floor before her. Resembling one of Earth's toy chemistry sets, it's one of the few 'games' we Mogadorians are permitted. I'm too weak to speak, still working moisture back into my desert of a mouth, so I watch in silence as the girl drags a scalpel down the belly of a wriggling earthworm. Then she fills an eyedropper with a clear solution and dribbles it into the worm's open wound.

The worm only writhes at first, but then its body begins to contort and change. Nubs of pliable flesh begin to protrude from the wound where the solution hit. The girl grabs a pair of tweezers and carefully stretches out the flesh, helping it to form into six spindly, spider-like legs. Haltingly, the tiny piken manages to get these legs under it, hefting the twisting remains of the worm's body. It scuttles a few steps across the floor, then collapses.

The girl watches, her head cocked, as the piken-worm tries to regain its footing. It can't, toppling onto what would be its back, legs kicking helplessly in the air. After a few moments of futile struggling, the piken's legs stop moving and it disintegrates into ash. The girl wipes up the ash with a damp washcloth and produces a new worm from a nearby box.

Something about this makes me feel incredibly sad. Not for the worm but more for the girl. It's disturbing to see how casually she alters and extinguishes the worm. It makes me uncomfortable to think how little my people value life. As soon as I have this thought, I get a strange, sick feeling in my stomach. It goes against everything written in the book; everything my people believe.

An image of One impaled on a Mogadorian blade springs to mind. I push it away.

I try to shift in the bed a little bit more, and it makes a

noise. The girl turns her head sharply, her eyes widening when she sees me watching her.

'You're awake!' she shouts, excited.

Kelly. The girl is my sister. But . . . she's grown up. When she springs to her feet, it's clear that she's almost a foot taller than when I last saw her, which should've been just yesterday afternoon, although it feels much longer. *Was* much longer, apparently.

'How –' I cough, my throat aching. 'How long?' I manage.

Kelly has already sprung to the doorway, shouting downstairs for our mother. She rushes back to me.

'Three years,' she says. 'By Ra, you've been sleeping for three years!'

12

I stare at myself in my bedroom mirror. I'm taller than I was. I'm skinnier, too, even though I didn't think that was possible. Whatever my parents had me hooked up to during my coma, it certainly didn't build any muscle. I suck in a deep breath and watch my rib cage protrude through my chest's too-pale skin.

Even standing in front of the mirror, examining my three-years-older body, takes a physical toll. I must look wobbly, because my mother grabs me by the elbow and leads me back to bed. She's been quiet since shooing Kelly and her rapid-fire questions from the room, giving me time to gather myself. I'm grateful for that. My mother has always been the gentle one in the family, often to the General's chagrin.

I can tell by the way she looks at me that she didn't expect me to wake up. She strokes my hair.

'How do you feel?' she asks.

'Strange,' I reply. It's true; my body feels weak and foreign, having grown up without me. But it's more than that. It feels strange to be back here with my own people, knowing what I do now. Even my mother, here stroking my hair, is a brutal warrior at heart, intent on killing the Garde.

I picture the Mogadorians swarming One, feel her fear

and anger anew. I can't help but see my mother's face on one of the soldiers. As she gently takes my hand in hers, I'm imagining my mother plunging a sword into One's back.

Suddenly I don't trust my own family.

'I don't remember anything,' I say, even though she didn't ask. 'The machine didn't work.'

My mother nods. 'Your father will be disappointed.'

I decided to lie when I was still living in One's memories, when we were sitting on the beach together. I won't be telling my people anything that I saw. Not that anything I learned would help Mogadore win its war anyway. What could I even say? That unlike Mogadorians, the Loric are allowed to develop individuality? That their freedom from doctrines like those in the Great Book is simultaneously their greatest strength and ultimate weakness? That I've seen what our people did to Lorien and that it looks like shit?

Yeah, that would go over big.

I'm grateful for the chance to practice this lie on my mother. When it comes time to tell the General, he won't be so gentle.

'Dr Anu will have to go back to the drawing board, I guess,' I say, probing a bit to see if she bought it.

'That won't be happening,' replies my mother. 'When you didn't wake up . . .'

She hesitates, but I don't need her to finish telling me. I can picture the General enraged, storming into Anu's laboratory and drawing his sword.

'Your father never liked Anu. Honestly, the way that old man talked, I'm surprised it didn't happen sooner.'

There are heavy footfalls on the staircase, approaching my room. So here comes the General at last. Here to debrief his only trueborn son, probably to rebuke me for not waking up sooner.

'What's up, skinny?'

Ivan leans in the doorway, grinning. How old would he be now – fourteen? He looks like he could play linebacker for a college football team. Like me, Ivan has grown taller in the last three years, but he's also grown wider in every conceivable way. I imagine all the strength and combat training he's been doing without me, likely coached by the General himself. I wonder how his Mogadorian theory grades have fared without me around to coach him.

'Did you have a nice nap?' he asks.

'Yeah,' I mutter. 'Thanks.'

'Awesome,' he says. 'Anyway, Father wants to see you downstairs.'

I feel my mother grow tense beside me.

Since when did Ivan start calling the General 'Father'?

'Adamus needs his rest,' says my mother.

Ivan snorts. 'All he's been doing is resting,' he says, then turns to me. 'Come on, get dressed.'

There is a familiar note of authority in Ivan's voice. He sounds very much like the General.

13

I'm expecting Ivan to lead me to my father's office, but instead we take the elevator down into the tunnels beneath Ashwood Estates.

'You woke up just in time for some action,' he says.

'Great,' I reply, struggling not to sound halfhearted. 'What's happening?'

'You'll see,' he says. 'Big shit going down.'

When the elevator doors hiss open, Ivan slaps me hard on the back. In my weakened state, I stumble forward a few steps. I'd probably have fallen right to the floor if not for Ivan grabbing me. He pulls me into a brotherly embrace, but in addition to an intimidating amount of strength, I feel a kind of menace in the way Ivan pats me roughly on the back. My palms begin to sweat.

'Seriously,' he whispers. 'So glad you're awake. Father's going to be pleased that his favorite son is finally up and about.'

Ivan leads me to the briefing room. There, two dozen Mogadorian warriors sit in a semicircle before the General. My father is as big as ever, his towering presence commanding the attention of everyone assembled, none of them even noticing when Ivan and I slip into the room.

Projected on the wall behind my father is the image of a red-haired man in his early forties. The picture is grainy; it looks as if it was culled from surveillance footage.

'This man,' my father intones, midbriefing, 'calls himself Conrad Hoyle. We believe, based on several tips from sources as well as extensive surveillance, that he is a member of the Loric insurgency. A Cêpan.'

My father clicks a button on the remote in his meaty hand. Conrad Hoyle's face is replaced by an image of a burned-down cottage in some rural area.

'One of our scout teams had an altercation with Hoyle at this location in the Scottish Highlands. We sustained heavy losses. Hoyle was able to escape.'

Another image appears. Conrad Hoyle, seated on a train, his face intent on a laptop screen. Whoever took this picture clearly did so with a camera-phone hidden a few rows ahead of Hoyle.

'A secondary scout team was able to pick up Hoyle's trail and has been following him ever since. We believe he and his charge, a priority Garde target we know to be roughly thirteen years old and female, have split up. It stands to reason that Hoyle and his Garde have a safe house where they plan to reunite.'

A city appears behind my father, and I recognize it from my studies of Earth's prime urban targets.

London.

'Conrad Hoyle is headed to London,' continues the General. 'There, we believe he will reunite with his Garde and attempt to disappear.'

My gaze drifts over the warriors in the room. All of them are paying strict attention to my father, yet something is off.

'We will follow Hoyle to London and wait for him to lead us to the girl. And we will terminate or apprehend them both. Preferably terminate.'

As the General makes this pronouncement, I notice her. She's sitting in the front row. Her blond hair stands out in this gathering of burly, dark-haired Mogadorians, but no one else notices her.

No one else can even see her.

Slowly, One turns around in her seat. She looks right at me.

'You have to stop them,' says One.

14

The briefing room has emptied out except for the General and Ivan. I'm seated at one of the desks previously occupied by a Mogadorian warrior. My head is swimming, just like it was when I first woke up.

My father looms over me, studying me. He sets a glass of water down on the desk and I drink greedily.

'What happened?' I ask.

'You fainted,' snickers Ivan.

My father spins on Ivan. 'Boy,' he snarls. 'Leave us.'

As Ivan sulks from the room, I think back to the briefing, to One appearing. Was I hallucinating? It felt so real, just like all those times when we spoke inside her memories. But all that was like a dream, a construction of my mind. She shouldn't be able to appear to me now. It doesn't make sense.

Yet somehow I know it wasn't a hallucination. Somehow One is still inside my mind.

I realize that I'm shaking. I put my head in my hands, try to focus, to steady myself. The General won't tolerate this kind of weakness.

My father's large hand comes to rest on my shoulder. I look up, surprised to find him staring at me with something approaching concern.

'Are you well?' he asks.

I nod and try to steel myself for the lies that come next.

'I haven't eaten,' I say.

My father shakes his head. 'Ivanick,' he growls. 'He was supposed to make sure you were ready before bringing you to me.'

The General lifts his hand from my shoulder, the brief moment of affection forgotten. I can tell by the return of rigidity to his spine that, just like that, he's back to business. Mogadorian progress. First and foremost. No matter the cost.

'What did you learn from One's memories?' he asks.

'Nothing,' I reply, meeting his hard eyes. 'It didn't work. I remember being strapped down, then darkness, and now this. Sir,' I quickly add.

My father mulls this over, appraising me. Then he nods.

'As I feared,' he says.

I realize that he never thought Dr Anu's machine would work. My father will believe my lie because he expected failure. Clearly he didn't care what happened to me in the process.

I remember Dr Anu's gamble with my father, wagering his life that his untested technology would succeed. It *did* work, and Anu was still killed.

The Mogadorian way.

'Three years wasted,' broods my father. 'Three years of you getting weaker, falling behind your peers. For what?'

My cheeks burn with humiliation. With frustration. With

anger. But what would my father do if I told him Anu's machine worked, that it gave me One's memories and, with them, doubts.

Obviously, I hold my tongue.

'This folly reflects poorly on our bloodline. On me,' continues my father. 'But it is not too late to remedy that.'

'How, sir?' I ask, knowing he expects me to respond eagerly to any opportunity to increase my honor.

'You will come with us to London,' he says. 'And hunt this Garde.'

15

The next twelve hours are a blur. My father has me fitted for a new uniform; my mother feeds me mammoth meals, like the kind athletes eat before big games – if those athletes had the appetite of full-grown piken. I am allowed a few hours sleep in my own bed, and later on the flight across the Atlantic. I'm almost thankful for this blur of activity; it leaves me no time to think of the Loric stowaway in my brain, or about what my father expects me to do.

We arrive in London the next morning. The General has brought Ivan along, as well as two dozen handpicked warriors, most of them trueborn.

As a Prime Urban Target, London is already home to a Mogadorian presence. The London-based Mogadorians have commandeered five floors in a downtown skyscraper to serve as their base of operations. They run a tight ship, but they've never been visited by a trueborn as high ranking as my father. They snap to attention when the General passes through the halls, even eyeing Ivan and me respectfully as we follow on his heels.

None of these loyal warriors detects the uncertainty I'm feeling inside. To them, I appear as one of their own.

My father assumes command of the London nerve center.

A wall of monitors manned by a pair of scouts provides a constant real-time feed of London's camera network. Another set of terminals crawls the internet in search of suspicious activity and certain Loric-related keywords. Before heading out to track Conrad Hoyle, my father wants to get the lay of the land. He orders the scouts to flip through various video feeds, the General quietly appraising several locations around the city for strategic advantages.

'Our unit trailing Hoyle reports he's on a bus nearing the city center, sir,' declares one of the scouts, relaying this information from his earpiece.

'Good,' intones my father. 'Then it's time for us to go.'

While my father was studying video and plotting bloodshed, I was collapsing into a nearby chair, still feeling light-headed. Ivan stands next to me, his arms folded sternly across his chest, looking more like a young version of the General than ever. When my father turns to face us, Ivan shoots me a sidelong glance.

'Forgive me for speaking out of turn, sir,' begins Ivan, 'but I'm not sure your son is up to this.'

My father's fist coils into a ball. His first instinct is to strike Ivan for his impudence. But then he looks at me, one eyebrow arched.

'Is that true?' he asks.

I know what Ivan's doing. He's spent the last three years worming his way into the General's good graces, calling him 'Father,' assuming my rightful place as his son. Figuring I was gone, Ivan's only concern has been his own advancement.

Before, I never would have given him an opportunity to make me look bad. Before, I'm not sure he would have tried. The thing is, I don't know how much I care about fighting back. During all that time spent in One's memories, and even now that I've woken up, I haven't once fantasized about my promised inheritance of Washington DC. How could I, now that I know the price that would be paid?

Ivan can have it.

'Perhaps he's right,' I say, meeting my father's steely glare. 'In my weakened state, I could be a liability to Mogadorian victory.'

Liability. Mogadorian victory. I know all the buzzwords to use on my father. Those haven't changed. He takes one last look at me, a hint of disgust in his face, before turning to Ivan.

'Come, Ivanick,' he says, sweeping from the room.

I'm left alone with the two techs. They ignore me, glued to their bank of monitors, watching as the bus containing Conrad Hoyle trundles through the city. I realize this is the first moment of peace I've had since waking up from my coma. I close my eyes and lower my head into my hands, trying to keep my mind blank, pushing away the conflicting feelings I've been having about my people. I'm relieved that I don't have to go on this operation. I don't know what I'd do if faced with the task of actually killing a Garde. But then, who am I? I was raised as a ruthless hunter.

'So that's your plan?' asks a familiar voice. 'To just sit here and do nothing?'

I look up to find One sitting next to me. I jerk back in my chair, nearly toppling over, eyes wide.

'Booga booga,' she says, wiggling her fingers at me. 'Seriously, dude. Get off your ass and do something.'

'Do what?' I snap. 'You think they'd hesitate to kill me too?'

One of the techs glances over his shoulder, frowning at me.

'Did you say something?' he asks.

I give him a blank look, then slowly shake my head. He turns back to his monitors. When I look over to where One was sitting, the chair is empty.

Great. Now I'm crazy.

'Look,' says one of the techs, 'something is happening.'

I turn my attention to the screen, where Hoyle's bus has jerked to a sudden stop. The doors fly open, and panicked passengers begin streaming off.

One of the rear windows explodes outward, a man flying through it. Before he can hit the ground, his body disintegrates into ash.

'He's onto us,' observes the other tech, both of them leaning forward to watch the action.

Bright flashes of gunfire pop across the screen, and then the back of the bus goes up in flames. As it does, I watch Conrad Hoyle emerge from the front doors. He's much larger than his picture indicated.

Hoyle holds a submachine gun in each hand.

'By Ra,' says the tech, sounding almost giddy, 'he's going to be a tough one.'

'We should be out there!' grumbles the other.

Most of the pedestrians are fleeing the scene of the flaming bus, like any sane person would. Except there are others that move towards the wreck: men in dark trench coats, shoving their way through the frightened crowd. The Mogadorian strike team has arrived. They're greeted by a hail of gunfire from Hoyle, and they quickly take cover before shooting back.

If my father and Ivan aren't out there yet, enduring Hoyle's fire, they will be soon. I should take pleasure in this noble combat, like the techs are, but I don't. I don't want to see Hoyle, a Loric enemy whom I've never even met, be murdered. Yet despite my conflicted feelings about the mission, I also don't want to see my father turned into a pile of ash.

My only choice is to turn away.

The techs are so absorbed by the action, they don't hear when the station monitoring internet activity chimes. I inch my chair over to the screen, squinting at a red-flagged blog posting.

It reads: **Nine, now eight. Are the rest of you out there?**

16

It takes only a few keystrokes to isolate the blog posting's IP address – it's here in London. The techs aren't paying any attention to me, especially now that calls for tactical support are coming in. Hoyle is proving to be one hell of a distraction.

A few keystrokes more and I've pinpointed the location to an address only a few blocks from the Mogadorian base.

I've discovered the location of a fugitive Garde. Not the General, not Ivan. Me. For a moment, I feel a swelling of pride. Take that, Ivan. I guess growing big and strong doesn't count for everything after all.

Now, what do I do with this information?

I should turn the Garde's location over to the techs, have them call my father back from battle. It would mean major glory for myself and my family, and another step for Mogadorian progress.

It's what I was raised to do. And I almost do it. But as soon as the thrill of discovery passes, I realize I don't want that at all.

I want to help this Garde. Maybe I can prevent another scene like Malaysia.

Wait. *Is* that what I want, or is that one of One's suggestions, a thought left over from traveling through her memories? If I'm hallucinating her, is there even a difference between One's thoughts and my own anymore?

'Deep stuff,' says One, peering at the computer screen over my shoulder. 'Maybe sort out your philosophical questions after we've saved this one's life, hmm?'

That settles it. I minimize the report before the techs have a chance to see it and slip out of the room. I run down hallways now empty of personnel, all of them having joined the ambush on Hoyle. The way I figure it, I've got only as long as Hoyle can keep fighting. After that, the techs will most certainly discover the blog post and relay the details to the strike team.

I'm already winded when I reach the street. I have to push myself. My leg muscles feel about ready to snap after years of disuse; my lungs are on fire, gray spots floating in and out of my vision.

Still, I strip off my coat, which marks me as a Mogadorian, and begin to run. Sirens sound in the distance, the local authorities on their way to the site of the battle.

It takes me ten minutes to get to the quiet backstreet where the building is. I can't believe the Garde safe house was right under our noses. If we had waited, Conrad Hoyle would have come to us, and all the mayhem on the streets could have been avoided. Of course, it's lucky for me that things played out like they did.

I'm gasping for breath as I stand at the doorway to the building. It's an old redbrick town house, now home to three apartments, according to the buzzers outside. Luckily, an old woman is just leaving to walk her white, puffy dog, and I'm able to catch the front door before it closes. I race to the second-floor apartment, the only one not to have a name stickered to the buzzer downstairs.

I pound on the apartment door, probably too hard. If I was a fugitive Garde, that kind of loud knocking would send me running for the fire escape. I hear startled movement inside the apartment, a TV being muted, and then silence.

I knock again, gentler this time, and press my ear to the door.

Muffled footsteps pad closer to the other side of the door, but the girl says nothing.

'Open the door,' I whisper, trying to keep my voice gentle and urgent. 'You're in danger.'

No response.

'Your Cêpan sent me,' I try. 'You need to get out of here.'

There's a lengthy pause, and then a small voice answers. 'How do I know you're telling the truth?'

Good question, but I don't have time for this. By now Conrad Hoyle has probably been overcome by the Mogadorian strike team. I could tell this girl that her Cêpan is as good as dead, that my people will be here soon. I could try breaking down the door, but I doubt I have the strength.

Just like that, One is standing next to me in the hallway. Her face is somber and distant.

'Tell her about the night they came,' says One. 'The night *your people* came.'

I think back to One's memory of the airstrip, the frightened faces around her, the mad dash towards the ship.

'I remember the night they came,' I begin, uncertainly at first but gaining confidence as I go. 'There were nine of us and our Cêpans, all running panicked. We saw a Garde fight off a piken. I don't think he survived. Then they pushed us onto the ship and . . .'

I trail off, recounting the last night of Lorien making me feel strangely sad. I glance to where One was standing, but she's disappeared back into my head.

A half dozen deadbolt locks are unlatched, and the apartment door swings open.

17

Her alias is Maggie Hoyle.

From what little I saw of Conrad Hoyle, I'm expecting Maggie to be a minimilitant in training. Instead, she is the polar opposite of her Cêpan. Maggie can't be more than twelve years old; and she's small for her age, mousey, with a mane of reddish-brown curls hanging on either side of a pair of thick glasses. The only sign of Hoyle's influence is the small handgun she's holding when I walk in, the kind of polite-looking weapon a rich lady might carry with her in a bad neighborhood. Maggie looks relieved to set the gun down as soon as the door is locked behind me.

'Is Conrad all right?' she asks me.

The muted TV in the corner of the small flat is tuned to a news report, a helicopter filming the burning wreckage of Hoyle's bus. It looks like the fight is over. We have to move quickly.

'I don't know,' I tell her, not wanting to say that I doubt her Cêpan survived. We need to get moving, and I don't want to upset her. There's no time for grieving right now.

Not only is she way younger than I expected, Maggie doesn't possess any of the bravado I thought came prepackaged with the Garde after spending years in One's memories.

She's fidgety and nervous, not cool and confident, and not at all ready to fight.

So that makes two of us.

I take in the rest of the apartment. It doesn't look lived in. Maggie probably moved in within the last week. A layer of dust still covers the empty mantel and countertops. There's a small suitcase open next to a half-deflated air mattress, with piles of clothes spilling out onto the floor around it, and a desk with a bowl of cereal on it, a couple of marshmallows still floating in the pink-tinted milk. I scan around the room, looking for the Chest that we've been taught all the Garde have, but I don't see it anywhere. Either she doesn't have it or she's found a good place to hide it.

Next to the cereal bowl is the laptop that brought me here. The computer is still open to the blog post, scrolled down to the bottom of the page where comments would go. The poor kid has just been sitting here waiting for someone to reply, and I'm the one who showed up.

'You shouldn't have done that,' I say, nodding to the laptop.

Maggie looks guilty, rushing over to the laptop to shut it.

'I know. Conrad would be mad,' she says, glancing over at the scene on TV. 'I was just worried he wouldn't come back and . . .'

Maggie stops herself, looking embarrassed. She doesn't have to finish; I know what she was going to say. That she was afraid she'd be alone.

Fear. Loneliness. It was a similar blend of feelings that caused One to take up with brain-dead surfers and start shoplifting. I don't really want to admit it, but they're the same feelings I've been having since waking up.

'What number are you?' she says.

'It doesn't matter now,' I say. I think back to my course on Legacy preparedness. Our instructors warned us about so many different powers the Garde might possess, and I try to think of one that might be helpful now. 'Is it too much to hope that you can teleport?'

'What?' she asks, not understanding.

'Your Legacies,' I explain.

'Oh.' She shakes her head. 'No. Conrad says I'm a couple of years from developing those.'

Maggie studies me as I walk across the room, kneeling down in front of her suitcase. 'Why?' she asks. 'What can you do?'

I don't answer. Next to her suitcase is a small backpack that I unzip to find filled with books, novels by human authors who I've never heard of. I dump out the books and begin stuffing handfuls of Maggie's clothing into the back-pack. We'll need to travel light. I don't pay attention to what I'm packing, only that it won't be enough to slow her down if we need to run.

'What're you doing?' she asks, still rooted to the spot next to the laptop.

'Packing,' I reply. 'Grab only what you need. Definitely leave the computer.'

Maggie doesn't make any move to help. I can feel her watching me, trying to figure out what's happening.

'I want to wait for Conrad,' she says, her voice small but firm.

'He won't be coming,' I reply, trying not to snap at her. She needs to start moving – now. I zip the backpack shut and stand. 'You have to trust me.'

'Winston trusted Julia and look how that turned out.'

Winston? Julia? I try to remember what little I can of Loric culture, thinking that this is some kind of Loric saying I'm unfamiliar with, or maybe they're some other members of the Garde I should know; but I come up with nothing. I decide to guess.

'I haven't seen them since we landed on Earth,' I say.

'Um, they're from Earth,' says Maggie. 'Also, they're not real.'

I stare at her, confused.

'*1984*,' says Maggie, seeing my confusion. 'George Orwell?' One of the books from her backpack. I shake my head. 'Never read it.'

'Who did you think I was talking about?'

'Uh –'

'You aren't Loric,' she says, examining my gaunt face, my pale skin.

'No,' I reply.

'And you aren't human either.' This sounds more like an accusation.

When I shake my head, Maggie inches towards where she set down her little gun. I don't make any move to stop her. She's perceptive. I can see the wheels turning in her head, analysing her situation. She knows there's trouble, but she's not sure if it's on its way or if it's already here.

'If you're one of them, why haven't you tried to kill me yet?' she asks. She reminds me of myself a little bit: small, intelligent and holding on to a belief that she can think her way out of problems.

'I don't know what I am,' I manage, realizing as I say this that it's the truth. 'But I'm not here to hurt you.'

I toss her the backpack.

'You need to run. It doesn't matter if it's with me or from me. Just run.'

Suddenly there's a sharp, breaking sound, the apartment's front door splintering as it is torn off its hinges.

Too late. Too late to run.

'Adamus,' snarls Ivan as he strides into the room. 'Fancy meeting you here.'

18

Streaming into the room behind Ivan are half a dozen Mogadorian warriors. Two of them stay posted at the door; the
others fan out, covering the windows, cutting off any possible escape route. They're a well-oiled machine, the protocol
in this situation clear. Contain the Garde at all costs.

I'm frozen in place. I'm not armed, having forgotten to grab
so much as a dagger on my way out of the Mogadorian headquarters. Even if I did try to fight – against my own people,
a concept I still haven't come to terms with – I wouldn't stand
a chance. At least that's how I justify my cowardice.

Maggie doesn't suffer from any of my uncertainties. She
might have given me the benefit of the doubt, but not Ivan
and his strike team. She knows she's in danger.

She executes a gymnast-caliber somersault towards the
table where she set down her gun. Maggie moves more
quickly than I expected, her fingers nearly closing around
the weapon.

But Ivan is quicker.

Before Maggie can grab the gun, he boots the table
towards her. The edge hits her right in the stomach, audibly
knocking the wind out of her. Maggie, the gun and the table
all go crashing to the floor.

Maggie recovers quickly, already desperately scrambling for the weapon when Ivan kicks it out of her reach. It skitters to a stop just inches from my feet.

Ivan steps on the back of Maggie's neck, grinding her face into the dusty floor. He must outweigh her by more than a hundred pounds. Maggie thrashes, screaming in frustration and pain, but Ivan keeps her pinned as he lifts up his shirt, examining his rib cage.

At first I don't understand what he's doing. But then I realize he's looking for bruises. If Maggie was still protected by the Loric charm, then the damage from when Ivan kicked the table into her would have been done to him. *Unless* she's next in line.

Ivan just confirmed that Maggie is Number Two.

'Number Two,' he says, a note of gruesome satisfaction in his voice. 'My lucky day.'

While Ivan has his shirt up, I notice a wound on his side. It looks like a bullet graze. Blood runs down his body, collecting in the waistband of his pants. He sees me looking and smiles proudly.

'Don't worry, buddy,' Ivan says. 'You should see the other guy.' He winks.

That's when it hits me. Ivan doesn't know what I was doing here. All he cares about is that the protocol of his mission has just changed from apprehend to eliminate.

Understanding that Ivan was referring to her Cêpan, Maggie begins struggling with renewed vigor. She manages to slip from under Ivan's boot, but only gets a hard kick in the chest for her trouble. The way Ivan kicks Maggie is as casual as the way I watched my sister build and snuff out a piken.

Maggie's down again, and this time Ivan presses a foot onto her back. She coughs raggedly, then cranes her neck up to look at me. One of the lenses of her glasses is shattered.

'You said you'd help me,' she gasps.

Ivan laughs. Some of the other Mogadorians in the room crack smiles.

'Is that what he told you?' exclaims Ivan, amused. 'Crafty Adamus! You always were the smart one. Come rushing over here all by yourself to claim all the glory, while the rest of us are out fighting.'

Ivan waves his hand at the gun at my feet.

'Go ahead,' he says. '*Help* her.' Sarcasm drips from his words.

I pick up the gun in a shaky hand and hold it loosely at my side. None of the Mogadorians in the room have weapons drawn. They really have no idea what I was doing here. Of course they don't believe Number Two. Why would they trust her over one of their own?

I glance around the room and force a smile. Ivan thinks he's just handed me a gift, and I know I need to play along. But what I'm really trying to figure out is how many I'd be able to kill before they returned fire? Two? Maybe three?

I'd start with Ivan, that much I'm sure of.

The small gun feels impossibly heavy. It's now or never.

But I can't do it. I can't kill my own people any more than

I could kill Maggie. I meet her eyes, large and pleading. I wish I could at least tell her how sorry I am, but the words won't come. I'm too afraid to even speak.

I drop the gun and look away.

'Don't have the stomach for it?' sneers Ivan, unsheathing his dagger. 'Whatever. You did your part.'

Ivan reaches down and grabs a handful of Maggie's hair, jerking her head back to expose her throat. I see a metallic glint around her neck: her pendant. A grin spreads across Ivan's face as he sees it too. He raises his dagger, and I can feel him staring at me. Does he think I'm a coward, or worse, a traitor?

'For Mogadorian progress,' Ivan shouts.

19

There are hundreds of pictures of the Irish countryside in Two's 'Photos!' folder. Even when it's rainy, the landscape is beautiful: lush and green, hills sprawling, mist sometimes rolling in. I click through until I reach a set of pictures dedicated to a goat, a scrawny little mongrel with brown patches of fur appearing like mud stains on his otherwise white coat. The pet Number Two had to leave behind when she and Conrad fled Ireland.

Here's a picture with her arms flung around the goat's neck. I wonder what the animal's name was.

I glance at the drying bloodstain on the apartment's floor, as if for an answer.

The other Mogadorians have left, some to celebrate, others to have their wounds treated from the battle with Conrad. I've been left alone here to go through Number Two's laptop. There won't be any memory download this time; rummaging through Two's private files will be as close as I get to knowing her.

There are few pictures of Conrad in Two's albums. Most of the time her Cêpan smiles indulgently, but other times the photographs are candid: Conrad reading a book next to a fire, Conrad chopping wood. I get the impression that they led a quiet life together, much less contentious than One and Hilde.

Besides the pictures, there are a few documents on the laptop. Two never kept a proper journal, but she wrote plenty. There is a long list of 'Books to Read.' There are frequently updated rankings of her favorite novels, and more specific lists like 'Strong Female Characters' and 'Villains Cooler Than the Heroes.' I read through these lists, although I hardly understand any of the references. I make some mental notes of books that I'd like to read. I think maybe Two would be happy that someone, even a Mogadorian, took some of her recommendations.

And then I think of the horror in Two's eyes as Ivan brought his dagger down, how I stood by and did nothing. What am I thinking? That I'll somehow make good on that by reading every title on the 'Books That Inspired Me' list? How stupid and hollow.

'Anything interesting?'

My father stands in the doorway. He made it out of the Conrad Hoyle fight unscathed.

'No,' I reply, closing Two's laptop.

The truth is, I've already deleted the only interesting thing on Two's computer. A reply to her ill-advised blog post. I deleted the comment along with the original posting, although I'm sure the techs back at headquarters already flagged it.

The General looms over me. Normally, we're supposed to snap to attention when he enters a room, but I can't work up the energy to go through the motions. I stay slouched in the chair, looking up at him.

'Ivanick tells me that you couldn't kill the Garde,' he says, disappointment and rebuke mixing in his voice.

'I *could* have killed her,' I clarify. 'Any of us *could* have killed her. She was a child.'

My father's face darkens. 'Your tone disagrees with me, boy.'

'Yeah?' I snap, suddenly reminded of the way One argued with Hilde. I want to say more, but then I think better of it. After all, look what happened to One. 'Sorry, Father,' I say in as even a tone as I can muster. 'It won't happen again.'

'That *child* would have killed you if the tables were turned,' my father says, and I can tell by the way the vein along his temple throbs that this effort to engage me in civilized conversation is requiring great self-control. 'She would see your entire people wiped out.'

That's what we've been taught. What Setrákus Ra has told us. But Two knew what I was, and she wasn't going to shoot me. Also, nowhere on her laptop files was there a list of 'Preferred Genocide Methods.' Once again my head starts to spin as everything I've been raised to believe is called into question.

'Father, I don't think that's true,' I say quietly.

'You doubt what I've taught you, boy? What we learn from the Great Book?'

I look up at the General. Meeting his gaze takes some effort, his eyes burning with his barely contained temper.

'Yes,' I whisper.

My father punches me in the face.

His fist is as heavy as a brick, even though I'm sure he pulled the punch somewhat or I'd be unconscious instead of merely toppling backwards out of the chair, my bottom lip split open. I feel blood trickling down my chin, taste it on my tongue. I know the smart thing would be to curl up, to avoid any further punishment; but instead I climb to my knees, chin raised, waiting for the next strike.

It doesn't come. My father stands over me, his fists clenched, staring into my eyes. I feel a heat that I haven't felt before – anger, righteous anger – and that emotion must reach my eyes, because my father's initial look of disgust suddenly betrays something else. A look I'm unfamiliar with.

It's respect. Not for my argument against killing Two – certainly not for that – but for being willing to take another punch.

'Finally,' growls the General. 'You've got some blood on you.'

I look down at my hands. They're pale, soft, and clean. I think of watching Number Two die. My hands should be covered in blood. And just like that, the anger leaks out of me and is replaced by something else, something worse.

Hopelessness.

'I'm sorry for defying you,' I say, keeping my eyes downcast. 'You're right, of course.'

I can feel the General watching me for a moment longer,

as if considering what to do with me. Then, without another word, he stalks out of the apartment, heedlessly walking through the spot where Ivan let Number Two bleed out.

I sink onto my hands and knees, feeling suddenly breathless. How long can I keep going like this, living among a people that I no longer understand?

20

Back at Ashwood Estates, they hold a banquet for Ivan.

All these planned suburban developments come equipped with community halls for neighborhood parties. It's been three years since One was killed, and our community hall hasn't seen use since then. People from the neighborhood spend a weekend cleaning out the dust, moving in a large table, and preparing food.

I wasn't awake for the last celebration. I wish I could sleep through this one.

The General gives a speech describing Ivan's valor in the field. Then he pins a medal shaped like a Mogadorian sword to Ivan's chest, Ivan grinning stupidly as my neighbors rapturously applaud. There's no mention made of my early arrival at Two's safe house, nor does my father spend even a moment memorializing the warriors that didn't return home, gunned down by Conrad Hoyle in the streets of London. No time spent on the weak.

I slip out, leaving behind a half-finished dinner, and I return to my house, enjoying the quiet darkness of my room. With the withering looks my father's been giving me since London, I'm sure he's glad I left early. Without me there, he can pretend Ivan is his trueborn son. They'll both love that.

It's a pleasant, breezy night, but I close my window, wanting to seal out the noise from the banquet. I gaze through narrowed eyes at the lights from the community hall, my neighbors enjoying their biggest celebration since coming to Earth thanks to the cold-blooded murder of an unarmed child.

When I turn away from the window, One is standing in the middle of my room. It's the first time that she's appeared to me since London. Her look is cold and accusing, far worse than the disdainful stares I've been receiving from my father.

'You watched her die,' she says.

I push my knuckles into my temples and squeeze my eyes shut, trying to will her away. When I open my eyes, One hasn't budged.

'Whatever part of my brain you're hiding out in,' I snarl, 'go back there and leave me alone.'

'You could've at least kicked the gun to her,' she says, ignoring me. 'Given her a fighting chance.'

It's a scenario I've agonized over: Two's silly little gun lying at my feet, her only a short distance away. I've played out the possibilities in my head and managed to rationalize the fear I was feeling at the time as strategic self-preservation. There was no way Two was getting out of that room alive, whether I helped her or not. But knowing that doesn't make me feel any less a coward.

'They still would have killed her,' I say, voice shaking. 'And then they would've killed me.'

'Which is what you're really worried about,' replies One, rolling her eyes. 'Saving your own skin.'

'If I die, what happens to you?' I ask, my voice rising. I want One to understand.

'I'm already dead, dummy.'

'Are you? Because it sure seems like you're here now, making me feel worse than I already do. I'm sorry I couldn't save Two, but –'

I'm interrupted by a soft knock on my bedroom door. I was so distracted by One I didn't even hear footsteps coming up the stairs. Without waiting for me to invite her, my mother slowly opens my door, looking concerned. I wonder how much of my conversation with my imaginary friend she overheard.

'Who are you talking to?' she asks.

I shoot a surreptitious glance to where One was standing a moment ago. She's gone now, retreated back into my brain.

'No one,' I snap, sitting down on the foot of my bed. 'What do you want?'

'I wanted to check on you,' she says, and gently takes my chin in her hands. She examines the yellowing bruise on my jaw, the scabbed-over spot on my bottom lip. 'He should not have done this.'

'I was being insubordinate,' I say, the token reply to one of the General's rebukes coming easily.

My mother sits down on the bed next to me. I get the feeling that she wants to say more but is having trouble finding the words.

'He told me what happened,' she begins, hesitating. 'With you and the Garde child. He wanted to send you to West Virginia, but I talked him out of it.'

There's a mountain base in West Virginia where intensive training classes take place. I've heard the 'training' is really endless hours of laboring in underground tunnels. For a true-born like me to be sent there would be the equivalent of a human teenager being sent to military school.

'Thanks,' I reply, not entirely sure why my mother is telling me this.

She stands up and goes to my window, looking out at the lights of the banquet.

'Get back to your studies,' she says quietly. 'Grow stronger. And the next time you have a chance to take down a Garde, do it.'

My mother kneels in front of me, cupping my bruised face in her hands. She stares into my eyes, her look beseeching.

I stare back at her in disappointment, sensing that there's something more she wants to say.

'Yes, Mother,' I reply. She opens her mouth to speak, but closes it without saying a word.

21

I am a model young Mogadorian.

I am dedicated to my studies. My understanding of Ra's Great Book is lauded by my instructors, my dedication to Mogadorian progress unquestioned. I finish top of my class in Advanced Tactical Planning, my final essay on how a Mogadorian guerrilla force could overwhelm a well-defended human city with a minimum of Mogadorian casualties trumpeted as something my father might have written in his younger days.

'Your son makes me certain that our military will continue to flourish well into the next generation,' I overhear one of my instructors tell the General. My father replies with only a grim nod. We have not spoken since London. It has been two years.

I keep my other tactical plans to myself. Secreted away in my room, I scribble out a plan for how a human army with proper strategic intelligence could repel a Mogadorian force. When I'm satisfied with the plan, I burn the pages in the bathroom sink and rinse away the ash.

Hand-to-hand combat is still not my strong suit. Ivan always chooses me as his partner for drills. Afterward, I'm always bruised and sore, and Ivan has barely broken a sweat.

He is bigger and stronger than any of the other students, and when we spar I see an emptiness in his eyes. It's the same dark look he gave me when standing over Number Two's body in London. It's like he thinks we're still in competition for the General's favor, even though I've long dropped out of that race. He's won, but he's too dense to realize it, still viewing me as a rival. When we train with blades, he 'accidentally' cuts my arm, the wound requiring three sutures.

'I'll toughen you up yet, Adamus,' he sneers, standing over me, blood squeezing through my fingers as I hold my arm. 'Make your father proud.'

'Thank you, Brother,' I reply.

What little free time I have, I spend in the capital. I don't bring Ivan along on these trips anymore, and I no longer waste time human-watching at the National Mall. I find a quiet bookstore where I entertain myself for hours reading what titles I can remember from Two's favorite books lists. I begin with George Orwell.

'Why did I have to get stuck in the brain of the universe's most boring Mogadorian?' complains One during a weekend trip to the bookstore. She visits me often, sometimes more than once a day. In a way, she's sort of my only friend. She teases me, but I know she doesn't mind these quiet periods of reading something other than the Great Book. During my Mogadorian classes, I can feel her mind growing restless inside me. Sometimes she manifests, commenting on how heinously pale my instructors are, or when I'm sparring with Ivan, how the discovery of deodorant would be a great step in Mogadorian progress. I've learned not to acknowledge her in public, to limit our conversations to the night, when everyone else is asleep.

It's then that we plan. I lie in bed, thinking. One paces around the room, anxious and bored.

'We should escape tomorrow,' she says. 'We could tell the president that there are a bunch of gross aliens planning war right in his backyard.'

'Not yet,' I reply, shaking my head. 'We'll know when the time is right.'

'What if the time is never right?'

I've spent two years like that, acting the part, waiting for an opportunity to make a difference. Even with their vast resources, my people are slow in finding the other Garde. There are successful operations from other cells: a mission in upstate New York yields a captive Garde. More often there are missions that never get off the ground because the target disappears, or the scout team does. I'm not sure how long the Garde can keep this up. I hope they manage to get organized soon, but I worry that One is right, that I'm biding my time for an opportunity that will never come.

And then, finally, word comes to us about Africa.

22

For the first time in years I'm invited into the General's briefing room.

'We have reliable intelligence that a member of the Garde might be hiding in Kenya,' says my father, handing out a printout of an article from a travel magazine. The article is a few months old, and considering its vague content, it is no wonder it took our techs so long to unearth it. In the article, while gushing about a small marketplace in Kenya, the writer describes a kid with a strange ankle branding that's unlike anything he's seen on other local tribespeople. The description bears a striking resemblance to the Loric charm.

'Has this been confirmed?' I ask, getting in my question before Ivan is even finished dragging his finger along the article's middle sentences.

'Obtaining confirmation using normal methods has proven an obstacle.'

'We can't exactly blend in with this kind of community,' I say, earning a sharp look of annoyance from my father, even though he knows I'm right.

'What's that mean?' asks Ivan, slow on the uptake as usual.

It is just the two of us being briefed by the General. Whatever my father has planned in Kenya, it will be the first time

Ivan and I will be out on our own. We both know what a prestigious and dangerous mission this is. I'm a little surprised the General chose me for this assignment – for any assignment, really. Could it be that he doesn't worry about placing me in harm's way anymore? I decide now is a good time to play the apt pupil, to demonstrate my commitment to Mogadorian progress.

'Assuming they're in an African village environment,' I explain to Ivan, keeping my words insultingly slow, 'it would make slipping in a scout team extremely difficult. They'd know we weren't locals, and we'd risk tipping our hand to the Loric prematurely. It's smart planning on the Garde's part. Isn't that right, Father?'

'Yes,' my father concedes, 'that is correct.'

'Why don't we just go wipe out this village?' asks Ivan. 'Who cares about blending in?'

I snort. 'How many incidents like London do you think we can have before the humans start asking questions?'

'So what if they ask questions?'

'You'd endanger the security of the entire war effort to massacre one village, then?'

'Adamus,' says the General, his voice a menacing rumble, 'would you like to run this briefing?'

'No, sir,' I reply. Ivan smirks.

'As for your question, Ivanick, subtlety is the correct course of action here.'

I feel Ivan deflate a little next to me. Subtlety is not something I'm sure Ivan even knows the meaning of.

'We have managed to secure you cover identities that will not unduly disturb the locals,' continues my father. 'You two will infiltrate this village and determine whether there is indeed a Garde presence. I will have a strike team mobilized in the jungle should you obtain confirmation.'

My father gives me a long look, sizing me up. Then he turns to Ivan.

'Ivanick, you will be in charge. You will report back to me directly.'

Ivan nods eagerly. 'Yes, sir. Of course.'

The General turns back to me.

'Adamus,' he says, 'do not disappoint me.'

'No, sir,' I reply.

23

Ivan watches the mosquito bite his forearm, shakily take flight and then plummet dead onto the hut's wooden floor. Our blood is apparently poisonous to the insects, although that doesn't stop them from trying. Ivan glowers at the swollen bites reddening his arms.

'We should've just wiped this place out,' he grumbles.

The three tanned Italian aid-workers in the hut with us pretend not to have heard him. I don't know who they think we are, what story they were told to convince them to let us pose as fellow volunteers, but I can tell they're afraid. I imagine they all have relatives locked in a place like West Virginia, that their complicity is part of some screwed-up deal my people forced on them. I wish I could tell them they weren't in danger, that this would all be over soon, but that would be a lie.

We arrived in the village yesterday, in a Jeep driven by one of the sullen aid-workers. The place is small, carved out of the encroaching jungle. It's comprised of huts around a single well and a modest outdoor marketplace. The village is on the road to Nairobi, so its marketplace attracts people from smaller nearby villages, here to trade with each other or sell goods to the tourists that pass by on buses twice a day. There is a small basketball court next to the hut the aid-workers live in, built by their predecessors to help them connect with the locals. Children sprint across the flattened soil, tossing a ragged, dark-brown basketball at the netless hoop.

Ivan and I are the perfect choices to be posing as aid-workers. We're the right age for it: idealistic teenagers come to volunteer their time between high school and college. It's the kind of activity that would look great on a kid's college application. Of course, for Mogadorians, assisting the less fortunate would be viewed as a waste of time.

'Humanitarian aid,' spits One, appearing at my side. 'Your people have a sick sense of humor.'

I shake my head. She's right, but I doubt the General realizes the grotesque irony of our cover. To my people, these aid-workers and the villagers are mere tactical assets, pawns to help us smoke out the Garde that might be hiding in the jungle.

Today the aid-workers have circulated word that they have a new shipment of vaccine for the village youths, something to fight against malaria. One by one the local children line up to grit their teeth and receive a shot.

When the children stop by our tent, Ivan and I study them. Most of them arrive barefoot or in sandals, but the ones wearing sneakers or socks are ordered by Ivan to take off their shoes and socks. None of them finds this strange. Humans are too trusting. There are many kids the age of the one we're looking for, but none of them bears the Loric scar. Every smooth ankle is a relief to me.

One of the kids receiving his injection stares at Ivan, then says something in Swahili. The other children in line laugh.

'What did he say?' I ask.

The aid-worker with the needle pauses, giving me a nervous look. Then, in shaky English, replies, 'He says your friend looks like pale hippo.'

Ivan takes a step towards the boy, but I stop him with a hand on his shoulder.

'The boy's right,' I tell the aid-worker, 'he does look like a hippo.' I flash the boy a thumbs-up, and the children laugh again.

'This is a waste of time,' seethes Ivan, and he stomps into the hut's backroom, where we've stored our equipment. I assume he's going to report to my father: no Loric found yet; Kenyan children hurt my feelings.

I step outside the hut, watching as the villagers go about a normal day. I can't help but indulge in a fantasy like I used to when observing Washington DC, about what kind of improvements could be made to this place. This time it's not a fantasy of conquest; it's one of assistance. With the technological advancements the Mogadorians are capable of, we could vastly improve these people's lives.

'Their lives would be most improved,' says One, 'if you just left their planet the hell alone.'

'You're right,' I whisper back, feeling stupid.

On the basketball court, teams are beginning to form up. A boy about fourteen years old sees me watching and waves. When I wave back, he jogs over and says something in what I think is Italian.

'I'm sorry,' I say, 'I don't understand.'

'Ah,' says the boy, and I see the wheels turning as he tries to place my language. 'English? American?'

I nod. The boy is fit, tall for his age. He is dark skinned, yet a few shades lighter than many of the other villagers, a smattering of sun-born freckles across his cheeks and nose. He looks somehow exotic. He is wearing a tank top and mesh shorts, a pair of worn basketball high-tops and striped high socks. High socks. My stomach drops as I realize who he is.

The Garde.

'Sorry,' he says in slow but perfect English. 'The other aid-workers speak Italian. My English is a little rusty.'

'No,' I say, swallowing hard. 'It's very good.'

He steps forward to shake my hand. 'I'm Hannu.'

'Adam.'

'Like the first man. That's good, but right now we need a tenth man for even teams.' He gestures over his shoulder at the other kids waiting on the basketball court. 'You want to play?'

What I want is to scream at Hannu to run. I glance over my shoulder, wondering where Ivan is. I can't make this too obvious, can't make a scene. If Ivan detects anything unusual, he'll radio in to my father right away. Hannu's only advantage right now is that my people don't know who he is. There's still a chance for him and whoever his Cêpan is to slip away undetected.

I need to get him away from the aid-worker's hut.

'Sure,' I say, although I've never so much as touched a basketball. 'I'll play.'

We haven't gone three steps before Ivan is jogging to catch up to us. The only way to describe his grin is shit eating.

'Adam,' he says, talking to me while sizing up Hannu. 'Who's your new friend?'

'Hannu,' replies the Garde, shaking Ivan's hand. I can tell by the way Hannu grimaces that Ivan's grip is vice-like. 'Another American. Cool.'

Everything about Hannu is easygoing, even the leisurely way he walks us over to the basketball court. He looks at home here, comfortable. Too comfortable. I wonder how long he's lived here – how often he's come to this court to shoot hoops. I think about the paranoid behavior of the other Cêpans, the nomadic life that One was forced to endure, the shut-in existence of Two. It seems like Hannu has had such a peaceful time on Earth that he's forgotten there's a war on.

Some of the younger children beam at Hannu as he passes by. He pats them on their heads, smiling back, joking with them in Swahili. I wonder how many languages he knows.

'Did you get vaccinated?' Ivan asks, blunt as ever. 'I don't remember you coming by.'

Hannu waves this away with a serene smile. 'Me? I'm strong like an ox. Save that for the kids that really need it.'

One of the other kids passes Hannu the ball, and he floats up a shot on a lazy arc. It drops through the basket without even brushing the rim.

'Have you lived here long?' I venture.

'All my life,' he replies. The kids pass the ball back to Hannu, and he flips it over to Ivan. 'Take a shot, big man.'

Ivan squeezes the ball so tightly that for a moment I'm afraid it will pop. Then he hurls it towards the basket in an ugly imitation of Hannu's stroke, the ball clanging wildly off the side of the backboard. Some of the kids, including the one who called Ivan a hippo, laugh.

'Good try,' says Hannu cheerily, winking at the laughing kids.

Ivan's expression darkens. I jump in, trying to direct the conversation in a way that will raise Hannu's dormant danger alarms without tipping off Ivan.

'Is it weird to have strangers just showing up at your village?' I ask.

Hannu shrugs. 'We get tourists on the bus sometimes.' He glances over at Ivan. 'I hope you guys packed sunscreen. Your friend is turning red.'

Ivan grabs my arm before I can form another awkward question. 'Come on, Adam. We have *work* to do.'

Hannu looks disappointed as Ivan drags me away. 'Maybe we'll play later, yeah?'

'I hope so,' I tell him.

As soon as we're out of earshot, Ivan hisses to me, 'That was him!' He looks thrilled. 'You might be worthless in a fight, but you can sniff out a Garde better than any of our scouts.'

I glance over my shoulder. Hannu has already put us out of his mind, helping some of the younger kids practice their form.

'We can't confirm that's him,' I say.

'Oh, come on, Adamus,' groans Ivan. 'I should've choked him right out there.'

'You don't want to waste the General's time until we can be sure,' I say, trying to buy time. 'Plus, even if that is our Garde, you don't know he's Number Three.'

Ivan sneers at me, and I can tell his mind is made up. When we get back into the hut, he grabs the nearest aid-worker by the shirt and pulls him over to the window.

'That kid,' he says, pointing at Hannu. 'Where does he live?'

The aid-worker hesitates, but I can see the fear in his eyes. 'Not sure,' he mumbles. 'Outside the village, I think. Near the ravine.'

'Good enough,' says Ivan, shoving the aid-worker away. He glances at me before disappearing into the backroom. 'I'll tell Father you say hi.'

So that's it. Soon the strike team will be here. I return to the doorway, watching Hannu dribble past a defender and flip a layup into the basket.

'He's dense,' observes One, suddenly standing next to me, looking at Hannu. 'You have to tell him.'

I nod. No more waiting around, no more planning, no more subtlety. There will never be a more perfect opportunity to defect. I've already watched one Loric die because of my uncertainty, because I failed to act in time. I won't let this one be captured, or worse.

'You're right,' I whisper back. 'Tonight, we escape.'

24

Night has fallen. The jungle around me is alive with strange noises. I should be worried about what kinds of animals are out there, snapping branches as they stalk me, hissing around my ankles. But there are other, more dangerous predators in the jungle tonight. Ones that I need to stop.

I run through the jungle with only a vague idea of where I'm going. Maybe running isn't exactly accurate – more like stumbling; it seems like every vine on the jungle floor has a mind to trip me. It's so dark out here, I'm practically blind. My knees and elbows are scraped from falls, my face cut from the branches slapping against it. Still, I press on toward the ravine.

The communicator on my hip buzzes with static. I swiped it before sneaking out of the aid-worker hut. My plan is simple, the best I can do under such circumstances. Get to Hannu and his Cêpan, tell them what's happening and use the communicator to monitor my people's movements. Hopefully, with Hannu's knowledge of the jungle, we'll be able to stay one step ahead of the soon-to-be-arriving strike team. It won't be easy – because of the remote location, my father has authorized a larger unit than normal, including a piken – but I know how my people think, how they attack. I can do this.

All I have to do is get to Hannu first. A task this thick jungle isn't making very easy.

When the jungle begins to thin out before me, moonlight shining through the canopy overhead, I know that I'm close. I can hear rushing water in the distance, the river coursing through the nearby ravine.

And then I see it. A single, solidly built hut. The jungle around it has been painstakingly cleared, leaving a flat expanse that's littered with angular mahogany equipment. As my eyes adjust, I realize the objects are some kind of homemade obstacle course. So Hannu does more training than just pickup basketball games in the village. That's good. He'll need to be agile for what's to come.

I approach the hut cautiously. The last thing I need is to spook Hannu and his Cêpan. If he's anything like Conrad Hoyle, Hannu's Cêpan might emerge from that hut with guns blazing.

I stop, stiffening, the hair on the back of my neck rising. Footsteps are crashing through the jungle behind me. I break out in a cold sweat despite the African heat.

I turn to see Ivan emerging from the jungle. In the moonlight, I see a trickle of sweat roll down his cheek, his face contorted in a humorless smile.

'Clever Adamus,' he sneers, 'thought you'd get away with this.'

He's on to me.

'With what?' I ask, stalling.

I glance over my shoulder at the hut. There's no movement inside, the sounds Ivan and I are making drowned out by the jungle. I'll stop Ivan if I have to, but I hope it won't come to that. Maybe I can still talk my way out of this.

I walk back towards the edge of the clearing, standing inches away from Ivan.

'Get out of here, Ivan,' I say, trying to sound as intimidating as possible.

He snorts, disbelieving. 'What? And let you try to steal all the glory? You'll probably freeze up again.'

And then I realize what dim-witted Ivan thinks I'm doing out here. He doesn't think I've come to warn Hannu; such treason isn't even a possibility to him. Ivan thinks I've come to capture or kill Hannu myself, just like he assumed I did with Number Two.

'You didn't even bring any weapons,' Ivan observes mockingly. 'Are you going to *talk* the Loric to death?'

He's right. I came unarmed, hoping it would help convince Hannu to trust me. Also, I never intended to actually fight my people, only evade them. I hoped that violence could be avoided.

With speed that surprises Ivan, I snake my hand forward and rip the dagger off his belt. His jaw drops when I hurl the weapon into the jungle.

'Adamus,' he exclaims, sounding hurt, like a kid who's had his favorite toy broken. 'What the hell? You better help me look for that.'

I grab Ivan by the front of his shirt and put my face in his. He's surprised again, not used to being manhandled. I stare into his eyes, trying to reach him. I know it's crazy, but Ivan used to be my best friend, despite everything. I have to believe that he'll still listen to me.

'Why do this?' I ask. 'Killing them won't heal our planet. It won't lead to Mogadorian progress. It'll only lead to more killing. More life wasted. Is that what you want?'

'What the hell are you talking about, Adamus?'

He stares at me, dumbfounded. I shake him.

'We don't always get along,' I continue, 'but you're like a brother to me. You trust me, don't you?'

Mutely, Ivan nods his head.

'Then trust me when I tell you that everything we've been told is wrong,' I say desperately. 'Our cause is unjust, Ivan. We can change that. You can help me work towards – toward *real* Mogadorian progress.'

I can see him trying to make sense of my words, confusion on his face. He looks away from me, over my shoulder, to the hut where Hannu and his Cêpan sleep. For a moment I allow myself to think that I've gotten through to him.

Then he shoves me away. He's finally realized what I'm up to, and it disgusts him.

'I always knew you were weak, Adamus,' hisses Ivan, 'but not a traitor too.'

That settles it.

I unclip the communicator from my belt and slam it into the side of Ivan's face.

25

I had hoped the blow would knock Ivan out. I should've known better.

Ivan is back on his feet before I can create some distance between us. He doesn't even register the trickle of blood from the cut I made above his eyebrow. That dead look I've seen in his eyes during a dozen training sessions comes on, and he's barreling towards me.

Ivan drives his shoulder into my stomach and lifts me, hurling me into a tree. The air explodes out of my lungs in a wet cough. Ivan grabs a handful of my hair and slams my head into the tree. Stars flash across my vision; I struggle to stay conscious.

Desperately, I kick at Ivan, my shin connecting solidly with his groin. He doubles over, retching, and drops me.

I stumble backward, into the jungle, shaking the cobwebs out of my head. Ivan is on me again before I have a chance to regroup, delivering a two-punch combination to my chest, followed by an uppercut that sends me tumbling over a fallen tree trunk. I scuttle backwards on my hands, running my tongue over the gap where my tooth used to be.

'You can do better than that,' says One, sitting cross-legged on the tree trunk.

'Shut up,' I mutter.

Ivan leaps onto the tree trunk, standing above me. He points over his shoulder, a wild look in his eyes.

'You want to fight me for *them*?' he snarls. 'For some Loric trash? You're choosing them over us?'

'Yes.'

'Then you can die with them!'

Ivan jumps off the log, intending to stomp my face. I roll away at the last moment, kicking him in the side of the knee as he lands. I hear something snap inside Ivan's leg, and he howls with pain.

I scramble to my feet. Center myself, regain my balance. Ivan lunges towards me, now limping slightly, but this time I'm ready for him. I deflect his punches — all straight ahead, angrily telegraphed — using his own momentum and speed against him. It's something I never tried in our sparring sessions, but it's exactly what Hilde had been teaching Number One.

Ivan comes at me again, frustrated, his blows more furious than ever. I duck under them and when he's off balance, drive the heel of my hand into his nose. His feet go out from under him.

I step down on Ivan's throat, thinking of Number Two and the way he stepped on her neck. Out of the corner of my eye, I think I see a flicker of light coming from the direction of Hannu's hut. But maybe it's just my imagination.

'Not so easy when someone hits back, huh?' I say.

Ivan shoves my foot away, but I catch his wrist in both of

my hands. He pulls me to the ground and tries to climb on top of me. He punches wildly at me with his free hand, but I'm in control. I whip my legs up and slip one leg under his chin, the other behind his head, then pull down on his head with both of my hands, choking him.

It takes a full minute for Ivan to lose consciousness, punching me in the ribs the whole time with decreasing force. When it's over, I shove his body away, lying on my back. I'm hurting all over, but I'm alive.

Around me, the jungle has grown eerily quiet.

But then I hear the hiss of orders broadcast across the half-broken communicator discarded in the dirt a few feet away, and I know what's coming.

I'm too late.

26

I manage to get to my feet and stagger towards the hut. I notice shadows lurking in the jungle around me, the scouts maintaining a perimeter.

In the hut's doorway, the crumpled body of a fifty-year-old man bleeds from a vicious sword wound. Hannu's Cêpan. Dead like the other Cêpans. Which means they must have discovered the boy is Number Three.

I feel like sinking to my knees, like giving up. I've thrown my entire life away tonight – I can never go home again; they'll know me as a traitor. I'll be spending the rest of my life running and hiding, hunted, just like the Garde. And for what? I didn't even manage to help Hannu. I was too late, took too long fighting with Ivan. I've accomplished nothing.

Suddenly the back wall of the hut explodes outward, splinters cascading in all directions. There is Hannu, alive, running – and running fast. Faster than humanly possible. He takes off before my people have a chance to close in, speeding towards the ravine.

There's still a chance.

There's no way that I can keep up with Hannu, but I run as fast as my body will allow, breath whistling painfully through my lungs. There are other pursuers nearby; I can hear them crashing through the jungle. Even with all the other scents in the jungle, I can still smell the acidic tang of piken breath as one charges towards the ravine. If I can only find a way to get to Hannu first, maybe I can still help him.

The sound of rushing water grows louder. I don't know how Hannu plans to cross the ravine. Maybe he's strong enough to jump it. Maybe he knows some secret way down. It doesn't matter, as long as he gets away. If he does, there is hope.

I see Hannu's silhouette nearing the edge of the ravine, maybe thirty yards from where I'm standing. There is a piken close on his heels. I'm afraid for him – he doesn't have anywhere to go – but when Hannu reaches the edge of the ravine he jumps, landing safely on the other side. It's a jump I could never make, and neither can the piken.

He's safe.

Except: my father is waiting for him on the other side of the ravine. There is nothing more Hannu can do. The General grabs the boy and lifts him easily. He cuts a striking image, like a Mogadorian hero culled right from the Great Book.

He hesitates for a moment, observing his prize, then tears what I know is the pendant from Hannu's neck and stuffs it into his cloak.

There's no way across the ravine. I can only watch as my father laughs, then pulls his sword from its scabbard. Its glowing shaft pierces the night before he plunges it through Hannu's chest and then drops him callously to the ground. He's dead.

One is screaming inside my head. Or is that me?

The General stares across the ravine. For a moment, our eyes lock.

I hear haggard footsteps approaching me from behind. I know what they mean, but I don't turn to face them.

My brief rebellion is at an end.

'Good-bye, Adamus,' hisses Ivan as he slams both his hands into my back, shoving me over the edge of the ravine, towards the rocks and water below.

27

The sun is warm on my face, in wonderful contrast to the cool saltiness of the ocean breeze. I relax back on my elbows and close my eyes. I turn my face up towards the sun, soaking in the California rays.

When I open my eyes, One is sitting on the sand next to me. She is so beautiful. Her blond hair is loose, brushing lightly across her bare shoulders. This is wonderful. Such a pleasant sensation. I can't ever remember feeling so content.

Why does she look so stricken?

'Adam,' she says, 'you have to wake up.'

'Wake up from what?' I ask, feeling not a care in the world.

I reach out and take her hand. One doesn't pull away; she just stares into my eyes with a pleading look.

'You have to wake up,' she repeats.

I feel a sudden chill. Somehow, my body is in two places at once. The other place is wet and cold. Painful. My body is tossed across rocks, buffeted endlessly by a forceful current. I can feel that some of my bones are broken, sharp pains slicing up and down my body.

I push that reality aside. I try to focus on California.

'Please, wake up,' One pleads.

'But it's so nice here.'

'If you stay here, you'll die.'

When I open my mouth to respond, muddy river water spills out. I gasp for breath, choking, struggling. The current is strong, pulling me downward.

But that doesn't make sense. I'm on a beach in California. All the pain is somewhere else, happening to someone else. One looks so sad and desperate, I have to turn away.

The sun is just beginning to set over the ocean, the sky turning orange and purple. Soon it will be dark, and I'll be able to rest.

'Wake up and fight,' begs One. 'Please, Adam.'

I don't know if I can.